Yasmina Khadra is the pen name of award-winning Algerian author Mohammed Moulessehoul. His novels include *The Swallows of Kabul*, *The Attack*, and *The Sirens of Baghdad*. In 2011 Yasmina Khadra was awarded the prestigious Grand prix de la littérature Henri Gal by the Académie Française.

Howard Curtis's many translations from French and Italian include works by Balzac, Flaubert, Pirandello, Jean-Claude Izzo, Marek Halter and Gianrico Carofiglio. For Gallic, he has translated four novels by Jean-François Parot.

The African Equation

The African Equation

Yasmina Khadra

Translated from the French
by Howard Curtis

Gallic Books
London

A Gallic Book

First published in France as *L'Équation africaine* by Éditions Julliard, 2011
Copyright © Éditions Julliard, 2011
English translation copyright © Gallic Books 2015

First published in Great Britain in 2015 by Gallic Books,
59 Ebury Street, London, SW1W 0NZ

A CIP record for this book is available from the British Library
ISBN 978-1-908313-70-6

Typeset in Fournier MT by Gallic Books
Printed in the UK by CPI (CR0 4YY)

2 4 6 8 10 9 7 5 3 1

1
Frankfurt

When I found love, I told myself, that's it, I've gone from just *existing* to actually *living*, and I swore to do whatever it took to ensure my joy would never end. My presence on earth now had a meaning, a vocation, and I had become someone special ... Before that, I'd been an ordinary doctor pursuing an ordinary career, leading a humdrum existence without any real appetite, having the odd passionless affair that left no trace when it was over, meeting friends for drinks in the evening or for pleasant hikes in the forest at weekends – in short, routine as far as the eye could see, with the occasional unusual event, as vague and fleeting as a sense of déjà vu, which had no more effect on me than some trivial item in a newspaper ... But when I met Jessica, I discovered the world; I might even say I gained access to the very essence of the world. I wanted to be as important to her as she was to me, to be worthy of her every concern, to occupy her every thought; I wanted her to be my groupie, my muse, my ambition; I wanted many things, and Jessica embodied all of them. The truth is that she was my star, she lit up the whole sky for me. I was as happy as a man could be. It was as if I just had to hold out my hand and summer would come early. A state of grace was a mere heartbeat away. Every kiss I received was like a vow. Jessica was my seismograph and my religion, a religion in which the dark side of things had no place, in which all the holy books could be summed up in a single verse: *I love you* … But in the past few weeks, doubt had crept into even those pious words. Jessica had stopped looking at me in the same way as before. I no longer recognised her. After ten years of marriage, I was aware that something was wrong with our relationship, and I hadn't the slightest clue what it was, had no way of locating the source of the problem. Whenever I tried to talk to her, she would give a start, and it would take her at least a minute to realise that all I was trying to do was break through the wall she had built around herself. If I insisted, she would put her arms up like a barrier and tell me that now was not the time. Every word, every sigh upset her, pushed her that little bit further away from me.

My wife didn't so much worry me as terrify me.

She had always been a fighter, had always battled for what she believed in, had always done all she could to make our lives better. Jessica and I had had ten wonderful years when everything had gone well, ten years of unbridled love, combining sensual passion and warm friendship.

I had met her in a brasserie on the Champs-Élysées in Paris. She was taking part in a seminar, and I was attending a conference. I fell in love with her the moment I saw her. I was near the front window, she was at the far end of the room, and we looked at each other in silence. Then we both smiled. She left first, along with her colleagues. I didn't think I would see her again. In the evening, our paths crossed in the foyer of the hotel where her seminar and my conference were both taking place, on different floors. Chance seemed to be on our side, so why not take advantage of it? … Within four months, we were married.

What was making her so distant? Why wouldn't she tell me any of her anxieties or secrets? In desperation, interpreting her attitude as the sign of a guilty conscience, I suspected an extramarital affair, a casual adventure that had driven her into a frenzy of remorse … But that was absurd. Jessica was mine. I couldn't remember ever seeing her look at another man.

Sometimes, sitting in the kitchen after a meal during which we hadn't spoken and she had avoided my eyes, I would reach out my hand to her. Instinctively, like a frightened snail, she would move her arm away and hide it under the table; I would keep calm, for fear of making matters worse.

Jessica was a beautiful woman. I was dying to take her in my arms; I was hungry for her, her warm body, her passionate embrace. The smell of her hair, her perfume, the blue of her eyes: I missed everything about her. I longed for her even though she was within arm's reach; I lost sight of her as soon as she turned away from me. I no longer knew how to get her back.

Our house was like a sealed mausoleum in which I was both a prisoner and a ghost. I didn't know which way to turn. I felt confused, superfluous, completely useless. All I could do was watch the lights going out one by one and darkness spreading from the wings to the stage, where my leading lady had forgotten her lines. No role matched her silences. She was merely a semblance of herself, as elusive as a memory that had lost its own story. What was she thinking about? What was worrying her? Why was she always in a hurry to go to bed, leaving me alone in the living room with a pile of questions?

I spent my evenings slouched in front of the television, even though it no longer amused me and I hopped listlessly from one channel to another. Wearily, feeling as if my head were in a vice, I would go to the bedroom and spend an eternity *listening* to Jessica sleep. She was magnificent when she slept, like an offering fallen from the sky, except that I was forbidden to touch. Freed from whatever obsessed her, her face regained its freshness, its magic, its humanity; she was the most beautiful sight I could hope for in the midst of the darkness that had seized my world.

By the time I got up in the morning, she was usually already gone. I would find traces of her breakfast in the kitchen, and a note on the fridge: *Don't wait up for me tonight. I may be back late* ... With a lipstick mark on the paper by way of signature.

Whatever the day brought, it was likely to be as dreary as my evenings.

I was a general practitioner. My surgery was on the ground floor of a grand-looking building, a few blocks from the Henninger Turm in the upper part of Sachsenhausen, in southern Frankfurt. My surgery occupied the whole floor and had a waiting room large enough to hold about twenty people. My highly efficient assistant was named Emma. She was a tall girl with muscular legs, the mother of two children she was bringing up alone after her husband had walked out on her. She kept my surgery as spotless as an operating theatre.

Two patients were waiting for me in the waiting room: a pale-faced old man in a tight coat and a young woman with her baby. The old man looked as if he had spent the night outside my surgery waiting for me to arrive. He stood up as soon as he saw me.

'I can't stand the pain, doctor. The pills you prescribed

aren't having an effect any more. What'll become of me if I can't find a drug that works?'

'I'll be with you in a minute, Herr Egger.'

'My blood's turned pitch-black, doctor. What exactly do I have? Are you sure you've made the right diagnosis?'

'I'm going by what the hospital has told me, Herr Egger. We'll have a look in a minute.'

The old man resumed his seat and huddled in his coat. He turned to the young woman, who was looking outraged, and said, 'I was here before you, madam.'

'Maybe you were,' she shot back, 'but I have a baby with me.'

I found it hard to concentrate on my work that morning. I kept thinking about Jessica. Emma noticed that I wasn't myself. At midday, she urged me to go and get some lunch and have a breather. I went to a little restaurant not far from the Römerberg. There was a couple that kept bickering in low voices at the next table. Then a family arrived with some noisy kids and I hastily asked for the bill.

I went to a little park not far from the restaurant and sat on a bench until a group of young tourists came and disturbed me. In the surgery, three patients were sitting twiddling their thumbs. They looked pointedly at their watches to indicate that I was more than an hour late.

At about five, I had a visit from one of my oldest patients, Frau Biribauer, who always deliberately chose to come towards the end of surgery so that she could tell me her troubles. She was a woman in her eighties, unfailingly polite and well dressed. But today, she hadn't put on any make-up and her dress hadn't been ironed. She looked downcast, and her withered hands were streaked with bruises. She began by making it clear that she hadn't come for any medical reason, apologised for constantly 'boring' me with her stories, then, after a pause for thought, asked, 'What's death like, doctor?'

'Come now, Frau Biribauer—'

She raised her hand to cut me short. 'What's it like?'

'Nobody has ever come back from the dead to tell us what it's like,' I said. 'Don't worry, we aren't there yet. All you have is a small benign tumour that'll disappear with the right treatment.'

I tried to put my hand on her shoulder, but she shrugged it off. 'The reason I came to see you, doctor,' she went on, 'isn't that monstrous thing that's growing under my armpit. I really do ask myself the question. It's the only thing I can think of lately. I try to imagine what it's like, that big leap in the dark, but I can't.'

'You should think of something else. You have an iron constitution, and lots of good years ahead of you.'

'The good years are those you share with the people you love, doctor. And what am I supposed to think about? What else is there?'

'Your garden.'

'I don't have a garden.'

'Your cat, your flowers, your grandchildren ...'

'I don't have anybody left, doctor, and I don't get any joy from the flowers on my balcony any more. My son only lives twenty kilometres away, but never comes to see me. Whenever I phone him, he says he's working every hour God sends and he doesn't have a minute to himself ... Whereas I have plenty of time to wonder what death is like ...' She wrung her hands. 'Loneliness is a slow death, doctor. Sometimes I'm not sure I'm still alive.'

14

She held my gaze for a moment or two, then turned away.

I reached out to take her hands, and this time she let me as if she no longer had the strength to resist.

'Try to forget your dark thoughts, Frau Biribauer,' I said. 'You're worrying unnecessarily. It's all in your mind. Keep your spirits up. You've shown great courage and a clear head. You have no reason to give in now. With its joys and pains, life deserves to be lived to the end.'

'But that's just it, doctor, what's the end like?'

'What does it matter? What matters is that you take more care of your flowers. Your balcony will look a lot more cheerful. Now, show me how our little tumour has reacted to the medication.'

She took her hands away and confessed with a sigh, 'I haven't taken the medication.'

'What do you mean?'

She shrugged like a sulking child. 'I burnt the prescription as soon as I got home.'

'You surely don't mean that.'

'Of course I do. Nothing matters when you have nobody left.'

'There are places that can help you, Frau Biribauer. Why not try them if you feel alone? You'll have company, you'll be well taken care of, and— '

'You mean an old people's home? Those are just places to die in! They're not for me. I can't imagine ending my days somewhere as grim as that. No, I couldn't stand people putting me to bed at a fixed time, taking me out into the fresh air like a vegetable, pinching my nose to make sure I swallow my soup. I have too much pride for that. And besides, I don't like relying on other people. I'll go with my head held high, standing on my own two feet, without needles in my veins or an oxygen mask attached to my face. I'll choose the moment and the manner for myself.'

She pushed my arm away and stood up, angry with herself. I tried to hold her back, but she asked me to let her go and left the surgery without saying anything else and without looking at anybody. I heard her open the front door of the building and slam it behind her. I waited to hear her walking down the street, but as she didn't pass my windows, as she usually did, I assumed she had gone in the opposite direction. A deep sadness took hold of me, and I quickly had the next patient shown in.

Night had fallen when Emma came and asked me if she could go.

'See you tomorrow,' I said.

After Emma had gone, I stayed in my consulting room for another half an hour or so, doing nothing in particular. As Jessica wasn't due home until late, I wasn't sure what to do with the time I had on my hands. I switched off the lights, leaving only my desk lamp on. That relaxed me a little. I loved listening to the silence of the building, a silence filled with shadow and absence that seemed to steady the things around me. People lived on five floors, along hushed corridors, and I never heard any noise from them. They shut themselves up in their homes as if in tombs. They were people of a certain age, well-to-do, of some social standing, and incredibly discreet. I'd sometimes pass one or two of them on the stairs, stooped, barely visible beneath their hats, in a hurry to disappear from my sight, almost apologising for being in my way.

It was eight o'clock by my watch. I didn't feel like going home to a darkened living room and sitting watching TV shows I wasn't interested in, checking the clock on the wall every five minutes and thinking Jessica was back whenever a car pulled up in the street. I glanced at my wife's portrait in its frame. It was a photograph taken on an Italian beach two years into our marriage: Jessica sunbathing on a rock surrounded by foaming waves, blonde hair flowing over shoulders so translucent they never tanned. She looked like a mermaid sitting on a cloud, laughing, her face radiant, her eyes bigger than the horizon … What had happened? Since she had been promoted to the post of deputy head of external relations at the multinational company she worked for, Jessica had changed. She travelled a lot, from Hong Kong to New York, from Scandinavia to Latin America, and worked flat out, sacrificing her holidays, bringing bundles of files home with her to go through in fine detail; sometimes she would shut herself up for hours in her tiny office, the door double-locked, as if she were dealing with top-secret material.

I grabbed my coat, wrapped my scarf around my neck, switched off the desk lamp and went out. In the foyer of the building, the lift was waiting patiently for someone to use it. It was a beautiful old-fashioned lift, encased in wrought iron, painted black and sparkling clean.

Outside, an icy wind was raking the walls. I put my coat on and walked up the street as far as the snack bar in the square. Toni the barman gave me a broad smile when he saw me come in. He poured me a tankard of beer and placed it, frothing over, on the counter. I was a regular customer for his seafood platter whenever Jessica was late home. Toni was a lively, humorous southerner, with fiery red hair. He loved playing to the gallery with his jokes that verged on rudeness. In the neighbourhood, he was known as the Sicilian because of his spontaneity and good humour. His excessive familiarity disconcerted some customers who weren't used to impromptu friendships, but they eventually got used to it. I liked Toni a lot, even though I was a little too reserved for his taste. He had a knack for making me loosen up, and enough tact to let it go when I didn't react to his slaps on the back.

'You're not looking too good, Kurt.'

'I've had a busy day.'

'Lucky you! You should be pleased.'

'I am.'

'You don't look it. I hope you didn't leave your smile on your stethoscope.'

I smiled at him.

'That's better. You see? It doesn't cost much to smile.' He gave the counter a wipe with his cloth. 'Hans has only just left, by the way. Didn't you pass him in the street?'

'No. When did he get back?'

'Three days ago. Hasn't he been to see you?'

'No.'

'Have you fallen out?'

'Not at all. If he hasn't been to see me, it must mean he has things to sort out ... So he's back from the Amazon?'

'Apparently, yes. We didn't have time to talk about it, but he seemed pleased with the expedition. Plus, he's tanned, and he's lost weight, which really suits him.'

Hans Makkenroth was an old friend. The heir of one of the richest families in Frankfurt, he ran several large companies specialising in medical equipment. But his fortune hadn't made him inaccessible. Quite the opposite: he was often seen in quite ordinary places, melting into the crowd and avoiding gala evenings and other social events like the plague. We had met ten years earlier at Maspalomas in the Canary Islands. Hans and his wife Paula were celebrating their silver wedding anniversary, while Jessica and I were on our honeymoon. We had adjoining bungalows close to the beach. Paula and Jessica became friends, in spite of the age difference. They would invite each other over for coffee in the evening and allow us, Hans and me, to join them. Hans was interested in boats, oceans, and remote peoples. As I was receptive, Hans took an interest in me too. We became inseparable.

Paula died of a sudden devastating bout of pneumonia four years later, and, since becoming a widower, Hans had travelled the world constantly, as if in an attempt to shake off his grief. He was an exceptional sailor, fascinated by far horizons. Every year, he would set off for the unlikeliest places, carrying aid to destitute peoples deep in the Amazon jungle, or in Africa, or in remote areas of Asia.

'Would you like something else?' Toni asked.

'I'm a bit peckish, but I don't feel like seafood tonight.'

'I have some delicious calamari.'

'I'd rather have meat. A starter should be enough.'

Toni suggested a carpaccio of beef.

On the plasma screen above the counter, a football match was in full swing. At the far end of the room, a family was having dinner in silence, gathered around an old man who was gesturing vaguely. Two young women were chatting at a table close to the window; the snack bar's neon sign spattered them with coloured light, adding gleaming highlights to their hair. One of the women stared at me before leaning towards her companion, who also turned to look at me. I asked for the bill and left, despite Toni insisting I have another drink. Out in the street, it had got colder.

I'd been planning to walk towards the river, in order to stretch my legs and clear my head, but the heavens opened and the rain forced me to go straight back to the car park where I'd left my car.

Because of the rain, there were traffic jams, and I didn't get home until about 10.30. I'd been hoping Jessica might be back, but the windows of our house were still dark.

A jacket of Jessica's lay on the chest of drawers in the hallway. I didn't remember it being there that morning when I left for the surgery.

In our room, the bed hadn't been disturbed.

I took off my coat, jacket and tie and went straight to the kitchen to get myself a beer. I sat down on the sofa, put my feet up on a pouffe and grabbed the remote. The first thing that came on was a political debate. I switched channels several times before coming across an underwater documentary showing sharks hunting in packs in a coral reef. Seeing the depths of the ocean had a calming effect on me, but I couldn't really concentrate. It was eleven minutes past eleven by the clock on the wall. By my watch, too. I started channel-hopping again frantically, and finally went back to the underwater documentary. Unable to focus on any one programme in particular, I decided to take a shower before going to bed.

As I switched on the light in the bathroom, I almost fell backwards as if hit by a gust of wind. At first, I thought I was hallucinating, but it wasn't an optical illusion, and was far more than a fleeting impression. *No*, I heard myself cry out. Paralysed, suspended in a celestial void, I grabbed hold of the washbasin to stop myself collapsing. My calves began to tremble, and the trembling rose to my stomach and spread through my body like a series of electric shocks. Jessica lay in the bath, fully dressed, the water up to her neck, her head twisted to the side, one arm dangling over the edge of the tub. Her hair floated around her pale face, and her half-closed eyes stared sadly at her other arm, which was folded over her stomach … It was an unbearable, nightmarish, surreal sight. Horror in all its immeasurable cruelty!

My house was swarming with intruders.

Somebody brought me a glass of water and helped me to sit down. He was saying something, but I wasn't listening. I saw strangers bustling around me, uniformed policemen, ambulance men in white. Who were they? What were they doing in my home? Then it came back to me. I was the one who had called them. There had been a brief moment of lucidity, followed by fog. Again I couldn't understand, couldn't find my way through the chaos cluttering my mind. Jessica … Jessica had killed herself by swallowing two boxes of sleeping pills. Two boxes … of sleeping pills … how was it possible? … Jessica was dead … My wife had committed suicide … The love of my life had gone … In an instant, my world had disintegrated …

I took my head in both hands to stop it falling apart. Impossible to get rid of that flash image in the bathroom, that *corpse* in the bath … *Jessica, come out of there, I beg you* … How could she come out of there? How could she hear me? Her stiffness, her marble-like pallor, her fixed, icy stare were irrevocable, and yet I had run to her, taken her in my arms, shaken her, yelled at her to wake up; my cries whirled around the room, smashed into the walls, drilled into my temples. As a doctor, I knew there wasn't much I could do; as a husband I refused to accept that. Jessica was merely a heap of flesh, a still life, but I'd laid her down on the floor and tried all kinds of things to revive her. Finally, exhausted, struck dumb with terror, I had huddled in a corner and looked at her through a kind of two-way mirror. I don't know how long I stayed like that, wild-eyed, prostrate with grief, overwhelmed by the calamity that had struck me.

The police finally left the bathroom, after packing up their equipment. They had taken photographs and collected any clues that might explain the circumstances of my wife's death. The ambulance men were given permission to remove the body. I watched them take Jessica out on a stretcher – Jessica reduced to a common corpse under a white sheet.

A tall man in a dark suit took me aside. He had a round face, white hair at the temples and a large bald patch. With a politeness that verged on obsequiousness, which for some reason irritated me, he asked if he could talk to me in the living room.

'I'm Lieutenant Sturm. I'd like to ask you a few questions. I know now is hardly the best time, but I'm obliged to—'

'No, lieutenant,' I interrupted. 'Now is definitely not the best moment.'

I could barely recognise my own voice, which seemed to reach me through an endless series of filters. I was furious with this policeman, and found his attitude inhuman. How dare he ask me questions when I didn't understand what was happening? What kind of answers did he expect from someone who had just lost his bearings, his faculties, his ability to think? I was in a state of shock, crushed by a storm that was sucking me into some kind of abyss …

There was only one thing I wanted: for my house to be silent again.

The lieutenant came back early the next day, flanked by two inscrutable inspectors I took an immediate dislike to. He introduced them briefly and asked if they could come in. I stood aside to let them pass. Reluctantly. I wasn't up to receiving visitors. I needed to be alone, to close the shutters over my windows, to wall myself up in darkness and pretend I wasn't in. My grief had replaced time, the world, the whole of the universe. I felt so small in its grip, so infinitesimal that a tear would have drowned me. And then there was that incredible tiredness. I felt shattered. I hadn't slept a wink all night. The more that macabre scene in the bathroom had come back to me, the less I could grasp it. It was like a recurring dream, like being chronically seasick. I think I threw up several times. Or maybe I had just felt nauseous a lot. I wasn't sure of anything. Jessica's suicide was a terrifying mystery … The truth was, I didn't want to sleep. Sleep would have been the worst torture. Why sleep? Just to realise, when I woke up, that Jessica was dead? How could I have survived the repeated shock of that brutal awakening? … No, the one thing I mustn't do was sleep … When the ambulance and the police cars had left the night before, I had switched off the lights and locked the shutters, then retreated to a corner of my room and kept sleep at bay until morning, conscious that no ray of sunlight would help me to see clearly in my grief.

I led the three police officers into the living room. They sat down on the sofa. I remained standing, not sure exactly what to do. The lieutenant pointed to an armchair and waited for me to sit in it before asking me if Jessica had any reason to take her own life. He had asked me the question almost reluctantly. I stared at him in bewilderment. After turning the question over and over in my head, I replied that I found it hard to believe that Jessica was dead, that I was still expecting her to wake up. The lieutenant nodded politely, and asked me the same question again as if my words were irrelevant and he wanted me to keep strictly to the facts, the reasons that might have led a person like Jessica to kill herself. From his way of looking at me, I realised that he was merely suggesting a preliminary hypothesis before moving on to another, more carefully thought-out one, because as far as he was concerned, there was nothing for the moment to prove that it was suicide. Becoming aware of his lack of tact, he straightened his tie and asked me straight out how Jessica had been lately. I replied that she had been nervous, evasive, secretive, but that never for a moment would I have thought her capable of such a desperate act. The lieutenant didn't appear satisfied with my answer: clearly, it didn't get him very far. After smoothing the ridge of his nose, he passed his hand over his bald spot, without taking his eyes off me, and asked me if my wife had left a note …

'A note?'

'Or maybe a recording,' he said, 'something like that.'

'I haven't checked,' I said.

The lieutenant wanted to know if my wife and I had been going through a 'rough patch'. He turned his eyes away as he asked the question. I assured him that Jessica and I had got on really well and never quarrelled. I began shaking, embarrassed at having to talk to strangers about my private life. Routine as this questioning was, there was a kind of shamelessness about it that I couldn't stand. It was as if the three policemen suspected me and were trying to catch me out. Their cold, unwavering pedantry exasperated me. The lieutenant scribbled some notes in a little book, then raised his fist to his mouth, cleared his throat and told me that according to the pathologist, my wife's death had occurred between 10 a.m. and 2 p.m. He asked me to tell them about my movements the day before. I told him I had left the house at 8.30 so as to be at the surgery by 9.15, that I had seen patients until 1, that I had gone out to have lunch before going back to work ... All at once, I was afraid. What if they asked me what I'd been doing between 1 and 3.30? How could I prove that I had been sitting alone on a bench in the park, without any convincing witnesses, while my patients sat twiddling their thumbs in the waiting room of my surgery?

The two inspectors were taking down my statement with false detachment, insensitive to the turmoil they were causing. I hated them for hounding me like this, for ignoring my grief and continuing to bombard me with questions, shamelessly rummaging in every nook and cranny of my married life. I was waiting stoically for them to leave, to get out of my sight. At the end of the interview, the lieutenant put his notebook away in the inside pocket of his trench coat and asked if he could help me in any way. I didn't answer him. He nodded and handed me his card, pointing out his telephone number in case I remembered any detail that might be of use to him.

Once the policemen had left, I took my head in both hands and tried to think about nothing.

Emma phoned to tell me that my patients were getting impatient. I asked her to apologise to them for me and to cancel all my appointments in the coming days. She asked if anything was wrong.

'Jessica's dead,' I said in a toneless voice.

'My God!' she exclaimed.

She was silent for a long while at the other end of the line, then hung up.

I stared at the receiver in my hand, not knowing what to do with it.

A few neighbours came round to see me. The previous night's flurry of activity hadn't escaped them. The arrival of the ambulance and the police cars with their flashing lights must have kept them awake. Now it was daylight, they wanted to find out what was going on.

About midday, alerted by Emma, Hans Makkenroth came to see me. He was deeply shocked by what had happened. 'What a tragedy!' he said, putting his arms around me.

We sat at the table in the kitchen and listened to the rain drumming on the window pane. Without saying a word. Without moving.

After a while, Emma arrived. She was appropriately dressed in a black tailored suit. It was clear from her red eyes that she had been crying. She was kind enough not to overburden me with her condolences, which might have proved awkward. Instead, she busied herself fetching us something to drink.

By the time night fell, the three of us were so lost in our own thoughts that it hadn't occurred to any of us to switch the light on in the room. We hadn't eaten anything all day, and our glasses were still full. I told Emma she should go home.

'My children are with my mother,' she said. 'I can stay.'

'It really isn't necessary.'

'Are you sure you don't need me?'

'I'll be all right, Emma.'

Before leaving, she reminded me that I had her mobile number and that I could call her whenever I liked. I promised her I would.

Then I turned to Hans.

'I'm not leaving you alone,' he hastened to announce in a commanding tone.

He called Toni and ordered dinner for us.

It was drizzling in the cemetery, and the greyness made the place all the more melancholy. The ceremony took place on a square of lawn demarcated by stony paths. The friends who had come to see Jessica to her last resting place huddled together beside the brown grave, some carrying umbrellas, others in raincoats. Jessica's father, Wolfgang Brodersen, stared intently at the coffin in which his daughter lay. He had arrived that morning from Berlin and had preferred to get in touch with the undertakers rather than contact me. From the way he was keeping his distance and saying nothing, I realised that he was angry with me. We had never been especially friendly. A former soldier, trained to be stoic, he spoke little and kept his opinions to himself. He had hesitated for a long time before consenting to Jessica marrying me, and hadn't stayed long at our wedding. I couldn't remember seeing him at the reception. A widower, solitary and stubborn, he avoided weddings and parties at all costs. On the rare occasions when Jessica and I had been in Berlin, he had given the impression that we were in his way. I had no idea why he was so hostile to me. Maybe that was how military men were: forced to live far from home, they developed a hard shell that made them resistant to the joys of family life. Or maybe, having no one else since his wife's death, he had felt possessive towards Jessica and hadn't looked kindly on the idea of someone taking his only remaining relative from him. I admit I hadn't blamed him or looked for excuses. Not that it would have changed much in our relationship. It was a pity, that was all. He loved Jessica. Although he hated showing his feelings, I just had to see him looking at his daughter to know how much he loved her. And Jessica loved him. In spite of her father's excessive reserve, she had no qualms about running to him and flinging her arms around him every time she saw him. He would stand there for a moment, his arms rigid at his sides, in the grip of an inner struggle, before returning her embrace.

Among the friends present at the funeral was Hans Makkenroth. From time to time, he would give me a sign of his support. Behind him, Emma shivered under her umbrella, the tip of her nose red with cold. Beside her, Toni was almost invisible behind the collar of his coat. To his right, Claudia Reinhardt, a colleague of Jessica's, kept wiping her tear-stained eyes with a tissue. She had been great friends with my wife and spent more time at our house than with her family. Claudia was a lively, funny girl. It was she who had urged Jessica to join a gym, and they had gone to aerobics classes together. She gave me a sad little smile, to which I responded with a slight nod, then plunged her nose back in her tissue and didn't look up again.

After the ceremony, people dispersed. Doors started slamming, and one after the other, the cars left the cemetery. I was aware only of the crunching of tyres on the gravel. When silence had returned, Hans Makkenroth came to me and said in a low voice, 'It's over, Kurt. Let's go.'

'What's over?' I said.

'What started one day.'

'Do you think it's as simple as that?'

'Nothing's simple in life, Kurt, but we have to make do.'

I threw a last glance at the grave. 'You may be right, Hans, but that doesn't tell us how to make do.'

'Time will take care of that.'

'I don't believe you …'

Hans raised his hands in surrender. The fact was, he had no answer for that, and realised that saying the wrong thing would only make things worse. He was sorry he hadn't found the words to comfort me, and was angry at himself for not keeping quiet.

Emma, Claudia and a few of my neighbours had come back to the house. Much to my surprise, my father-in-law, Wolfgang Brodersen, was there too, sitting slumped on a chair near the balcony. I had been thinking he had already left for Berlin. He stood up, put his glass down on a chest of drawers and waited for me to approach him before he opened the French window and suggested I follow him onto the balcony. He began by looking up at the coppery sky, as if trying to get his thoughts into some kind of order, then turned his piercing eyes on me and let me have it: 'How could you have allowed her to get into such a state of despair?'

'I can assure you I didn't see it coming.'

'Precisely,' he said, 'precisely ... You should have been paying attention. If your mind hadn't been elsewhere, you might have been able to avoid this tragedy. There are signs we can't ignore. People don't kill themselves on a whim. Jessica was a strong character. She wouldn't have given in to some stupid little problem. She was my daughter. I knew her better than anyone. She was a fighter, she always got back on her feet ... What could have driven her to such an absurd, violent end?'

'I don't know.'

'That's not the answer I expected from a husband. You were the person who was closest to her. She must have given you some kind of warning. Of course, she wasn't the kind of girl who would panic over just anything, but she was intelligent enough to confide in her husband. If you didn't see it coming, it was because Jessica was suffering in silence. You had your mind on other things, I assume, and that's what led her to such a monstrous act.'

'How can you possibly know that?' I said, outraged at his insinuations.

'I was married too. My wife didn't need to draw me a picture.'

'That's enough!' I interrupted. 'Jessica was my wife and I loved her more than anything in the world. I understand your grief, I feel it just as much as you do. I don't know what Jessica was hiding from me. I don't know what was wrong with her. Not a minute goes by when I don't ask myself why she did what she did.'

Wolfgang looked at me in silence. On the balcony, his breathing replaced the murmur of the rain. He unclenched his fist and stood there facing me, his eyes fixed on mine. 'May I ask you an indiscreet question?'

'You might as well. Go ahead.'

'Will you answer me honestly, man to man?'

'I have no reason to lie to you.'

He took a deep breath. 'Were you cheating on Jessica?'

The bluntness of his question came like a slap in the face. But what broke my heart was the tone in which he voiced his suspicions: it was thick with such suffering, such helplessness, such fear that I felt sorry for him. The Wolfgang I had known, the rock-solid ex-soldier, was crumbling before my very eyes, right there on the balcony, which had suddenly taken on the dimensions of a battlefield. I was certain that if I'd touched him with my finger it would have gone right through him.

I waited for him to recover a little of his composure and said, 'No ... I wasn't cheating on Jessica. I had no reason to look elsewhere for what I had within reach.'

His eyes grew moist. He leant on the rail and struggled to hold back his tears. He took a deep breath, nodded and said in a hoarse voice, 'Thank you.'

He went back into the living room and out through the hallway. From the balcony, I saw him leave the house and walk back along the street, heedless of the rain. He was dragging his feet, as if weighed down with a heavy burden. It was the first time I had seen him defeated: in spite of his age – seventy-five – he had always made it a

31

point of honour to stand erect, and to give the impression in all circumstances that he could withstand any tragedy, any hurricane.

My neighbours and colleagues started to take their leave. Someone whispered, 'I'm with you all the way, doctor.' It was kind of him, but I didn't believe it. What did he know of my solitude? My grief was too personal to be shared; it made me insensitive to all such expressions of sympathy, all those customary phrases and actions that bear no relation to the situation at hand. Grief is a parallel universe, a horrible world where the sweetest words, the noblest gestures seem absurd, inappropriate, clumsy, stupid. I was irritated by those sympathetic little taps on the shoulder which reverberated inside me like hammer blows. *I'm with you all the way, doctor* ... For how long? Once my guests were gone, my house would close over me like a fist; I would hold out my hand, searching for support, for a shoulder to lean on, and find nothing but empty air.

Evening arrived. In the darkening living room, only Hans, Emma, Claudia and I remained. The two women finished collecting the glasses and paper plates left scattered by the guests. They tidied the living room, put away the dishes and took out the bins, while I walked from room to room without knowing why. Wolfgang's words throbbed in my temples ... *Were you cheating on Jessica?* ... *Were you cheating on Jessica?* ... Now that Jessica was gone, would our paths ever cross again? Would we end up making peace? Were we actually at war? I had the feeling I'd failed in my duty as a son-in-law, that I'd missed an

opportunity for a possible reconciliation with Wolfgang …
I tried to get a grip. What was I inflicting on myself now?
Why add an illusory guilt to my widower's grief? Even
if I had fallen short in my behaviour towards Wolfgang,
there were surely more important things to worry about
while I was in mourning.

I went back on the balcony. I needed fresh air. The
cold lashed my face. I leant over the rail and gazed at the
streams of water in the gutters. Every now and again, a
car passed. Watching it move away, I had the impression it
was taking a little of my soul with it.

Claudia joined me, a glass in her hand. 'Drink this,' she
said. 'It'll buck you up.'

I took the glass and lifted it to my lips. The first sip felt
like a trail of lava, the second shook me from head to toe.

'You should eat something,' Claudia said. 'You haven't
touched a thing since we got back from the cemetery. I'm
amazed you're still standing.'

'I'm walking on my head.'

'I can imagine.'

'Can you?'

She placed her hand on mine, a gesture that made me
feel ill at ease. 'I'm really sorry, Kurt. I haven't had a wink
of sleep in the last few nights.'

'I'm only just starting to wake up. And I don't
understand what I see around me.'

She strengthened her grip on my fingers. 'You know
you can count on me, Kurt.'

'I don't doubt that. Thank you. You were great with the
guests.'

'It's the least I could do.' She took her hand away,
leant back against the rail, and sighed. 'You think you're

prepared for anything, and when it happens, you realise how wrong you were.'

'That's life.'

'I still can't believe that Jessica could have done something like that. Over a promotion … Just imagine! Over a job … A job she would have got one day anyway.'

An electric shock couldn't have given me a greater jolt … Promotion? … Job? … What was she talking about? Claudia's choked voice immediately sobered me up.

'What job? What's all this about a promotion?'

Claudia looked at me in astonishment. 'Didn't she tell you?'

'Tell me what?'

'Oh, my God, I thought you knew.'

'Please just tell me.'

Claudia was completely thrown. She knew she had gone too far to pull back. She looked around in panic, as if searching for support. I wouldn't let her avoid my gaze; I needed an explanation. I grabbed her by the shoulders and shook her angrily. I knew I was hurting her, but I wouldn't let go.

'For heaven's sake, tell me.'

She said, in a tone that seemed to emanate from somewhere deep inside, 'The board of directors had promised her she'd be put in charge of external relations. Jessica had been working towards the position for two years. She wanted it more than anything. And she really deserved it. Our CEO even name-checked her during an EGM. Jessica was the kingpin of the company. She went well beyond the call of duty. She was the one who'd negotiated the biggest contracts in the last few years, with great success. All our colleagues agreed on how efficient she was … I thought you knew all about this.'

'Please go on.'

'Three months ago, our marketing director, Franz Hölter, also started campaigning to be head of external relations. He's a careerist, ambitious, willing to go to any lengths to leapfrog his way to the front. He knew Jessica had a head start on him, and he did everything he could to catch up with her. He even torpedoed a couple of projects to discredit her. It was like a war to the death. At first, Jessica had no problem handling the competition. She knew her subject. But Franz had managed to win over the CEO and was starting to gain ground.'

'So that's why Jessica wasn't herself these last few weeks?'

'That's right. She was very worried. Franz did whatever he wanted. A real shark operating in dirty waters. He put every obstacle he could in her way. It's no surprise Jessica ended up cracking under the strain. Her final negotiation, with a Chinese group, broke down because of a file that had supposedly disappeared. The board were furious. And Jessica realised she had made a fatal mistake. A week ago, the verdict was delivered, and Franz was appointed to the position she'd wanted so much. When I went to comfort Jessica, I found her sitting crushed in her office. The blood had completely drained from her face. She told me to leave her alone and went out to get some air. It was about nine in the morning. She didn't come back. I tried to reach her on her mobile, but all I got was her answering machine … My God! … It's so unfair.'

The last bastion keeping me a tiny bit sane had fallen.

I felt a tightness in my throat, and couldn't utter a syllable. Torn between indignation and anger, incredulous and dazed, I didn't know which way to turn. Jessica had taken her own life because her board of directors hadn't promoted her! I found it inconceivable, inexcusable. It was as if Jessica had just killed herself for the second time.

My house became a funeral urn filled with ashes. All my hopes, all my certainties had gone up in smoke.

Time seemed to have stopped. Everything around me was clogged, unable to move. I would get up in the morning, botch my day's work and return home in the evening as if to a labyrinth, trying to shake off the ghosts of those no longer with me. I didn't even feel the need to switch the lights on. What good was a lamp against the shadows that were blinding me?

At the surgery, I found it hard to concentrate on my work. How many times did I prescribe inappropriate treatments before realising, or before being picked up on it by my patients? Emma saw that things couldn't go on like this ... I was forced to entrust my surgery to Dr Regina Hölm, my usual replacement when I was on holiday. I went home to pack my bags. It had occurred to me that spending some time in the country, where I had a second home, would allow me to get back on my feet. I hadn't gone fifty kilometres before I did a U-turn and drove back to Frankfurt. No, I wouldn't have the strength to be alone in that little stone house perched at the top of a verdant hill. It had been our nest, Jessica's and mine, our retreat when we wanted to get away from the city's pollution and noise, its constraints and anxieties. We would go there for weekends, to recharge our batteries and make love with the passion of teenagers. It was a lovely spot, camouflaged by tall trees, where only the odd hiker ventured and where the wind singing in the leaves would dispel our worries. There was a fireplace in the living room, and a sofa on which we would lie in each other's arms, blissfully happy, and listen to the wood crackling in the hearth. No, I couldn't go there and trample on so many wonderful memories.

For two days, I shut myself up in my house in Frankfurt, with the blinds down, the lights off and the phone off the hook. I didn't open the door to anybody. I kept asking myself how a beautiful, much-loved woman with a fabulous career ahead of her could disregard all the chances she had and take her own life ... *If your mind hadn't been elsewhere, you might have been able to avoid this tragedy*, Wolfgang had said. His reproaches reversed the roles, swapped the perpetrator and the victim, confused the crime and the punishment. Had Jessica given me a sign I hadn't recognised? Could I have changed the course of events if I had been more vigilant?

One night, in pouring rain, I went out and wandered the streets. I walked past red lights blinking at the intersections, little parks, neon signs, advertising hoardings appearing and disappearing in the darkness, empty benches. The noise of my footsteps preceded me. Tired of walking, soaked to the bone, I stopped on the banks of the Main and gazed down at the shimmering reflections of the street lamps on the river. And there too, try as I might to forget, to shake off my pain, the image of Jessica lying lifeless in the bathtub emerged from the waves and shattered any respite I'd hoped to grant myself.

I went back home, shivering and exhausted, and stood

by the window, a blanket around my shoulders, waiting for day to dawn. And dawn it did, draped in white, as if it were merely the ghost of night.

'You have to get a grip on yourself,' Hans Makkenroth said, 'and fast.'

He had been round several times. When I refused to open the door, he had threatened to call the police. The state in which he found me shocked him. He ran to the phone to call an ambulance, but I persuaded him not to. Cursing, he pushed me into the bathroom. What I saw in the mirror terrified me: I looked like a zombie.

Hans dragged me back to the living room and forced me to listen to him. 'When I lost Paula, I thought I was finished. She'd been everything to me. All my joys I owed to her. She was my pride, my glory, my happiness. I'd have given anything for one more year, one more month, one more day with her. But there are things we can't negotiate, Kurt. Paula's gone, just as every day thousands of people who are loved or hated die. That's how life is. All kinds of things happen, we may be stricken with grief, we may be bankrupt, but the sun still rises in the morning and nothing can stop night from falling ... Paula has been dead for five years and thirty-two weeks, and every morning when I wake up, I expect to find her lying beside me. Then I realise that I'm alone in my bed. So I throw off the sheets and go about my daily business.'

I don't know if it was Hans's words or the vibrations of his voice that reached down into the depths of my being, but all at once my shoulders sagged and tears ran down my cheeks. I couldn't remember having cried since I was a small child. Curiously, I wasn't ashamed of my weakness. My sobs seemed to clear away the blackness that had been contaminating my soul like a poisonous, putrid ink.

'That's it,' Hans said encouragingly.

He forced me to take a bath, shave, and change my clothes. Then he bundled me into his car and took me to a little restaurant just outside the city. He told me that he had come back to Germany to settle some issues with the Chamber of Commerce and launch a project that meant a lot to him. This would take two or three weeks, after which he would sail to the Comoros, where he was planning to equip a hospital for a charitable organisation he belonged to.

'Why not come with me? My yacht is waiting for me in a harbour in Cyprus. We'll fly to Nicosia then set off for the Gulf of Aden ...'

'I can't, Hans.'

'What's stopping you? The sea's wonderful therapy.'

'Please, don't insist. I'm not going anywhere ...'

2
Blackmoon

1

Hans hadn't been exaggerating. Out at sea, stripped of their symbolism, all points of reference were reduced, so that each thing found its true significance. I certainly found mine: I was merely a single drop among a billion tons of water. Everything I had thought I was or represented proved to have no substance. Wasn't I like the wavelets born from the backwash and then merging with it, an illusion that emerges out of nothing and falls back into it without leaving a trace?

I thought about my patient, Frau Biribauer. *What's death like?* ... If it was like the sea, then everything might be forgiven. Then I thought about Jessica, and caught myself smiling.

I felt a little better, washed clean of my wounds. Like getting out of the bath after a day filled with confrontations. My grief was allowing me a semblance of respite; there was no space for it in the kingdom of shipwrecks, where sorrows drowned without arousing any dismay.

We had been travelling for two weeks, the wind in our sails, on board a twelve-metre boat. We had left Cyprus at dawn, in glorious weather, and crossed the lustral waters of the Mediterranean, sometimes pursued by excited seagulls, sometimes escorted by pods of dolphins. Every day was a new blessing, and when night removed us from the chaos of the world, I closed my eyes and took a deep breath of the odours emanating from the depths like so many reminiscences flooding back from the dawn of time. I felt as if I had regained my inner peace.

I loved to perch on the side of the boat and peer at the horizon. It was something I never tired of. It would free me of my anxieties, as if I were being reborn: a forceps birth of course, but a determined one. The sea tore my grief apart like waves hitting a reef. Of course, when the water receded, rocks would emerge amid the foam, but I could deal with that. I clung to the rigging of the foresail and offered my chest to the wind. I sometimes spent hours on end without thinking of anything specific. The lapping of the waves against the hull cradled my soul. Occasionally, a passenger liner would pass in the distance, and I would follow it with my eyes until it had faded into the sea spray; occasionally, too, through a curtain of mist, I would glimpse a surreptitious shore – was it the Farasan Islands, or the Dahlak Archipelago, or else a mirage? What did it matter? The only thing that mattered was the emotion it aroused.

Hans no longer interrupted me. Whenever he joined me on deck and found me in a kind of ecstatic communion with the naked sky and the sea, he would back away.

Two weeks spent gliding over the calm waters. Only once had a storm whipped the midday breeze into a frenzy, after which a heavy swell had slowed us down; the next day, the Mediterranean had unrolled before us a mother-of-pearl carpet on which the first glints of daylight sparkled. Towards evening, shimmering streaks lashed the surface of the water and, with the sunset and its fires, we witnessed a breathtaking spectacle in which red and black fused in a fresco worthy of the northern lights. To crown our wonder, dolphins leapt from the waves, as rapid as torpedoes, proud of their perfect fuselage that propelled them into the air like fleeting gleams of crystal. At times, fascinated by their lavish choreography of synchronisation and magic, I had the impression my pulse was adjusting its rhythm to the waves that they unleashed.

Intoxicated by nature's generosity, I joined Hans in the recess that served as a dining room. Above a leather sofa set in glistening wood hung a portrait of Paula. I supposed there were others on the boat ... How did he manage to live with a ghost and keep a cool head? ... Hans smiled at me as if he had read my thoughts. He pushed his glasses back up onto his forehead and shifted on his seat, pleased to have company at last. I felt embarrassed to have made him wary of what he said to me. I sensed that he turned every word over in his mind before risking it out loud, for fear of hitting my weak spot, convinced that the mere mention of Jessica's name might plunge me back into my unhappiness, which wasn't necessarily the case.

'Land in sight?' he asked.

'I haven't checked,' I said.

'Come and sit down ... How about a drink before dinner?'

'I'm already drunk on space and wind.'

'You should put a hat on. It isn't sensible to stay bare-headed in the sun for too long.'

'The wind blew mine away yesterday morning.'

'I have others, if you like.'

'No, thanks, don't worry about me. I'm fine, honestly.'

'Happy to hear you say so.'

Running out of ideas, he drummed on the table. He must have exhausted his favourite subjects. Since we had left Cyprus, every evening after dinner, he had told me about his humanitarian expeditions. He knew everything there was to know about the primitive tribes of the Amazon. He had made it his life's work to fight on behalf of these dispossessed and defenceless populations, chased from their lands by excessive deforestation and unregulated poaching, and forced to wander the jungle in search of shelter from which they would be driven again and again until they perished, uprooted and destitute. To illustrate his stories, he would show me photographs he had taken at the 'scene of the crime'. There he was, in shirt and shorts, posing with naked women and children outside straw huts; holding an old shaman in his arms; pointing at a giant anaconda that had died trying to swallow a crocodile; sharing an ancient peace pipe with a tribal chief who looked like a totem; standing in the path of monstrous machines that were devastating a clearing; protesting against local administrators ... Hans travelled relentlessly. Since Paula's death, he had delegated the running of his businesses to his two sons and stalked human misery all over the world. As he put it, maturity lay in sharing, because the true vocation of man was to be useful.

Tao, the cook, had made us a particularly delicious Oriental meal. He served us at eight on the dot and immediately withdrew. He was a short man in his fifties, with a complexion like overripe quince. Close-cropped jade-black hair crowned his ascetic face with its high, prominent cheekbones. He was discreet and efficient, always appearing and disappearing noiselessly, always on the lookout for the least sign from his employer. Hans liked him a lot. He had met him five years earlier in a hotel in Manila and had hired him on the spot. Tao was the father of a large family to whom he sent all his earnings. He never talked about his family, never complained about anything, eternally hidden behind a vague smile as calm as his soul. I had barely heard him say a word since we had been on the boat.

After dinner, we went back up on deck. A meagre fog was doing its best to envelop the boat, but its stringy embrace unravelled in the wind and formed a kind of unstable, ghostly vault above our heads. In the bluish sky, intermittently, you could see the stars glittering gently, like dying fireflies. Apart from the lapping of the waves, there was not a sound to be heard. The silence seemed to be one with the darkness.

Hans leant on the capstan and lit his pipe. He gazed at the glow in the bowl of the pipe, from which tiny sparks escaped, and asked me if I had ever swum in international waters.

'Never more than a hundred yards from the beach,' I replied.

'That fear of cramp again?'

'Exactly. It takes hold of me as soon as I go out of my depth.'

'A childhood trauma, I suppose.'

'Not necessarily.'

'What, then?'

'I don't like taking pointless risks.'

He nodded, puffed at his pipe, a distant smile on his lips. 'Living means running risks every day, Kurt.'

'That depends in which direction you're running.'

I didn't care for the turn the conversation had taken. My situation didn't lend itself to existential questions. Hans realised that and pretended to check the rigging, then, after an exaggerated puff at his pipe, said, 'When I was young, I often came here to go deep-sea diving. My father loved it. I remember he would put on his diving suit faster than a sock and throw himself into the water before the instructor. He was such a stolid man usually, inflexible at work and in his private life. But as soon as he smelt the sea, he'd become as excited as a hungry kid at the sight of a chocolate waffle.'

'I can imagine.'

'He put me to shame, he really couldn't keep still. And often, when he dived, the instructor had to go down and force him to come up again. My father was quite capable of following a ray or watching for a moray eel in its hole until he fainted. My mother was always worried sick about him. She wouldn't let him take me to see the corals up close … I get goose pimples just from thinking about it. They were wonderful days … Later, with Paula, I came back here to revive those memories. But Paula wasn't a born diver. She suffered from claustrophobia and couldn't spend more than thirty seconds underwater.'

I don't know why I said to him, 'I envy your gilded childhood. My father never even took my mother and me to the seaside. He hated water, even tap water.'

I had embarrassed him. I was aware of how out of place my words were, and yet, driven by some need to be unpleasant, I hadn't been able to hold them back. Hans stared at the bowl of his pipe, smoothed his well-tended beard with his other hand, pondered for a few seconds, then raised his head.

'It's true, I had a dream childhood, and above all the privilege of knowing my grandfather. He was an exceptional man who'd been a famous playwright in the 1920s. I was twelve years old and, at that age when you get all kinds of ideas in your head, I wanted to be a novelist. One day, when we were walking together in the woods, I asked him how to become a writer. My grandfather pointed to a ruin and said, "You see that stone? How much do you think it weighs? At least a ton, don't you think? Well, it was a dwarf who carried it here on his back from the quarry over there." I told him that was impossible, that it would take at least twenty circus strongmen to shift the stone one centimetre. To which my grandfather replied, "That's pretty much what literature is. Finding a story for each thing and a way to make it interesting ...".'

He stopped to see if I had understood what he was getting at. Hans had always been modest: whenever he wanted to put someone in his place, he preferred subtlety to a full-frontal attack.

Realising that I didn't see the connection, he concluded, 'I didn't become a novelist, Kurt, but I learnt to find a story and a meaning in everything.'

'I don't follow you.'

'It's not me you have to follow, but your own path. The most solid foundation we can find is in each of us. You can lift any stone with any lever as long as you convince yourself that the stone only exists in your head. Because everything happens in here.' And he tapped his temple with his finger.

'What stone are you talking about, Hans?'

'You know perfectly well what I'm referring to.'

At last I understood. I had done everything I could

to avoid the thorniest of subjects, but now I had fallen in head first. Hans had probably been waiting for this opportunity since we had left Cyprus. He had been tactful enough not to provoke it, but he had hoped for it, and now I was offering it to him on a plate. I pretended to peer at the few gaps in the fog and, in order to change the subject, asked, 'Where exactly are we?'

Hans looked at his watch. 'We passed the strait of Bab-el-Mandeb some time ago, and by dawn we should have left the Red Sea for the Gulf of Aden. If you like, we can put in at a little port I know, south of Djibouti. Not just to take on fresh supplies.'

'You're the captain.'

'It's up to you, Kurt. If you don't feel like it, it doesn't matter. We have enough to see us through the next ten days … I love the little fishing ports in this region, and their bazaars filled to the brim with plastic dishes and pointless fake chrome utensils. The people are really nice around here even when they're trying to flog you cheap rubbish at exorbitant prices. They think every tourist is as rich as Croesus and stupid enough to take a rusty old teapot for Aladdin's lamp. You'll see, their spiel is such fun, you almost want to let them relieve you of your last cents just for the hell of it.'

I shook my head. 'To be honest, Hans, I didn't much like it when we put in at Sharm el-Sheikh or at Port Sudan.'

'Why?'

'Too many people and too much noise.'

Hans burst out laughing. 'I see … Your wish is my command: no stopping before the Comoros.'

We chatted for a long time on deck, talking about this and that, steering clear of unpleasant topics. Ever since we had embarked, it was Hans who had led the conversation. I was content to listen to him, interrupting only to encourage him, especially when he got on to seafaring. I knew almost nothing about the subject, couldn't steer or read a compass, let alone find my position on a map. With his encyclopedic knowledge, Hans loved to hold forth about the sea and about ships, from the most ancient to the most state-of-the-art. He was very proud of his boat, which he had decorated himself. Whenever he took the controls, he gave the impression he was taking charge of his own destiny. The first few days, laid low with seasickness, I would spew my guts out over the hawsehole, then collapse on a seat, wrap my arms around the bulwark, and watch Hans through the window of the control room. He would be standing erect like a conqueror, his white beard held high, like an older but wiser Captain Ahab. At first, he had invited me to the helm and explained the workings of the different dials on the control panel, showed me the radio, the radar, the tracking system, the navigation instruments, then, realising that I wasn't taking much of it in, he had stopped 'bothering' me. My mind was elsewhere and his teaching bored me. I preferred to spend most of my time scanning the horizon and listening to the sails flapping in the wind.

Although we avoided mentioning Jessica, Paula's name came up again and again. Hans spoke about her as if he had left her early that morning and was sure he would go home to her that night. I could tell he missed her, but he had the gift of managing things so that she remained omnipresent in his heart and mind.

'It's starting to get chilly,' I said, energetically rubbing my arms.

He nodded. 'One last drink?' he suggested.

'I don't think so.'

I took a shower before going to bed. As on the previous nights, I planned to switch off the lights and stare at the darkness for an hour or two. I had started to read Musil on the plane taking us to Nicosia. That night, I realised that I was still on the first chapter. Incapable of concentrating on the text, I started again from the beginning. Like the night before, and the nights before that, I put on a little music, the same piece of Wagner, then, in the middle of a sentence or a metaphor, the book faded away and I found my mind wandering. And there, in the muffled silence of my mahogany-lined cabin, amid the platinum joints and the paintings on the walls, Jessica's ghost caught up with me. I closed my eyes to dismiss it, but in vain. What I dreaded more than anything was waking up – the first thing that would come into my mind was Jessica's death – every time I woke up I would experience the exact same emotions I had felt in that bathroom where the love of my life had slipped away from me. It was terrible. Would I ever get over it? … I wondered above all how I managed to get up, shower, shave, drink my coffee and go back up on deck to see the sea replace time … Day being merely a respite, night would find me in bed again and would spread its blackness into my thoughts and whisper in my ear, just before I drifted off, asking if I was ready or not to face the moment of waking that stood on guard, waiting for morning.

I took a sleeping pill.

As I did every night.

*

I was woken by the noise of something falling. The pill I'd taken had dulled my senses, and I wasn't sure where I was. I looked for my watch, couldn't find it, consulted the one built into the bedside table: 4.27. Someone was yelling at Hans in the next room. Suddenly, the door of my room was flung open, and a torch was shone right in my face. I didn't have time to react before a shadowy figure rushed at me and placed something metallic against my temple. A second figure came into the room, searched for the light switch and turned it on. The ceiling light revealed two excited black men. The first was in his thirties, solidly built with shaven head and shoulders like a weightlifter's, a brute naked from the waist up, with amulets around his arms and venom in his eyes, screaming orders at me in an unknown language. The other intruder was a slender teenager, with slashes on his face, and eyes that shone like a drug addict's. He was pointing some kind of firearm at me, maybe a sawn-off shotgun or a home-made carbine.

The older man was a real giant and too strong for me to put up any resistance. He tore me from my bed and threw me against a wall. I was no sooner on my feet than I received a blow with a rifle butt in my stomach which bent me double. The second intruder grabbed me by the hair and forced me to kneel. His blood-red eyes travelled over my body like two man-eating ants. I had never met anyone like these two in my life. The younger man seemed to be waiting for an excuse, any excuse, to shoot me dead ... The giant rummaged in the drawers, turned the mattress over to see what was underneath, and took down the paintings in search of a hidden safe. Whenever he came across anything interesting – my watch, my sleeping pills, my wallet, my mobile phone, my belt, my sunglasses, my book – he threw it into a small, dirt-stained jute sack. The search over, he came back to me, looked into my eyes in the hope of detecting some detail that might have escaped him, lifted my chin with the tip of his Kalashnikov and yelled something at me in his language. He repeated the same question three times, in a guttural voice that made the veins on his neck throb. Not getting any answer, he hit me and pushed me out into the corridor.

In the control room, four armed men stood with guns aimed at Hans and Tao. They were all yelling at once. A fifth barred the stairway that led up on deck, moving the blade of a sabre back and forth across the palm of his hand, as sinister as an executioner getting ready to behead his victim. There was an unhealthy gleam in his eyes, and his fixed grin chilled my blood. Puny-looking, with a bony face and unusually long arms, he gave the impression of not being entirely of sound mind, especially with the grotesque pair of glasses without lenses he was wearing so casually.

Our attackers were young, some barely out of puberty, but they seemed to know exactly what they were doing. After lots of yelling and bursts of spittle, they ordered us to put our hands in the air. Hans, who had only had time to put on a pair of trousers and one sock, tried to calm them down, and was ordered to shut up and keep still.

'No other passengers?' a tall, thin man with bronzed skin asked the younger of the two men who had come to get me.

'No, chief.'

The chief turned and looked at me, lingering over my underpants, my bare legs. With his revolver, he shoved me against the wall. My Adam's apple scraped my throat. I found it hard not to close my eyes, expecting a gunshot at any moment. I was seized with terror, and I clenched my fists to push it back.

'Are you the pilot?' he asked me in English.

'No, I am,' Hans said. 'What do you want with us?'

The chief laughed, revealing a gold tooth, and without taking his eyes off me retorted, 'These damned whites! They always need everything spelt out for them.' He went up to Hans and looked him up and down. 'Is this your boat or did you hire it?'

'It's my boat.'

'Great! ... French, American, British?'

'German.'

'Are you in business or some kind of scam?'

'They're spies,' the giant with the amulets said.

'That's not true,' Hans said. 'My friend's a doctor. And I'm in humanitarian aid. I'm supposed to be equipping a hospital in the Comoros ...'

'How touching,' the chief said ironically, turning to Tao. 'And the chink?'

'He's Filipino.'

'The skivvy, I assume. He cleans, does the cooking, wipes your arse, attends to your every need ... How much would a Filipino cook fetch on the market, Joma?'

'You probably couldn't give him away,' the giant said.

'In other words, a bad investment,' the chief said, walking around Tao.

Tao did not flinch. He held himself erect, his face inscrutable, revealing nothing of what he was feeling.

'Sorry,' the chief said, 'I'm going to have to dispense with your services. I hope you can swim.'

Immediately, the giant with the amulets took Tao by the waist. Hans tried to intervene, but a blow with a rifle butt knocked him to the floor. Tao didn't struggle. He didn't understand what was happening. His small body was engulfed by the black giant. I stood there petrified, in a daze, unable to react. I watched the giant take Tao up on deck. Not a muscle responded.

'Kurt, don't let him do it!' Hans screamed at me from the floor.

His cries brought me to my senses. I rushed to the stairs, swept aside the boy with the sabre. There was a kind of flash inside me, followed by blackness …

Water was thrown over me. I emerged from a fog. There was blood on my vest, my boxer shorts and my thigh. I lifted my fingers to my temple: I was the one who was bleeding.

The giant with the amulets put the bucket down on the wooden floor and dug his shoe into my side. 'This isn't a hotel.'

The chief crouched beside me. He was young, in his early thirties, quite good-looking, with fine features and a straight nose. He wore his fatigues like a banker wearing a suit, with a self-assurance that was meant to be as seductive as it was intimidating. From his affected airs and graces, it was clear he was a product of the local middle class, someone who'd had a future at the head of his community but had turned bad.

Holding our passports in one hand, he waited for me to come back to my senses and then said, 'Excuse our methods, doctor. We work in the traditional way around here. With the means at our disposal.'

I looked for Hans. He was behind me, in a corner of the control room. His eye had disappeared beneath a purplish swelling.

'Let me explain the situation,' the chief said in perfect English. 'The ball is in our court, but the rules of the game belong to you and your friend. You behave yourselves and we'll treat you well. You try to be smart, and I can't guarantee anything.'

'Why did you throw Tao in the sea?' Hans screamed, beside himself.

'You mean the chink? That was a question of logistics.'

'You killed a man, for heaven's sake!'

'People die every day. That's never stopped God from sleeping soundly.'

Hans was disgusted by the chief's words. His face was trembling with anger and his breathing was laboured. He bit his lip to restrain himself.

'Did I say something stupid?' the chief asked, cynically.

'Are you trying to make me believe you don't have any regret, any remorse?' Hans cried, his voice throbbing with indignation.

The chief gave a toneless laugh and looked at Hans as if seeing him for the first time. After a silence, he opened his arms wide in a theatrical gesture and said, 'To feel regret or remorse, you need to have a conscience. And I don't have one.'

Hans was so disgusted, he didn't say another word.

'What are you going to do with us?' I asked.

The chief pursed his lips and thought over my question. 'I'll be frank with you,' he said. 'I don't really care if you live or die. It's entirely up to you if you return home safe and sound or end up in a ditch with a bullet in your head … But from now on, you're my prisoners. What you own belongs to me, apart from your family photographs. You can already say goodbye to your boat. The spoils of war.'

'It's my boat,' Hans protested. 'I'm not at war with anyone. I'm just passing through. You have no right …'

'There are no rights here, Mr Makkenroth. And there's only one law: the law of the gun. And tonight the guns are on my side.'

'What are you going to do with my boat? Sell it off cheap? Strip it?'

'The real question is: what are we going to do with you? Am I to understand that you're more concerned about what happens to your boat than to you? … You're my hostages, my meal ticket. I don't care about the Geneva Convention or UN resolutions, I'll treat you as I see fit. From now on, I'm your god. Your fate is closely linked to my moods, so if I were you I'd try to keep on the right side of me.'

We were forced to get dressed, our wrists were tied, and we were shut up in the room that Tao had occupied, down in the hold. The boy with the lensless glasses came and took up position in the doorway. He leant one shoulder against the door frame, tilted his head to one side and began watching us in a strange way. The stupid grin on his face sent a chill down my spine.

'Are you all right?' Hans asked me.

'I think so. How about you?'

'I'll be OK … Do you realise? They threw Tao overboard!'

'Do you think he'll make it?'

'He can't swim.'

'They have us at their mercy. They didn't need to do that.'

'It's their way of showing they're in control. People's mindset is different in this part of the world. The life of a man and the life of a mosquito are the same to them. These people are alive now, but they come from another time.'

The guard kept moving his greyish tongue over his lips. The stillness of his eyes accentuated my sense of unease.

'Where did they spring from?'

Hans shrugged. 'I don't know. I heard an engine coming closer. I thought it was the coastguard at first, but they aren't allowed to operate in international waters. Tao came and told me that a felucca was heading straight for us. Something hit the hull. Within a fraction of a second, these maniacs were coming on board. I couldn't do a thing.'

'Who are they?'

'No idea. This area's full of all kinds of predators: rebels, mercenaries, pirates, terrorists, smugglers, arms dealers. But I never imagined they were capable of venturing so far from their bases. I've done this stretch of water twice before, the last time only six months ago, and had no trouble ...'

He paused for breath. When he spoke again, his voice was heavier.

'I'm sorry, Kurt. You have no idea how sorry I am to have got you mixed up in all this after what you've been through.'

'It's not your fault, Hans. It's the way of things: it never rains but it pours.'

'I really am sorry.'

'Shhhh!' said our guard in a whistling voice, raising his finger to his lips.

Again, his glassy eyes sent a shiver through me.

Hans and I were flung unceremoniously in the felucca, to be guarded by the giant with the amulets and three of his associates. The leader and the rest of the gang remained on board the yacht. As our new craft set sail for whatever fate had in store for us, we watched the boat make a series of clumsy manoeuvres before moving away in the opposite direction to ours. Hans had tears in his eyes; I saw the resentment well up in him. When the boat had faded into the darkness, he placed his chin on his bound fists and withdrew into himself.

The felucca pitched on the waves, throwing us from side to side. In the silence of the night, the noise of the engine was like the moans of a dying pachyderm. I began feeling seasick and my migraine was getting worse. I threw up over my knees.

The crossing seemed endless. Far in the distance, the first blood-red marks of dawn sprinkled the horizon. The wind froze my arms and knees. My back felt itchy. I couldn't scratch myself or rub myself against the worm-eaten wood of the boat, from which big splinters as deadly as knives stuck out in places. Every now and again, the giant kicked me in the shin to stop me sleeping. Facing me, the boy with the lensless glasses was watching me constantly, a strange smile on his granite face.

The cries of seagulls … I had dozed off. The sun had risen; the felucca threaded its way through the jagged edges of a reef, glided along a narrow, meandering passage filled with silt, and sailed up the lagoon as far as a tiny, gravelly beach. The giant threw us to the ground. The others pulled the boat out of the water and dragged it into a blind spot, where they covered it with a tarpaulin to camouflage it. We immediately set off on foot. A *thalweg* led us into a creek that we had to go around in order to advance further inland. After an hour's walking, we reached a basin thick with undergrowth, where an armed adolescent stood guard. He was a short boy with stunted legs, his forehead riddled with pustules. He was wearing a dirty pair of trousers and a torn vest. The giant spoke to him in a local language, pointed to a hill and dismissed him. We retraced our steps over several kilometres. From time to time, we glimpsed the sea. I tried hard to memorise the places we were going through because I had only one idea in my head: to seize the first opportunity that presented itself to Hans and me to escape … Poor Hans! He limped in front, his shoulders sagging, his face distorted by his swollen eye. A trail of blood stuck his shirt to his back. He kept moving forward like a sleepwalker, his chin on his chest.

We reached a cave oozing with damp and filthy with excrement and the traces of meals. It was a dark, fetid hole, its uneven roof covered with bats' nests, its bumpy floor strewn with trails of wax as if thousands of candles had melted on it. There were rusty iron rings on the walls, some still with age-old chains through them, their joints eaten away by time and sea salt. Here and there, leftover food had blackened in the midst of crushed cans, tattered cloths and assorted rubbish. A sickly-sweet odour emanated from the corners of the cave, depleting the air. Disturbed by our arrival, flies rose in a buzzing fury and began attacking us in close-packed contingents.

The giant ordered his men to chain us. Too exhausted to do anything, Hans let them. He could barely stand. I tried to resist the arms crushing me; some kind of handcuff rapidly closed over my wrists and I was thrown to the ground.

'This is your hotel now,' the giant announced.

'You can't leave us here,' I protested.

'Why not?'

'My friend is hurt. This place is unhealthy and may make him worse. Can't you put us somewhere else?'

'Yes. I can tie you to a tree, or plant you in the sand, but you won't find a better place to see Africa from up close. That's what brings you here, isn't it? Exoticism, wild spaces, nostalgia for lost empires ...'

'We aren't tourists.'

'Of course not. In Africa, there are no tourists, only voyeurs.'

He ordered his men to follow him outside. Immediately, the flies took possession of the place again; their buzzing made the stench of the cave even more oppressive. I was nauseous, but there was nothing left in my empty belly to spew up. Hans lay down on the shit-stained ground and tried to sleep. His giving up worried me as much as his eye.

'You have blood on your back,' I said.

'I was cut with a sabre as I tried to go up on deck. I wanted to throw a lifebelt to Tao.' His face creased at the memory of the scene on the yacht. 'When I think of Tao,' he said, 'you don't know how angry I am with myself.'

'There's no point feeling guilty. We have to keep our spirits up. The sea isn't far. We need to know where we are. I have no intention of rotting here.'

'Shhh!' said the boy with the lensless glasses, still standing guard over the entrance to the cave.

Night fell like the blade of a guillotine. I had drifted off to sleep. Outside, there wasn't a sound; the boy who had been mounting guard had disappeared. I listened out: apart from the noise of the sea, nothing. At that precise moment, while a cold sweat froze my back, I became fully aware of the gravity of the situation.

'Have they left?' I asked Hans.

Hans didn't reply. I nudged him with my knee; he didn't react. For a second or two, I thought he was dead. I bent over him, pinned my ear to his side; he moaned and rolled over.

I was racked with hunger and thirst, but I didn't care. A tension I had never known was choking me. There was nothing inside me but dark thoughts and dread. I sensed that I was in danger. I didn't want to go back to sleep: I wanted to look into the darkness and assume it was night, a moonless, starless night like those I had known in Frankfurt in winter; I wanted to keep my eyes wide open and familiarise myself with what I couldn't see; this was perhaps the last time I could cling to something that kept me alive … Hans had given up. I disturbed him when I spoke to him; he would answer reluctantly, out of politeness. I imagined him struggling with Tao's ghost. But I needed to talk, to say something, no matter what, to ask questions to which I wouldn't demand answers; Hans's silence left me defenceless. Silence is the cruellest medium for panic; it turns doubt into an obsession, darkness into claustrophobia. What were they going to do with us? Death was prowling around us; I could have touched it but I was afraid to provoke it. I listened out for a voice or an animal cry that would burst through that awful, crushing silence, but it was pointless. Outside, the night was like a sarcophagus; it stank of mustiness and rotting flesh. I was scared ...

In the morning, a teenage boy brought us something to eat: a kind of thick, lumpy soup. The smell alone made me nauseous.

'What is this?' I asked.

'Here we eat and don't ask questions. It isn't every day we have something to get our teeth into.'

The boy seemed bored, as if he was being forced to do tasks he hated. He was very tall, with prominent shoulder blades, an angular face and a tuft of frizzy hair cut into a diamond shape in the middle of his shaven skull. A tattoo showing a girl's face and the letter f adorned his right shoulder. I turned and held out my arms so that he could untie me. He stepped back warily.

'How can we eat with our hands behind our backs?' I said.

'Does sir need a trolley?' the giant grunted, appearing suddenly as if emerging out of the stone. 'A chrome-plated trolley with embroidered white place mats, silver cutlery and crystal glasses?'

He chased away the boy, who left without hurrying, then pushed the pan in my direction with his foot.

'If you really want to feel Africa at its most authentic, you just have to smell your meal. Of course, it looks like vomit, but isn't it already a foretaste of the great journey of initiation?'

'How can we possibly eat with these chains?'

'By licking the pan, like animals.'

He walked over to Hans, who was still lying on his side.

'He's been hurt,' I said.

The giant bent over Hans and pulled up his shirt to see the state of the wound. 'I've seen worse,' he muttered. 'He'll get over it.'

'I'm a doctor. I need to examine him.'

'I tell you it isn't serious.'

'And I tell you his wound will get infected if—'

With one hand, he grabbed me by the throat, stifling the rest of my protest.

'Don't raise your voice to me,' he said, opening wide his huge white eyes. 'I hate that.'

His fingers closed over my carotid artery; their throbbing reached my temples.

'You're in Africa … you're in my home, and here, I'm the master. When you talk to Joma, you take care what you say … And stop looking at me like that or I'll gouge your eyes out with a toothpick.'

My brain was starting to lack air.

'Have you got that?'

Spit from his mouth spattered my face. Scornfully, he pushed me away.

'I don't like you,' he said, wiping his mouth with the back of his hand.

He made as if to leave the cave, then turned back, shaking with suppressed rage as if an age-old resentment, silenced for centuries, had caught up with him and overwhelmed him. In his massive face, as black as coal, his nostrils quivered in time with the spasms making his cheeks twitch.

'You must be wondering what kind of creature I am, not enough of a primate to be tamed, nor human enough to be moved.'

'I don't know what you're insinuating.'

His hand landed on my cheek, so hard that my skull bounced off the rock. In a sudden surge of pride and revolt, I stood up again to confront him. Our breaths met. He raised his arm. I defied him, my neck stretched to breaking point. Unable to make me back down, he gave up on the idea of hitting me again and left the cave like a devil deserting the body of a possessed man.

On the second day, it was the boy with the lensless glasses who brought us our food. Again, that rancid, sticky goo that left a rotten aftertaste on the palate and made us belch for hours on end. At first, I didn't think I could swallow a mouthful without throwing up, but hunger masks nutritional horrors the way spices conceal bland food … The boy gave a start when I pushed the pan away with my foot. Not grasping the meaning of my gesture, he didn't take much notice of it; he was only surprised that I could turn down a meal. He sat down on a bump in the ground and, with his sabre between his thighs, looked at me with a curious stare. Since the attack on the yacht, this boy had intrigued me. His gaze was an enigma; there was no way to guess what was brewing behind it. His eyes were small – light brown, surrounded by a sandy white, the edges of the irises gnawed by tiny milky pellets – but inscrutable, and so fascinating that they almost overshadowed the rest of his face. They were the only things you saw above a puny body, two arms barely thicker than broomsticks and two legs straight as crutches ... Eyes as troubling as a sudden, inexplicable sense of dread.

'Joma isn't easy to get on with,' he said suddenly. 'It's best not to tease him. He goes crazy sometimes for no reason.'

Unsure where he was trying to lead me, I refrained from reacting. Seeing him there with his sabre, while Hans and I were defenceless, didn't exactly fill me with confidence.

'Are you really German?'

I didn't reply.

My silence offended him. His jaws clenched. He was barely containing his temper. He adjusted his lensless glasses, examined his nails, sniffed and muttered, 'Do I look like a spy?'

'What do you want me to say?'

'Do I look like a spy?'

'I never said you were.'

'Then why don't you answer me? I'm not trying to grill you.'

Again, I said nothing. I was afraid that a clumsy remark on my part might upset him. The look in his eyes, the way he fiddled with his glasses and worried about his fingers, his various facial expressions, sometimes vague, sometimes more defined, suggested how deeply unstable he was.

'Joma says you're either mercenaries or spies.'

I didn't reply.

'Of course, the others don't believe him. Joma reads too many books; he sees the bad in everyone. Plus, he's allergic to white people.'

'If the others don't agree with him, why don't they let us go?' Hans asked, still lying curled up, without turning.

'They're not in charge. Joma isn't either. It's Chief Moussa who gives the orders.'

'Where is Chief Moussa?' I said.

'Don't know.'

'When will he be back?'

'When he feels like it. He has to get rid of the boat first …'

He scratched his back with his sabre, embarrassed. He wanted to talk, but had run out of ideas. I needed him to talk, in order to know who his accomplices were, what they were planning to do with us, where we were; above all, I needed to get an idea of our chances of getting out of here, to believe in them with the force of desperation, just as a condemned man who has exhausted every possibility and refuses to give up believes in a miracle. I thought there was a chance I could get through to the boy. Who was to say? Surely there was no such thing as a criminal completely resistant to emotion; as long as he had something resembling a soul, however deeply buried it was in his animal-like nature, it was still possible to reach him provided you could find a chink in his armour.

'Are you also allergic to white people?' I asked, in order to encourage him to continue.

'Not especially,' he replied, pushing his spectacles up towards his eyebrows. 'I don't meet them often. The first time I saw a white person for real was three years ago. It was a guy from the Red Cross. For Joma, the Red Cross is a modern version of the missionaries. You know, those guys in cassocks who used to spread the good word among the tribes. Joma is convinced they're the same bunch of spies, except that the white fathers had the Bible, and the medics have vaccines.'

'That's ridiculous,' I objected. 'How can he say something as stupid as that? The Red Cross is a non-governmental body. It takes action where you live and where we live too. A lot of people working for it have paid with their lives for the help they gave others. They're everywhere where people suffer, without distinction of colour of skin or religion. They don't baulk in the face of war, dictatorships, epidemics, or imprisonment. Your friend is being unfair and way off the mark. If he can't recognise one of the most generous acts of our time, it's because he's blind and heartless.'

'Personally, I don't give a damn. Whether they're spies or mercenaries isn't going to change anything in my life. And besides, I'm not into politics.'

'This Joma, is he the big guy with the amulets?'

'They're real amulets from a great marabout. Each one has a special power. They protect him against fear, bad luck, betrayal and bullets.'

'Be that as it may, Joma is wrong. He should wear an amulet against prejudice.'

'That's in his nature. It's the way he is, and that's all there is to it.'

He listened out, went and made sure that nobody was near the cave and came back and sat down next to me. There was a more moderate look in his eyes now.

'Why do you always carry that sabre with you?' I asked, trying to win him over. 'We're chained up and we have no desire to fight.'

He shook his head. 'It isn't a sabre,' he said cautiously, 'it's a machete.'

'It's a formidable weapon.'

'It's a piece of old iron. It's the way you use it that makes it formidable.'

Outside, the giant started yelling at his men. The boy gave a small enigmatic smile and shrugged his angular shoulders.

'So you're really German?'

'Yes.'

'Wow! ... Do you know Beckenbauer?' he asked suddenly.

The change of subject was so incongruous, I wondered for a few seconds if I had heard correctly. 'Franz Beckenbauer?'

'Yeah ... Have you met him?'

'No.'

'Don't you live in Germany?'

'Yes.'

'It isn't possible. You can't live in the same country and not have met him.'

'Oh, yes, you can. There are people who live in the same building and never meet their neighbours.'

'That's crazy. Here, everybody knows everybody ... My father would have given anything to meet Beckenbauer. He was a fan of his. The only poster we had in the house was of Beckenbauer dribbling past an opponent with his arm in a bandage. It had been pinned to the wall a long time before I was born. And whenever my father stood in front of the poster, he'd shake with excitement ... There were no other pictures in the house. Not of grandfather who died by falling down a well, or grandmother who I didn't know …'

I couldn't quite follow him.

He was biting his nails like a rodent.

'I think I heard the name Beckenbauer before any other,' he said enthusiastically. 'My father wanted to be called the Kaiser, but in the village, everyone, young or old, called him Beckenbauer. It's true, he had class, my father. He was tall and cool-headed, and he played for the local club. It wasn't really a club, more a bunch of idlers running after a punctured ball on a dusty stretch of waste ground all day long. Whenever anyone scored a goal, he'd jump up and box the air then wave to the "stand". The stand was a handful of kids and a few goats grazing in the bush … My father played centre back. He wore a captain's armband even though he wasn't the captain of the team, and a white shirt with a big number 5 on the back that he'd drawn with a felt-tipped pen. His shorts he'd cut out of a pair of trousers and soaked for days in a dye he'd made himself to turn them black. He loved wearing the colours of the German national team, a white shirt and black shorts. The shirt was okay, but for the black shorts, my father had got the formula and quantities wrong when he made the dye. After the match, he started getting spots on his buttocks and around his genitals. And the next day, he was really sick and walked around as if he'd shit in his pants.'

I found it hard to comprehend the fact that you could tell amusing, heart-warming stories in the same part of the world where a man could be thrown in the sea like a cigarette end being flicked away.

'And who are you a fan of?' I said.

He shrugged, losing interest. 'There's Messi, Ronaldo and lots of others, except that Joma says an idol doesn't have to be a white man. So I went for Drogba, Eto'o and Zidane.'

'Zidane's white.'

'Only white-skinned. He's African at heart.'

'Do you play football?'

'I'm rubbish at it.' He looked at his toes sticking out of his worn-out espadrilles and wiggled them. An unexpected sadness came over his face. 'I've never been good at anything,' he sighed.

'You should have stayed at home.'

'There wasn't anything at home. I was like an old boat in a disused harbour, taking in water while waiting for a buyer. Except that nobody was buying. Nobody where I lived had any money. They couldn't even afford a rope to hang themselves with. I was fed up with taking in water. After a while, I told myself, if I was going to sink, I might as well sink at sea. At least, nobody would see. So I raised anchor and set sail.'

'You chose the wrong sea.'

'Maybe the sea doesn't exist, maybe it's just a mirage. In any case, I don't see the difference. Here or somewhere else, it's all the same.'

'No, it isn't.'

'For me it is.'

'I'm sure you're a good person. Your place isn't among these people. What they're doing is a serious crime, and they don't realise. They kidnapped us and kidnapping is against the law. They'll be severely punished.'

'They don't give a damn about the law. They don't even know what it is. All they know is how to kill and loot, and they seem to enjoy that.'

'Don't you agree with what they're doing?'

'I don't have an opinion. Nobody asks me anyway.'

'So why join them?'

'It's just the way it is.'

'There's such a thing as choice.'

'I don't have a choice.'

'Yes, you do ... Nobody's forcing you to go along with this bunch of ... of reckless idiots ... What's your name?'

My question threw him. He thought it over, frowning and pulling at the tip of his nose, which was thin and straight, then lifted his chin and said bitterly, 'What's a name? A trademark, that's all. My family's name doesn't even mean anything. I've learnt to get along without it. I sometimes forget it ... Here, they call me, "Hey, you there!"' He took off his glasses and wiped his face on his vest. 'That doesn't make me much of a person either ... But I'm patient. One day, they'll give me a combat name. There's no reason why not. I'm a warrior and I risk my life like the others ... Everyone has a nickname – why not me?' He started biting his nails again. 'I'd get a kick out of having a nickname,' he added in a feverish breath. 'That would make me someone ... A nickname that sounds good, that you can't easily forget ... Blackmoon, for example ... I'd like that, Blackmoon. Plus, it sounds like me.'

'Well, Blackmoon, you're not someone who's good for nothing.'

'You don't know me.'

'You don't need to spend lots of time with people to know them. I'm sure you're a reasonable person.'

'It's true, I'm not wicked. The bad things I've done were to defend myself. It isn't that I have regrets or that I'm trying to clear myself. I'd have liked things to happen differently, but what's done is done, and there's no point bringing it back.'

'I agree, except that you can also redeem yourself.'

'What do you mean?' he asked with a frown.

'You can be of use to us. You can help us to escape.'

He shook his head as if he had just received an uppercut to the chin. 'What?' he said in a choked voice. 'Help you to escape? What are you talking about? What do you take me for? I talk to you for a while, and you immediately think you've got me in your pocket. I was only having a chat. Here, apart from Joma, nobody says a word to me. And even Joma doesn't talk to me, he just tells me off ... Why do you take me for a sucker?'

'Don't take it badly. I wasn't—'

'Shut up!' he yelled, getting to his feet, his sabre at the ready. 'I try to be nice to you, and you try to trick me. Why should I help you to get out of here? What's in it for me? What will I do after that? And who'll help me when the guys get their hands on me? We're in Africa, damn it! Wherever you hide, they always track you down. And besides, do I look like a traitor?'

He was incensed. His sabre hovered above the back of my neck.

Taken aback by the violence of his about-turn, I no longer knew how to react. His cries echoed in the cave like explosions. I was afraid the others would hear and come to see what was going on. Suddenly, in the same way as he had lost his temper, he calmed down. In a flash, he was again the boy who liked football. I was flabbergasted.

Who was I up against? Who were these people who were furious one moment, placid the next. I looked at the boy in amazement, at the sabre he had now lowered, and his eyes which were recovering that disturbing acuteness that had made me so ill at ease.

He threw me even more when he said, in a moderate, even conciliatory tone, 'You mustn't take me for an idiot. It isn't good. I may not look up to much, but I have my self-respect.'

'I'm sorry. I wasn't trying to be unpleasant—'

'Shut up. Just because I'm not shouting doesn't mean I'm not angry. Stop amusing yourself by taking me for a fool. Joma says that white people think Africans have mush for brains. But they're wrong … We're just as intelligent as you, even if you're more calculating than the devil.'

He sat down again, placed his sabre on its side, brought his knees up to his chest, folded his arms over them and was still. Only his jaws continued to move. I wondered if he was entirely in his right mind or if he was a brilliant actor.

After a long silence, he looked up and said, 'Do you think Beckenbauer's still alive?'

I thought it best not to restart the conversation.

The following day, it was another boy who brought us food. Blackmoon didn't set foot in the cave again. I saw him from time to time, passing the cave entrance, but not once did he lift his eyes in my direction.

In the afternoon, Hans at last emerged from his lethargy. Standing on his unsteady legs, shivering with fever and hunger, he tried desperately to free himself of his chains.

'What's the matter?' I said.

He was unable to utter a sound. He stared in terror at a corner of the cave while his Adam's apple leapt in his throat. His voice emerged, quavery and unrecognisable.

'A snake ... There's a snake over there ...'

I thought he was hallucinating, then, following his gaze, I noticed a shadow moving a few paces from us. My blood froze. A conical head the size of a hand glided over a stone; a snake more than three metres long, plump and hideous, had wriggled out of a crack, its eyes shining through the gloom. Hans started screaming for help.

'Whatever you do, don't move!' said a guard alerted by Hans's cries for help.

The snake slid over a bump on the ground and, attracted by the cries, came towards us, its tongue quivering. I was petrified with horror. The reptile lifted its head as far as Hans's belt, then recoiled; I closed my eyes, my heart pounding fit to burst ... Nothing happened. I opened my eyes again; the snake slithered towards a hole, slid into it and disappeared.

'Get us out of here!' Hans screamed, his nerves at breaking point. 'Get us out of here!'

Two of our kidnappers cautiously approached the crack through which the snake had vanished. Joma joined them. All three stood looking at the hole.

'We won't stay a moment longer in this nest of madmen!' Hans cried.

'I have nowhere else to put you,' Joma said.

'But there's a snake,' I said, beside myself.

'It wasn't a snake, it was the spirit of the cave,' he said, with a seriousness that left us speechless. 'It's the guardian

76

of the place. If it had wanted to harm you, it would have gobbled you up like two hard-boiled eggs.'

With this, he ordered his men to block up the hole and, without another word, abandoned us to our fate.

2

Four days spent waiting for the return of Chief Moussa!

On the first night, I had a dream: I was on a tree cutting a branch with a saw. Below, my mother was playing with an orange medicine ball. She was only a little girl with golden hair, but in the dream she was my mother. She was running after the ball and humming a tune. Suddenly she stopped hitting the ball. There was a strange silence. Blood was gushing from the top of my mother's head, over her bare shoulders, and down to her feet. She looked up at the tree and turned white. *Kurt*, she cried, *what are you doing?* ... I shifted my attention to what I was doing, and realised it wasn't the branch I was sawing off, but my arm ... A sudden pain woke me; my chains were digging so hard into my wrists, they'd almost cut them.

The second night, I dreamt about Paula. We were sitting at the table on the veranda of our bungalow in Maspalomas. Hans was doubled up with laughter. I couldn't understand why he was laughing. Paula was performing an acrobatic dance, her red dress fluttering around her like a poppy. There was a closed door standing on its own on the edge of the veranda. Paula opened it and a stream of blinding light flooded the veranda. Hans ran to the door, yelling at his wife to turn back. Paula continued walking into the

78

light, dissolving into it bit by bit. Hans yelled and yelled; the wind had blown the door shut, so firmly that I had hit my head on the rock ...

On the third night, I dreamt about Jessica, but I can't remember anything about the dream.

Four days!

Four days and nights heavy with uncertainty and anxiety, spent shivering at night in the coolness of the sea spray and suffocating by day in the corrosive humidity of the cave ... Four interminable days and nights spent scraping my bones on the rough ground, forced to perform a thousand gymnastic manoeuvres to scratch myself, and a thousand others to relieve myself; drinking my bitterness to the dregs and chewing over my powerlessness like a poisonous herb ... Four days as sleepless as the nights, four nights as shadowy as our kidnappers' plans for us, wondering when I would finally wake up and emerge from this sordid dream that had relegated my grief to the background ... I was angry with these maniacs conjured by some evil spell who had broken into my life, turning my mourning upside down and in one fell swoop destroying the faith I had in mankind. I felt like screaming, tearing out the ring that kept me chained to the wall and dented my self-respect, and lashing out at random with my shortened arms. I felt sick in my flesh, sick in my being, and sick everywhere my thoughts took me. Why was I being confined in a foul-smelling cave, in the middle of nowhere, with these incessant swarms of flies drinking from the corners of my lips and driving me mad? What right did these bandits have to divert us from both our route and our destiny? I was furious. Hatred rose in me like molten lava, secreting in my mind a blackness I didn't think I was capable of.

The more I observed our kidnappers, the angrier I got. Everything about them disgusted me – their filthy language, their single-mindedness, their absence of humanity – while here I was, reduced to a mere piece of merchandise with an uncertain fate, chained up, depersonalised and forced to lick my cold soup out of a disgusting can. The whole universe appeared to me devoid of logic, lacking in purpose, vile and absurd, something almost to be renounced. Frankfurt seemed light years away, belonging to a period suspended between mirage and sunstroke. Had I really been a doctor? If I had, was it yesterday or in a previous life? … I had become nothing overnight – worse, a piece of junk, a contraband product to be traded on the black market, a hostage playing Russian roulette with his own future … It was appalling! I was ashamed of my complaints, my indecision, my hollow fury that had nothing to hold on to, no resonance, that turned round and round in a void like a simulated belch, too improbable to come out into the open air … And I was angry with myself … I was angry with myself for every pain that afflicted me, every question that tormented me, every answer that refused to come … I was angry with myself for suffering the blows of fate without being able to react, as resigned and wretched as a sacrificial lamb …

Four days and four nights! … How did I manage to hold out?

Headlights lit up the cave. I twisted my neck to see what was happening. Two pick-up trucks and a spluttering jeep had just come to a halt in the yard. Armed men jumped to the ground, yelling in loud voices. Orders were given.

Our guards came running. The campfire projected their turbulent shadows on the sand. Doors slammed, then the lights and engines went off. I made out the chief from his silhouette. He was carrying an automatic rifle across his shoulder. Joma approached him and asked him if everything was all right. The chief pointed to a form lying on a stretcher and joined the rest of his men, who had disappeared inside a tent.

A few minutes later, they came to get me. I found it hard to stand up. My bones felt weak, and my knees stiff. I was frogmarched to see a sick man laid low with fever. He was very thin, with a muddy complexion. Lying in a fetal position on the stretcher, his neck straining back and his hands stuck between his thighs, he was moaning and shivering, insensitive to the water-soaked cloth that a boy was pressing to his forehead. From the smell he gave off, I realised he had urinated on himself.

The chief was walking up and down inside the tent, his hands on his hips. He appeared very bored. Standing at a slight remove, Joma was holding a storm lantern at arm's length. He paid no attention to me. The chief at last consented to notice that I was there. He clapped his hands in embarrassment, approached me, and was surprised to see me in such a bad state. He looked to Joma for an explanation. Joma didn't react.

'Are you in pain, doctor?'

I found his question absurd, almost cynical. If I'd had any strength left, I would have thrown myself at him. He pointed to the patient.

'He has malaria. Try to do something for him. He's a great guy.'

In my mind, I refused to approach the patient, felt

reluctant even to touch him. My aversion squirmed inside me like a reptile, sharpening my senses and what remained of my fighting instinct. I was shocked, outraged even, that they should call on my services after what Hans and I had been put through. I looked at the chief and found him as pitiful as his patient. I wasn't afraid of him, felt only disdain for his authority, disgust for the paranoid monster hiding behind his lantern, and cold hatred for this whole gang of degenerates who had been released into the wild like virulent germs in a pandemic …

Curiously, by some kind of professional reflex, I crouched, took the patient's hand, felt his pulse, examined him: he was in a bad way.

'Do you have any quinine?' I asked.

'Not even so much as an aspirin,' the chief retorted.

'And what do you expect me to do?'

'Treat him.'

'With what?'

'You'll manage. You're a doctor, aren't you?'

I stood up and faced the chief. Again, his smugness, his affected airs stoked my aversion. Our noses were almost touching; my eyes were boring into his. I had never thought myself capable of such violent animosity. I took a step back, repelled by his drunken breath, and in a voice throbbing with scorn declared, 'I'm a real doctor, not a witch doctor. My profession's not about going into a trance or invoking the spirits of the ancestors to ward off evil. Your man needs drugs, not a voodoo session.'

'Careful what you say!' Joma threatened.

The chief quickly raised his hand to put him in his place. After pondering my words, he took my chin between his thumb and index finger, then turned away, much to the

82

annoyance of Joma, who cried, choking with indignation, 'What! Are you really going to let him get away with speaking to you like that?'

'He's right, Joma. Ewana needs drugs, and we don't have any.'

'That's not the point!' Joma protested. 'This cretin has no right to talk down to us. Does he think he's dealing with cavemen or what? What was all that about voodoo? If I were you, I'd grab a car jack and teach him to swallow his arrogance.'

'That's enough!' the chief said. 'It's been a tough journey and I'm exhausted. Take the doctor back.'

With a weary hand, he dismissed us.

Once outside the tent, Joma jabbed his rifle butt into my back to make me walk faster.

'You're a tough guy, aren't you?'

I didn't reply.

He grabbed me by my shirt collar and twisted me round to face him.

'Well, I'm an old cooking pot. A cauldron straight out of hell. We'll soon see how tough you are. I'm going to cook you on a low heat until you melt in my mouth.'

He showed his teeth in a fierce grin.

I looked at him dejectedly, turned towards the pale sky and searched for my star among the thousands of constellations, which all seemed oblivious to my prayers tonight. A vague premonition took root in me: I'd just made myself a sworn enemy.

When I woke up, I found the chief crouching by my side. He was in his fatigues, his eyes hidden by his sunglasses.

He hadn't expected to find Hans and me in such a terrible state. He stood up, paced up and down the cave angrily, and kicked a tin can, which rolled into the shadows with a clatter. Then, unable to contain himself, he turned to Joma and screamed, 'Have you been keeping them tied up all this time?'

'I don't have enough men to keep an eye on them,' Joma said grudgingly.

'I never asked you to chain them like that.'

Joma didn't like the way he was being scolded. 'What did you want me to do, Moussa? Mollycoddle them? We didn't have anything to eat, and the joker you put in charge of looking after the hideout wasted the drinking water and let the cans of rations go off in the sun.'

'I'm talking about the hostages, Joma. They aren't prisoners of war, damn it.'

'Is there a difference?'

'Yes, a big difference!' the chief cried, exasperated by his subordinate's attitude.

Joma gave a shudder. 'If you have a problem with me, Moussa, talk to me in private. I don't like being lectured in front of strangers …'

'I don't care if you like it or not, Joma!' the chief spat, and left the cave.

A few minutes later, we were untied. Electric shocks went through me every time I moved a finger or a toe. My wrists were covered in blackish scabs, and my hands were grey and pale. Hans had to put himself through a crash course in order to learn to push himself off the ground and get to his feet. His joints had stiffened up and he couldn't put his arms in front of him. The bloody patch on the back of his shirt had turned black. We were dragged to a reservoir of stagnant water, not far from the cave, to wash our faces and our clothes, which we let dry on our bodies. Hans began to sway on his stiff legs, and was shaken with convulsions; he complained of stomach pains and dizziness, but our kidnappers forbade me from going near him. After the makeshift bath, we were taken back to the cave and given a piece of fish and a slice of pancake. The brackish, polluted water from the reservoir had merely aggravated our wounds, which, now that the scabs had come off, bled and caused great excitement among the flies.

In the afternoon, Moussa ordered his men to get ready to evacuate the place. The tent was immediately taken down and the pirates' kit was wrapped and loaded into the vehicles along with bags of provisions. Hans and I were shoved onto two separate pick-ups, and the little convoy set off. I was so relieved to be leaving the cave that I didn't even think to wonder what other hellhole we were being transferred to.

We drove for hours without coming across a living soul. Towards evening, we stopped in a gorge whose ridges were crowned with undergrowth. The pirates called the place 'the station' – I would later discover that stations were hiding places scattered around the countryside where smugglers and rebels kept supplies of fuel and water when they were on the move. The drivers filled up the vehicles and checked the state of their tyres and the level of water in the radiators, and then, after a basic supper, we spent most of the night driving.

Very early the next day, the convoy entered an area

of scrub where the paths were impassable. The ground was hard and uneven, and the vehicles bounced over it, almost knocking us senseless. We passed between narrow ravines, and the branches of the thorny shrubs rustled on the sheet-metal bodywork and scratched our backs. If one of the boulders had fallen on us, we'd have been done for. Joma drove without a thought for those of us in the back. All he knew how to do was press his foot down on the accelerator, move the wheel wildly from right to left and crank the gear stick back and forth. He didn't care about the engine speed, or how much we were being shaken about, or the dust being thrown in our faces by the shovelful. Curiously, his clumsiness amused his associates, who burst out laughing every time a heavy jolt threw them against each other.

With my wrists tied, I held onto the seat. I could feel the knocking of the axles reverberate right through my body.

Judging by the position of the sun, we were heading due west.

The ordeal eased after a hundred kilometres. There weren't even any ruins around to suggest anyone had ever settled in the area. A valley covered in varicose scrub stretched to infinity, anonymous, totally devoid of distinguishing features – if you were trying to figure out where you were, or if you were thinking of escaping and wanted to know which direction to go, it was a depressing prospect.

The convoy halted at the foot of a mountain shrouded in dust. It was the only thing approaching a landmark for miles around. I asked the boy who brought me food if the mountain was sacred and if he knew its name. Joma, who I hadn't seen behind me and who had guessed where I was going with this, retorted that it was Kilimanjaro: with global warming the snow had melted, and all that was left of the legendary mountain that Hemingway loved was a mere boulder stuck in the middle of a crater, so insignificant that it would inspire neither budding griots nor visionaries at odds with authority. The boy burst out laughing, and Joma pointed two fingers at me and went 'boom', delighted to have scored a point.

During the stop, tied as I was to a root, I didn't manage to catch a glimpse of Hans.

A ragged man was crouching at the top of a hill – God knows where he'd come from. At the sight of the convoy, he picked up his bundle and ran down the slope, gesticulating wildly … The pick-up swerved to the side and headed straight for him. He had now reached the edge of the track. Instead of slowing down, Joma accelerated and charged at him. Surprised by the vehicle's sudden detour, the stranger just had time to move back to avoid being hit. He fell backwards. Around me, the pirates shrieked with laughter and slapped their thighs … The poor man started to pick himself up from the dust, and at that moment the jeep, which was behind us, now also left the track and hurled itself at him. At first dumbfounded, he realised that he wasn't out of trouble yet and still, by some extraordinary reflex, had to perform a superhuman feat of acrobatics to dodge the wheels passing a few inches from his head. Disoriented, he dropped his bundle and set off at a run straight up the hill, without turning. His headlong flight merely increased my kidnappers' hilarity. There was something so indecent in their exaggerated laughter it was beyond my understanding. They were laughing proudly, as if the impunity they allowed themselves instilled in them an overwhelming sense of courage and invincibility. They were also laughing because they noticed that their attitude shocked me as much as their murderous attempts to knock a man down. Much to my despair, I realised that these men who held me captive, these men who would decide my fate, these men devoid of conscience, weren't content with trivialising the deliberate act of killing, they also claimed it as a right.

My eyes went from the kidnappers to the poor wretch clambering up the hill. I was incapable of distinguishing the horror I felt from the pity. At that moment, the pirates and the man were part of the same human misery. Any protest on my part was doomed in advance: there was nothing I could say or do ... I thought of my previous life, so delightful and easy that it seemed like a joke. A sanitised life, as well timed and ordered as a musical score, where every day began and ended in the same way: a kiss when I woke, another when I got back from work, another before switching off the light in the bedroom, with *I love you*s at the end of every phone call and text message – in short, the ordinary happiness you take for granted, as unquestionable as a fait accompli ... Oh, that happiness, the philosopher's stone, the domestic dream, the earthly paradise of which you're both the baleful god and the privileged devil ... that damned happiness that rests on so little but overrides all other ambitions and fantasies ... that happiness which, when you come down to it, has only its self-delusion as protection and its innocence as an alibi ... Had I suspected how vulnerable it was? Not for a moment ... Then, one evening, one *ordinary* evening, no different from any of the thousands of evenings that went before it, everything turns upside down. What you've built, what you were sure was yours, suddenly vanishes in the blink of an eye. You realise you were sleepwalking along a wire. Overnight, the dashing Kurt Krausmann who used to be so concerned that the creases in his trousers were straight, the solemn and serious Dr Krausmann wakes to find himself in the back of a clapped-out pick-up, surrounded by ragged-looking killers, in the middle of an unknown country where the death of a man is worth no more than the act that causes it … How sad it all was!

The sun was just starting to go down on that second day when we reached a plateau from which the rays ricocheted off as if from a mirror, dotting the surrounding area with false oases. It was a stony, charcoal-grey land, that was turning completely into desert. Strips of undergrowth indicated the place where a river had once flowed. There were a few scrawny trees here and there, their branches lifted to the sky like arms raised in surrender, but still no villages anywhere to be seen.

We spent the night in a ravine, and very early the next day the convoy headed due west to a new station. This time, the hiding place seemed to have been discovered and looted by other bandits, leaving nothing but empty jerry cans and sacks that had been ripped open. As the place was no longer safe, Moussa ordered his men to carry straight on to the next station. A blazing sun pursued us all the way there. The pick-up was like a furnace. I was dripping with sweat, my back burnt by the slatted sides and my feet by the floor. Exhausted and discouraged, forced to continue on their way without food or drink, our kidnappers resigned themselves to the bumpy terrain. Some dozed, their mouths open, their weapons between their thighs. As for Blackmoon, he remained on alert, keeping a close eye on me as if I were the only thing that mattered.

Coming out of a stony maze, the jeep overtook us and forced the two pick-ups to fall into line behind it. Chief Moussa got out and lifted the binoculars to his eyes. He pointed to something in the distance. Joma took the binoculars from his hands, looked through them for a long time, then nodded. 'Village at nine o'clock!' Moussa said, getting back in his jeep. The three vehicles veered south and headed straight for the village, which was actually nothing but a ragged settlement.

Alerted by the humming of the engines, swarms of kids emerged from the huts and started running at top speed towards a stony column to take shelter. The youngest of them, naked from head to foot, stumbled and fell. He must have hurt himself badly because he lay there on the ground without moving. Two small boys stopped and yelled at him to get back on his feet then ran back to help him up, and disappeared again quickly behind the rocks. The pirates' three vehicles moved into a small open space surrounded by half a dozen huts, most of them deserted. Moussa was the first to get out. He fired in the air to flush out the inhabitants, but without success. His men plunged into the huts, screaming like animals. Some came out empty-handed, others with wretched pieces of booty: a foul-smelling pancake, an opened sachet of powdered milk, an old blanket. An old man was sitting outside his hut, his body propped up on an ancient stick. Dressed in an overcoat as old as the world, his skull hairless, his expression opaque, there he sat, calmly, paying no heed to this bandit raid, as if he had spent his whole life being robbed. Beside him, on a tattered mat, an old woman was watching the agitation around her without really seeing it. In her ageless face, her two eyes were so eroded by trachoma they were almost extinguished. The loincloth she was wearing barely concealed her nakedness. Her withered breasts, which seemed to have suckled whole generations, hung over her skeletal sides like two dried marrows. In the poverty of their configuration, there was a kind of topography of misfortune. Two of the pirates rushed into the hut and brought out a bleating goat. The old couple didn't move, didn't even turn to look. They sat there, immutable, like two stuffed animals.

I was shocked by the shameless way the thieves were robbing people as destitute as these, and even more by the old couple's detachment as they watched themselves being relieved of their only goat, probably the only thing they owned, without saying a word, without making a gesture, as if it were the slightest of misfortunes, a mere formality.

Moussa ordered his men to withdraw. The vehicles drove around intimidatingly in the middle of the empty huts, a few shots were fired in the air to celebrate this pathetic raid, and the convoy set off again. I don't know why, but when the pick-up drove past the old couple sitting dazed on the threshold of their hut, I showed them my tied wrists – maybe I was trying, through this superfluous reflex, to ask their forgiveness for being the reluctant witness to such a despicable act. One of the pirates, who had noticed my gesture, gave an ironic grin, as if to say: What could you have done if your hands had been free, except hide your face?

*

On the fourth day, we came out onto a plateau of cosmic emptiness, without a trace of greenery, without one drop of water, without a single patch of shade: an expanse of burning stones, where the reflections were as sharp as a razor, a land from just after the Big Bang, still engorged with fire, which had kept its original ochre hue like the first layer of sediment from before the first rains, the first grass, the first stirrings of life.

Two birds of prey were whirling in the sky. The false majesty of their circling did not augur well. On a bare hillock, a group of vultures were swarming around a shapeless form. Was it an animal or a human being? The vultures took turns dipping into their prey, as calmly and shamelessly as partygoers savouring a well-deserved meal. The largest of them turned to the convoy, in no way bothered, even though the track was very close. I clearly made out its hairless neck and blood-smeared beak. Suddenly, I thought I saw an arm move amid the wings.

'There's a man there,' I yelled at the driver. 'Stop, there's a man being eaten by vultures, and he's still alive …'

My kidnappers woke with a start and instinctively grabbed their weapons, expecting an enemy attack. Joma just kept on driving.

'Stop, please! I tell you there's an injured man …'

Joma glanced at me in the rear-view mirror and tapped his temple with his finger.

'I'm not imagining things. I saw him move. He's alive … Stop right now …'

On the hillock, the vultures moved their wings in a

dance of death, and again I thought I saw the arm move. I threw myself at the back of the cab, and knocked on it.

'You have no hearts. You're monsters. Stop, stop, you bunch of savages …'

Joma braked so sharply that the jeep behind us nearly crashed into us … The word 'savages' had slipped out. I couldn't take it back or downplay it. I only became aware of how serious it was when it rang out over the noise of the pick-up, bearing as it did centuries of tragedy and trauma. I didn't think it for a second but, through some dormant mechanism, I had said it. And Joma had heard it … He jumped out, ran along the side of the vehicle, grabbed me by my shirt collar and pulled me over the side. I fell on my stomach, face down. He took me by the hair and lifted me up. His face was distorted with anger and hatred.

He pushed and kicked me towards the hillock, without saying anything.

'What's going on, damn it?' Moussa asked, coming to a halt by the side of the road. 'Where's he taking him?'

When we got within twenty metres of the hillock, Joma crushed the back of my neck between his fingers.

'Where do you see an injured man? Where is this guy we *savages* are abandoning to the birds?'

The shapeless form in question was the carcass of a jackal. As for the arm I thought I'd seen move, it was only the jackal's paw, which one of the vultures was busy tearing to pieces.

'So, who's having visions now?'

Joma fired a shot into the air, and the vultures flapped their wings but didn't fly away – they were far too hungry to give up their feast.

'Is there the body of a man in there, mister doctor?'

'No.'

'I didn't hear that,' he said, putting his hand to his ear.

'I'm sorry. I thought …'

'You thought what? That there was a man being eaten by birds or that you were surrounded by heartless savages?'

'I was wrong.'

'All down the line, cretin, all down the line. You don't understand a damned thing about our continent … You're in Africa now, and in Africa, you're the savage.'

'I'm sorry.'

'Too easy. You can apologise to me on your knees. I did warn you: if you don't want me to walk all over you, become invisible. Now get down on your knees and beg my forgiveness.'

I didn't do as he said.

'On your knees, you son of a bitch, or I'll blow your brains out.'

The chief's jeep left the track and came towards us.

Joma stuck the barrel of his rifle under my chin. I didn't give in. I had no desire to give in. I heard Moussa shouting orders; Joma wasn't listening. His eyes bulging, his mouth wide open, he was trembling with anger. The jeep came level with us and stopped. The chief jumped down, and put his arms out to calm his subordinate.

'Don't be a fool, Joma.'

'The son of a bitch has to realise that the days of colonialism are long past.'

'Put down your Kalashnikov.'

'Not before he's on the ground.'

The chief didn't dare come a step closer. Joma's finger was on the trigger. Sweat was pouring down his forehead.

'On your knees!'

'Do what he asks,' Hans yelled at me in German. 'The man's not in his right mind.'

I couldn't blink or swallow. But I wasn't scared. I think my nerves must have given way, because I no longer had any awareness of the danger I was in. Let him get on with it, I said to myself, resigned. The situation was beyond my understanding, and I was tired, convinced that, sooner or later, this madman would shoot me. Everything in him condemned me. He had promised to cook me on a low heat until I melted in his mouth. And he would keep his word. His hatred was a programme he would not deviate from.

'Please, Kurt!' Hans cried. 'Do as he says!'

The chief tried to approach, but Joma pointed his weapon at him and forced him to retreat.

'Don't interfere, Moussa. This is between him and me.'

'Let me remind you he's my hostage.'

'I don't give a fuck about that. I took up arms to defend principles, not to line my pockets. I guarantee that if he doesn't grovel at my feet, I'll settle his hash right now.'

The chief urged me to comply. I shook my head. The barrel this time was aimed at my forehead. A deep silence fell over the hillock. The men in the pick-up were standing, waiting to see my skull explode. Hans was petrified; his cries had exhausted him. Further down, on the track, the rest of the gang were motionless. Things were clearly getting worse and they were waiting to see how it was all going to end. In the sky, the two vultures circled in slow motion, their shadows skimming the ground like a bad omen.

'I'll count to three,' Joma boomed. 'One ... two ...'

Blackmoon, whom I hadn't seen come up behind me,

kicked me hard in the shins and forced me to kneel. The irregularity of the procedure didn't seem to bother Joma. All he cared about was seeing me on the ground.

'You see?' he said. 'It isn't complicated.'

'What's got into you, Joma, damn it?' Moussa exclaimed.

'I'm teaching this bastard about Africa. He needs to know that things have changed.' He grabbed me by the throat, squeezed hard and said, 'No one race is superior to any other. Since prehistoric times, it's always been the balance of power that decides who's master and who's slave. Today, the power's on my side. And even if to you I'm nothing but a stupid nigger, I'm the one who calls the shots. Knowledge, social rank and skin colour don't mean a thing when you've got a gun shoved in your face. You thought you were God's gift? I'm going to prove to you that you're nothing but a little runt like the rest of us, born out of the same arsehole. Your university qualifications and your white man's arrogance don't matter in a place where a simple bullet's enough to do away with all your privileges. So you were born in the West, were you? You're lucky. Now you're going to be reborn in Africa and you'll understand what that means.'

He pushed me away and walked back to the track like an ogre vanishing into the shadows.

'What's your problem with this man?' Moussa yelled after him.

'I don't like his blue eyes!' Joma shouted back.

Arms grabbed me round the waist and lifted me from the ground. I was paralysed. Everything seemed insubstantial, grotesque, improbable. I had come close to disaster, just like the hitchhiker the other day, except that I don't think I'd even realised how bad it had been. It was a strange feeling that scared and overwhelmed me: it was as if my mind was numb.

Moussa fired into the air to re-establish his authority; the shots did nothing to sober me. I was helped onto the track and then into the back of the pick-up. As I was hoisted on board, Blackmoon whispered in my ear that if he hadn't forced me to kneel, Joma would have shot me down … Shot me down? I found it hard to grasp those words. Did they have a meaning? If so, what? And to whom, the attacker or the victim? How could I resign myself to the idea that a person could be shot down as easily as a tree being felled? And yet, hadn't Tao been thrown in the sea like a cigarette end being thrown on the ground? … Yes, you ask yourself too many questions when you're trying to convince yourself that what you're seeing isn't a hallucination, that the nightmare you're living through is one hundred per cent real. The truths you've been avoiding blow up in your face; the ordeals you thought were meant for others become yours with such clarity you find it hard to bear. Are they premonitory signs of the End, of a time when the dark ages and the modern world come together to give birth to destructive androids and show mankind the shortest route to its own extinction?

My kidnappers had stopped laughing. They were staring at me in silence as if I'd returned from the dead. Unwilling to look at them, I turned away and gazed beyond the two vehicles that were following us, beyond the dust they raised, far, far away, where the earth and the sky merged and formed a line as tenuous and fragile as the thread holding me to life … Life? … Was I alive? … I had the sudden conviction that I was merely living on borrowed time.

3

The scrub was starting to grow scarce and, as the convoy plunged further inland, the desert became more marked, the few clumps of vegetation vanishing as if by magic. Apart from the vultures and the odd animal startled by the roar of the pick-ups, the area was like a deserted planet, deadly in its monotony, given over to heat and erosion. A jagged line of grey dwarf hills extended across the plain, like the spine of some fossilised prehistoric monster. To the north, a boulder-strewn *reg* stretched to infinity; to the south, the earth fell away abruptly, crisscrossed by a jumble of dried-up rivers. All at once, huddled in the shade of a low hill, there appeared a ruined fort surrounded by barbed wire. This was our kidnappers' rearguard. They were delighted to have returned to the fold, filthy and exhausted, but safe and sound. A broken gate led to a parade ground presided over by a long-unused flagpole. On either side, lines of squat barracks, some completely collapsed, others partly burnt and covered in tattered tarpaulins and sheets of iron; a well with a pulley, a rubber bucket on the coping; an enclosure for a few bored-looking goats; a water tank rusted on the outside; a lorry with its bonnet torn off next to a sidecar motorcycle straight out of the last world war; and finally, opposite a hovel with wire netting around it, a clumsily whitewashed rat-trap above which flew an unidentifiable rag that was meant to be a banner: this was the 'command post'. A group of bandits were waiting for us on the front steps – doubtless, the commanding officer's praetorian guard, a dozen armed eccentrics, standing stiffly to attention in a way that was meant to look military but was sadly lacking in credibility. Some wore paratroopers' uniforms with boots and berets pulled down over their eyes, others threadbare civilian clothes, with misshapen trainers, espadrilles or sandals with straps – they all raised their hands to their temples in a regulation salute when a knock-kneed officer emerged from the command post to greet our convoy.

Moussa ordered his men out of the vehicles, lined them up in a row facing the command post and presented arms to the officer, who returned the salute with a smug look on his face. There was an exaggerated obsequiousness in this almost theatrical protocol that would have made me smile if Hans hadn't just collapsed in front of me. Joma pulled him to his feet and held him upright.

The officer reviewed his troops, without paying any attention to Hans or me, listening distractedly to the report that Moussa delivered to him in a local language. He didn't seem very interested in what his subordinate was saying. He was very dark-skinned and as solid as a rock, his shaven skull screwed to his shoulders with no neck and no chin. His face was almost featureless, just a dented sphere with dilated nostrils and protruding eyes that flashed like lightning. He wore a tunic open over his belly and an American army belt around his neck. He at last deigned to look at us. Chief Moussa handed him our passports, took a few steps back and lined up with his men.

The captain leafed through our documents, looked from our photographs to our faces, wiped the corners of his mouth with his thumb then came and examined us closely.

'I'm Captain Gerima,' he announced. 'And this is my kingdom. I have the power of life and death. I just have to give the order … It's fate that brought us together. You have nobody to blame but yourselves. When a fly is trapped in a web, it can't blame the spider. That's how life is. The world has always functioned like that, since the dawn of time. Actually, since the dawn of time, it's always been night. The dawn of humanity isn't quite ready to rise yet …'

Impressed with his own rhetoric, he made sure his men were too, then continued, 'I don't know how long you're going to stay with us. I must warn you that nobody escapes from here. If you keep your heads down, you'll be well treated. If you don't, well, I won't go into details.'

He came to a sudden stop, as if he had run out of ideas, or maybe he'd lost the thread of his speech, which he must have fine-tuned the previous night specially for us.

He turned on his freshly polished boots and disappeared back into his lair.

Two men pushed us into the hovel with the wire netting around it opposite the command post, untied us and withdrew, leaving the door open. Hans shuffled over to a mat that had been laid on the bare ground and tried to take off his shirt, but without success. I tried to help him and noticed that, in drying, the wound had closed over part of the cloth.

'Put water on it,' a voice suggested. 'It'll soften the scab.'

A white man we hadn't noticed emerged from beneath a mosquito net in the corner. A beam of light revealed his hermit-like face: he was a man in his fifties, thin, with long grey hair tumbling over his shoulders. He had a frayed beard and was bare-chested, with prominent ribs and a sunken belly. His eyes shone like a sick man's.

'French?'

'German.'

He looked pityingly at Hans. 'Is he hurt?'

'A sabre blow. He's burning up.'

'Put water on the wound. It'll make him feel better.'

'I'm a doctor,' I said, making it clear to him that I could look after my friend without anyone's help.

He took a metal flask from a heap of miscellaneous objects and came up to us. 'This is my water ration,' he said. 'Everything's rationed here, even prayers ... Your friend's in a bad way.'

Without waiting for my permission, he trickled small quantities of water on Hans's wound, made sure the material and the scar absorbed it, then pressed delicately on the wound with his finger.

'Journalists or aid workers?'

'We were just passing. These pirates hijacked us out at sea ... And you?'

'Anthropologist ... at least, I think so.'

'Have you been here long?'

'Forty years ... In Africa, I mean. I love Africa ...'

Hans submitted to his care. The water was doing him good. In places, the scab over the wound was coming away and starting to release a few threads of the cloth.

'Don't move,' the stranger advised, 'or it'll start to bleed ...' He poured a little more water on the part of the shirt that was stuck. 'Sorry to have to say this, but I'm glad I have company at last. I was seriously starting to go crazy … What did you think of the big man?' he asked, referring to the captain. 'As a braggart, he has no equal … He's made himself an officer and thinks he's at the head of a real fighting force with those ten alley cats of his. I know him well. He was a sergeant-major in the regular army before he was court-martialled for smuggling. He'd been stealing from his unit's stock of canned rations and selling them on the black market. He managed to get out of prison by greasing a few palms, and since then he's gathered a gang of morons around him and carried on his little trade under cover of the civil war.'

'Who are these people?'

'Whoever they are, they're dangerously fickle. Sometimes they call themselves resistance fighters, sometimes revolutionaries. What cause do they claim to uphold? None of them can be bothered to answer. Whenever they get an ideological thought in their heads, they invent a slogan for themselves and get drunk on it until they lose the thread. The fact is, these maniacs don't know if they're coming or going. They don't think, they take aim. They don't talk, they shoot. They don't work, they loot. They can't see the end of the tunnel. They've forgotten how things turned bad for them and have no idea how it's going to end … You must think me very talkative, don't you? You can't blame me. I haven't had anyone to talk to for a long time now, and although the walls may have ears, they're sadly lacking in repartee.'

All at once, he held out his hand.

'I'm sorry, I haven't introduced myself. You soon lose your manners around here … My name's Bruno, I'm from Bordeaux in France.'

'This is Hans, and I'm Kurt …'

'Pleased to meet you, even though the circumstances and the place are not ideal ...'

I helped Hans to take off his shirt and laid him on his stomach. The cut on his back was a large one, going across half his hip. Now that the scab had softened, you could see the wound bed; it was bad, hatched with tiny blood vessels oozing pus, the lips dark brown at the edges and turned out; the tissue around it had turned pale and was starting to get thinner along a strip of at least a centimetre while a purplish-grey patch spread on either side of the cut, from the vertebrae to the top of the groin.

'Not a pretty sight,' the Frenchman observed.

'I need to clean the wound and also find something to lower the fever.'

The Frenchman went back to his straw mattress to get a little plastic sachet and a bottle filled with a disgusting-looking ointment. 'Spread that on the wound.'

'What is it?'

'A powder made from medicinal plants which disinfects and heals at the same time. And the ointment reduces itching.'

'That's out of the question. There are enough germs in the wound already—'

'Please,' he interrupted me calmly. 'There are no drugs here. You make do with what you can get. Trust me if you really want to stop your friend getting gangrene.'

Reluctantly, almost humiliated at being forced to opt for what I thought of as a quack remedy, I took the sachet, then hesitated. Bruno asked me to let him do it. Without waiting for my approval, he bent over Hans's wound.

'It'll make him feel better, you'll see,' he promised, clearly trying to make up for having stepped on my toes.

No sooner had Bruno finished treating Hans than Joma appeared. He was tipsy. His body filled the doorway, and he had to bend his head to get through. He swayed in the middle of the room, his hands on his hips, muscles throbbing in his bare chest. He looked me up and down and kissed the amulets around his biceps – two leather pouches embroidered with multicoloured threads and tied to his arms with thin strips.

'You still haven't apologised to me,' he said, twisting his neck like a wrestler.

The disgust I felt for him changed suddenly into an uncontrollable, debilitating dizziness.

'Oh, yes,' he went on, 'even savages have self-respect.'

Bruno tried to intervene, but Joma raised a finger to stop him.

'You stay out of this, or I'll pull your haemorrhoids out through your ears.'

Having put Bruno in his place, Joma opened his arms wide, delighted to have me to himself.

'What gives you the right to call us savages? Did you pick us off a baobab tree? I'd really like to know what makes us savages. War? Your wars are beyond cataclysmic. Poverty? We owe that to you. Ignorance? What makes you think you're more cultivated than I am? I'm sure I've read more books than the whole of your family combined, starting with you. I know Lermontov, Blake, Hölderlin, Byron, Rabelais, Shakespeare, Lamarck, Neruda, Goethe and Pushkin by heart.' He was getting excited now, ticking the names off on his fingers while his voice grew louder. 'So, Dr Kurt Krausmann, what makes me a savage and you a civilised man? What is it you see in me? Somebody black even to the whites of his eyes?'

'I'm sorry if I offended you,' I said. 'That wasn't my intention. I'd have called any man who ignores someone in distress a savage.'

'The thing is, I didn't ignore someone in distress, Dr Krausmann, but a dead jackal.'

'I understand.'

I didn't recognise my own voice. I was hypnotised by that murderous gaze that went right through me. When nothing is certain, when right and wrong have cancelled one another out, fear becomes the most exaggerated form of surrender. Without being fully aware of what was happening, I found myself giving up. Was it fatigue, hunger, a desire to be left in peace? Or all three factors? It didn't really matter. I didn't want to argue with this brute. What was the point of arguing anyway? Where would it get us? You can't negotiate with people inured to strong-arm methods and perfectly aware of their own immunity. With such people, you had to make concessions. It was pointless trying to reason with them; their convictions were elsewhere. Joma was nothing but a torturer, and even if it diminishes his temporary power a torturer readily accepts his victim's resigned submission.

Joma was taken aback. He had come to attack me, and my unconditional surrender left him with a sense of disappointment. He hadn't expected it and was upset to have to put off his speechifying to later. To save face, he pointed his finger at me and said, 'You're making progress, doctor. You're starting to understand what being African means.'

And he walked out.

'Phew!' Bruno said, fanning his face with his hand. 'That doesn't happen often. Joma usually hits anyone who gets in his way. What could you have said to him?'

I preferred not to answer.

Bruno didn't insist. 'Anyway, you got out of it brilliantly.'

'Have you had dealings with the man?'

'Not personally. But I've seen him at work. If you want my advice, avoid him.'

'Is he vindictive?'

'Worse than that, he's crazy. Nobody likes him around here. Not his comrades in arms, nor his guardian angels. He's like a crushing machine that's out of control. Apparently he gets everything he says from books. He loves making speeches. But as soon as he opens his mouth, everyone tiptoes away.'

'Do you think he'll leave me alone?'

'I don't think so. He's too bored with the others.'

Hans took off his shoes and held his bruised feet in a ray of sunshine. Indifferent to what was going on around him, he wiggled his toes in the light and massaged his ankles; his movements were abnormally limp.

Bruno could see that there was something not quite right with my friend's head, but he modestly refrained from lingering on the subject.

'How long have you been here?' I asked him.

'I've stopped ticking off the days, because I don't have a pencil ... Maybe three or four months ...'

'What?' I cried in astonishment.

'Well, the market for hostages has been saturated lately,' he explained. 'They're waiting for things to settle before they restart negotiations. Ransom demands may be revised upwards ... As far as I know, your government has previously given in to blackmail by pirates in order to free its subjects. It's going to be hard to persuade it to pay out any more money, at least in the immediate future.'

'Who are our kidnappers exactly? Al-Qaeda, rebels, soldiers?'

'Subcontractors.'

'What does that mean?'

'Exactly what it says: they subcontract. It's just like any other business. There are big companies, and there are subcontractors. The people holding us are common adventurers. There are no more than twenty of them, all told. Not being powerful enough, or well enough equipped to go it alone, they subcontract. Whenever they get hold of a hostage, they offer him to a stronger group, which in turn sells him on to another, tougher gang, and so on up to the criminal or terrorist organisations that have a solid enough structure to negotiate with governments.'

'I don't understand,' I admitted, out of my depth.

Bruno scratched his temple, thinking. 'Well, for example, I was kidnapped with a correspondent from Italian television. I know sub-Saharan Africa and the Sahel like the back of my hand, and I sometimes act as a guide to Western journalists. I've even managed to get them interviews with particular warlords and local underworld bosses. A criminal gang grabbed us just outside Mogadishu. They sold us for five thousand dollars to a group of rebels. Then some terrorists bought us for twelve thousand dollars. They let the correspondent go because his TV channel agreed to pay the ransom, and I was handed over to some smugglers in exchange for a case of ammunition and three antipersonnel mines. Then the self-styled Captain Gerima got me from the smugglers for two hundred litres of drinking water and a second-hand crankshaft, and since then I've been waiting for my next buyer.'

'That's absurd.'

'Tell me about it.'

'Shhh!' ordered Blackmoon, who had come to stand guard outside our jail, with his sabre in his hand.

They brought us food. Rancid pancakes and shreds of dried meat.

When Hans fell asleep, Bruno went back to his bed, put on a battered pair of glasses, leant back against the wall and opened a dog-eared old book, which he spread on his knees.

'Have you ever tried to escape?'

Without looking up, he gave a little smile. 'Where would I go? The nearest water source is eighty kilometres further south. Behind the hill, the country is flat. In front is a bare valley. We're as unlikely to pass unnoticed as a cockroach on a tablecloth. Plus, there are guards around the camp, and they have itchy trigger fingers.'

'Where are we exactly?'

He put his book down on the floor and turned to me. 'Somewhere in hell on earth. Somalia, Ethiopia, Djibouti, Sudan, I don't have the slightest idea. We're constantly on the move, often at night. This is just a stopping-off point. After three or four weeks, they'll move to another hideout. Not to cover their tracks, but to avoid being slaughtered. There are plenty of gangs of degenerates operating in the area, and they don't see eye to eye. The zones of influence aren't clearly marked, and every gang wanders about according to the situation. The logistics are random; if you don't have allies, you're screwed. This area is controlled by rebels and bandits. The regular army aren't strong enough to venture far out of their camps. The proof is that this fort our kidnappers are squatting in used to be an army outpost. It was evacuated after a rebel incursion, and since then, it's been abandoned. There's a village a hundred kilometres to the east, and as there are no more garrisons in the sector, its inhabitants have fled.'

Hans asked us to be quiet.

Bruno obeyed. He buried his head in a cloth that he used as a pillow and crossed his hands over his belly. After a few minutes, his breathing settled down and he started snoring.

Outside, three guards were telling each other stories and laughing. They were speaking in their dialect, but I guessed that they were talking about raids, skirmishes, ambushes and death. They made 'bang!' and 'rat-tat-tat' sounds to represent machine-gun fire, aped their victims' supplications, and laughed out loud at the fear one of their cronies had shown.

Then silence fell like a guillotine.

A breeze started hissing through the gaps in the sheet metal. Hans's eyes were open. How did he plan to get to sleep with his eyes open? Slowly, fatigue overcame me and I drifted off.

Late in the night, Hans woke me. He was sitting up; his ghostly silhouette could be seen clearly in the half-light.

'I think Tao got away,' he whispered in a toneless voice. 'I'm convinced of that now. You remember when they put us in the felucca? I took a good look at my boat, there was no lifebelt on deck. Tao must have grabbed it as he was being thrown overboard. I'm sure of it. Tao's quick. He wouldn't have let them get away with it.'

'It was pitch-black, Hans. You could hardly see the boat.'

He frowned and lay down again, his eyes wide open.

Guilt was gradually driving him to a state of total denial.

In the morning, through the door with the wire netting, I saw a ribbon of dust above a mass of stones that had once been the rampart of the fort. It was the sidecar motorcycle coming back from somewhere or other. It parked outside the command post. The rider got off and helped a man out of the sidecar. The passenger was a middle-aged, almost light-skinned mixed-race man, quite frail and stooped, his ovoid skull balding at the front; he was wearing a crumpled suit and prescription glasses and holding a threadbare bag to his chest. Captain Gerima shook his hand warmly and motioned him to follow him into his office. A few minutes later, Joma came to fetch Hans. I asked him where he was planning to take my friend. 'To the infirmary,' he retorted. I reminded him I was a doctor; Joma laughed and made the ridiculous statement that in Africa, all you needed was a witch doctor. Two men lifted Hans and dragged him to a shack behind the command post.

I waited for Hans all morning and all afternoon, but he didn't come back. When I asked after him, all I got was insults.

'He's a good doctor,' Bruno reassured me. 'He tended my dysentery. At least he has proper drugs.'

'Is he a real doctor?'

'I think so. I don't know where he lives, but the captain sometimes sends for him when someone is seriously ill.'

Night fell, and I still hadn't seen Hans again.

The next day, and in the days after that, no sign of Hans. I started to panic and asked to speak to the captain. He wouldn't see me, but sent Joma to make it clear to me that a hostage would do better to behave himself if he wanted to get home in one piece. I dismissed these threats and demanded to know how my friend was. All I got in return was a string of curses and mimed throat cutting.

On the fourth day, the sidecar motorcycle left the fort, with the doctor on board. Hans remained in the 'infirmary'. It was only after a week that I saw him, a bandage around his chest, escorted by Blackmoon as far as a sheet-metal sentry box which served as the latrines.

'Why are they isolating him?' I asked Bruno, dreading a serious infection that the pirates were trying to hide from me.

'We're the ones they're isolating, Monsieur Krausmann,' he said. 'If our kidnappers are giving your friend such special treatment, it must mean they've struck a deal for him.'

I didn't understand. He sat down next to me and explained. 'When I was seized with the Italian journalist, we were held with a third hostage in a horrible cellar for weeks. In the dark. Tied up like sausages. Then the journalist was transferred to a separate cell, and they started to treat him better, giving him nicer food and allowing him to wash and shave. Some time later, he was released. I think your friend is going to be freed soon. You have to know how things work around here: even though

111

these criminals don't seem up to much, they're well organised. They have contacts in town and among officials who communicate anything that might interest them, in real time. And then there's the internet. They type in the names of their hostages, and in a second or two they have all the information they need. That's what they've done with you and your friend. Your name can't have told them much. Your friend's, though, probably came with a lot of tempting details ... I've been a prisoner for four months and I've learnt to sense when the wind is changing. The captain seems enthusiastic. That's an unmistakable sign. Usually, he's as moody as a pitbull ... What exactly does Monsieur Makkenroth do?'

'He's in humanitarian aid.'

'There must be something else.'

I hesitated, made sure that no prying ears were around, and admitted, 'Hans Makkenroth is a leading industrialist in Germany, and is very rich ...'

'That explains it. Captain Gerima may already be negotiating with several groups interested in your friend. Depending on how much the "merchandise" is likely to fetch, the auction can reach an astronomical figure.'

A thousand questions were jostling for position in my head, but I was too exhausted to put them in any kind of order. I didn't know how this kind of negotiation worked or how long it would last and, frankly, I was less and less able to see the end of the tunnel. In two weeks of captivity, I had lost my sense of judgement. My sleepless nights had exacerbated my anxieties, and every minute that passed lessened my presence of mind. I had become someone else. My voice had changed and my reflexes had grown dull. I had lost weight; an unkempt beard was engulfing my face, and the disgusting food we were served had made me ill. At this rate, I was certain I'd end up cracking or being put down like a dog.

The world was tightening around me like a straitjacket. It was a world of thirst and sunstroke where, outside the fort, nothing ever happened. Apart from the swirls of dust that the wind unleashed and abandoned immediately, and the vultures screeching in the arid sky, it was an implacable realm of silence and stillness. Even time seemed crucified on the sinister rocks that stood out against the horizon like presages of doom.

I went to take a breather by the door, which the guards left open during the day. Bruno and I were allowed to stretch our legs in a small yard marked off by a roll of barbed wire attached to posts; this was our 'solarium', a space of less than a hundred square metres adorned with a dead tree, at the foot of which I sometimes spent hours on end observing our kidnappers going about their business or practising quick marching, with debatable enthusiasm, beneath a leaden sun. It was after one in the afternoon; many of the pirates had retreated to their barracks while those few on fatigue duty bustled here and there. From the height of his lookout post, the sentry kept watch, his finger on the trigger. In the shade of a zinc canopy, Blackmoon sat like a plague victim in quarantine, sharpening his sabre on a pumice stone, his grotesque lensless glasses held together on his face with sticky tape. Ewana, the man who had been suffering from malaria, was smoking a joint behind a row of empty crates. He was wearing two baseball caps pulled down over his skull, one with the peak in front and the other with the peak flat against the back of his neck. Now that he had recovered, he would only appear when it was

113

siesta time, hide in a corner and indulge in such virtual excursions. On the steps of the command post, a young boy was washing the captain's linen; he was the 'orderly', who spent his days rinsing the officer's underwear, mending his socks, polishing his shoes and his weapons and wiping his cheap stripes … Looking at these maniacs who took themselves for warlords just because they were so good at terrifying people, listening to them shouting at each other in an unintelligible dialect and laughing their heads off over some trivial thing, I couldn't help pinching myself. On what planet had the irony of fate dumped me? What lesson was I, a newly bereaved husband, to draw from being cast adrift in this death-haunted land? … What disturbed me about my kidnappers wasn't their offhandedness, nor the destitution to which their status as a rebel band condemned them; but there was a glaring lack of awareness in the way they went about their day-to-day lives that made their dangerousness as natural as a snake bite, and just sensing them around me, I felt I was in a kind of purgatory where it wasn't necessary to have sinned, since the mere fact of ending up there constituted a crime.

Bruno joined me in the doorway. He placed a sympathetic hand on my shoulder; his gesture irritated me, but I didn't move away.

'It'll work out,' he promised. 'Everything works out in the end.'

'Do you think they'd kill us if they didn't find a buyer?'

'They'd already have done away with me. Nobody's asking for me and I don't have the slightest market value.'

'They haven't released you either.'

'I'm sure they'll let us go when they've amassed enough money to go home. Gerima's a rogue. He can't wait to blow all his money on whores, as far as possible from here, because he knows that if he stays here, sooner or later he'll get caught. He's clever. The only thing he's interested in is lining his own pocket. At the first opportunity, he wouldn't hesitate to get shot of these idiots who are following him blindly. It's always been like that around here. I know lots of bandits who, after crisscrossing the bush and getting themselves talked about in the media, suddenly vanished into thin air. Where are they, do you think? In Kenya or Chad, or some country at peace where nobody knows them and they can have an easy life on the money they've made. They grease a few palms here and there, get hold of new identity cards, and probably a new reputation because everything can be bought in this region, including the gods and patron saints, and they start a new life, as respectable as a marabout.'

Bruno took his hand away; he must have felt my muscles contract in his grip.

'The hostage trade has become an industry in Africa,' he went on. 'In the old days, I drifted from Mali to Tanzania, and it was a piece of cake. Wherever I ended up, I just had to knock at a door, any door, whether it was a house or a hut, and I automatically had board and lodgings. Those were great times. But ever since the first dollars were paid to kidnappers, the cobblers have put away their nails and their glue, the porters have given up carrying baskets for housewives, and any down-and-out imagines he's hit the jackpot as soon as he comes across a foreigner ... Governments shouldn't have yielded to the kidnappers' demands. At first, it was only jihadists targeting the odd aid worker. Now, it's open season for all kinds of chancers: ex-convicts, idlers, brainwashed kids from all over the world who come to claim their visa for paradise … The groups have proliferated; some are connected with Al-Shabaab, others operate on their own account, and nobody knows what to believe any more.'

I asked Bruno to stop and went back to my straw mattress.

In the evening, the guards placed a grille over the door of our jail and padlocked it. The confinement added an extra layer of depression to the sickly smell of the room. To get a little air, I went to the window, which was just a hole in the wall with thick iron bars across it. I wanted to gaze at the sunset, to escape for a moment from the thoughts that were tormenting me. I have to hold out, I told myself. When the sun had disappeared, the darkness threw itself on the shadows like a predator on its prey, and a senescent night, totally lacking in charm or romance, and worn down by age, prepared to make the desert its tomb. I didn't know much about the African night, yet I knew it would remain, for me, as devoid of meaning as the chance that had led me to this godforsaken spot. I thought about the nights I had known in the old days, in Frankfurt, Seville, Las Palmas, the south of France, Istanbul, Salonica; saw again the terraces with their white balconies, the gleaming shop windows, restaurant bars lined with mirrors and made mysterious by subdued lighting, the places that had filled me with awe, the streets that led me through a thousand little ordinary joys, the small parks where children played, the benches in the shade of the birches to which old people and lovers came to hear themselves living, the tourists taking photographs of each other at the foot of the monuments; I heard their singsong voices, the bursts of music drifting out of the clubs, the coaches setting off for the sun, and those nights seemed to me as subliminal and full as moons. It was amazing that a man deprived of his freedom, whose future was so uncertain, could revisit the life that had been stolen from him with such clarity, and that the small details to which he had paid no attention should come back to the surface with incredible precision and fill his heart with a nostalgia whose splendour was equalled only by the depth of his grief. So I closed my eyes and searched for the slightest little gleam that could alleviate my unhappiness; a shrill laugh, a quick run, a furtive glance, a smile, a handshake, anything that could fill my solitude with untold presences. Of course, Jessica was everywhere; I made out her perfume in the stench of my jail, recognised the swish of her dress in all the rustling around me; I longed for her in the midst of these shadows that were taking over my thoughts. Her absence left me naked, impoverished, mutilated; and there, standing by that damned window with the burning-hot bars, facing that night that had no story to tell and on which both rocks and men turned their backs, I made myself a solemn promise, a promise as unbreakable as a vow, not to weaken and, whatever happened, to get out of here and find my way back to my towns and my streets, my people and my songs, the places I had loved, the beaches where my tenderest memories lay, all my weaknesses and all my habits and all my countless illusions!

4

The third week of my captivity ended with a sandstorm
that lasted three days and three nights. I thought I was
going to choke to death. With a *cheche* around my head, my
eyes swollen and irritated, I felt as if the dust was getting in
through my pores. I'd never seen a sandstorm before, and
I discovered this extraordinary phenomenon in a kind of
delirium. It was like a malevolent flood, as if a Pandora's
box had unleashed on the world incessant gusts of wrath
and evil spells. The sky and the earth had disappeared in
a pandemonium of noise and obscurity; I could no longer
tell day from night. All you could hear were the torrents
of sand rolling across the desert and moaning elegiacally
in the crevices. Then the storm suddenly abated and, as if
by magic, everything went back to its accustomed place.
The heat resumed its obsessive hum and the horizon its
frustrating emptiness.

I had only glimpsed Hans twice since we had been
separated. He was walking a little better now. Blackmoon
let me know that my friend was getting special treatment
and that in the evening he was taken for a walk behind
the hill to help him recover. The atmosphere in the fort
was fairly relaxed; the captain was in a good mood and
Chief Moussa, who had left with his henchmen to plunder

the nearest villages, had come back, the two pick-ups overflowing with provisions.

Bruno and I were crouching by the door of our prison. Blackmoon stepped over the little barrier and walked to the foot of the dead tree, with a book in his hand and without his sabre. It was unusual for him to appear without it; it was as if he were missing a limb; he seemed different, an ordinary young man, calm, pleasant to look at. Without even glancing at us, he sat down on a clod of earth and immersed himself in his book, which remained obstinately open at the same page.

'What have you done with your sabre, Chaolo?' Bruno asked.

Blackmoon pretended not to have heard. When Bruno asked him the same question again, he looked around as if the Frenchman had been addressing someone else, then pointed to his own chest and said, 'Are you talking to me?'

'Yes, of course.'

'My name's not Chaolo.'

'Oh, really? Since when?'

Blackmoon shrugged and went back to his book. 'It isn't my name any more,' he said after a pause, and gave me an exaggerated wink, as if asking me to enlighten Bruno.

'He has a combat name now,' I said. 'It's Blackmoon.'

'Impressive,' Bruno said, concealing a smile behind his hand. 'Is that why you got rid of your sabre?'

'It isn't a sabre, it's a machete,' Blackmoon said with a hint of irritation. 'I lent it to the cook. He needs it to cut up the animal.'

Bruno passed his swollen fingers through his beard, scratched his cheek and, ignoring the signals I was making to avoid things turning nasty, ventured, 'Now that you have a combat name, they're surely going to let you have a sub-machine gun.'

Blackmoon seemed happy to play the Frenchman's game. He pushed his glasses back towards his forehead and said, 'The only time they put a gun in my hands, it went off by itself, and the stray bullet hit Chief Moussa's dog and killed it. Captain Gerima, who's a bit of a sorcerer, told me the spirit of firearms is incompatible with mine. Since then, I've carried a machete.'

He fell silent while a young pirate walked past pushing a wheelbarrow.

Bruno waited for the rest of the story, but it didn't come. 'What are you reading?' he asked to restart the conversation.

'I can't read.'

'What do you mean, you can't read? You've been looking at that book for ages.'

'I like looking at the words. For me, they're better than drawings. They have so many mysteries. So I look at them and try to decode their secrets.'

'You can spend hours on end engrossed in a book just to look at the words?'

'Why, do you have a problem with that?'

'Not necessarily.'

'It doesn't bother me. I sit down under a tree or on a rock, I open my book, I look at it and I feel fine … The only thing I regret is that I never went to college.'

'What job would you have chosen if you had?'

'Teacher,' he said without hesitation. 'There was one in my village. He was distinguished, and people treated him with respect. Every time he passed our house, I stood up to be polite. He had style, that teacher. My father said it was because he possessed knowledge, and nothing's above knowledge.'

'Is that why you wear glasses? Because it makes you look like a teacher?'

'There's no law against dreaming, is there?'

'Of course, it's the one right there's no law against … I assume you followed Moussa because he possesses knowledge?'

Blackmoon gave a scornful grin. 'Moussa doesn't possess anything. Joma says he's an intellectual, and an intellectual is a big talker who shows off like a circus horse. A poser, that's all Moussa is. He doesn't believe a damned word of the speeches he bores us with.'

'In that case, why do you stay with him?'

'I'm not with him, I'm with Joma.'

'Is he a relative of yours?'

'Joma doesn't have any family. He says he came into the world directly from the sky, like a shooting star.'

'And why do you stay with Joma?'

'I like him. He isn't easy to get on with, but he's straight. I've known him for years. He was a tailor in the market in my village and I was his boy.'

'What does that mean, his boy?' I asked Bruno.

'It means I did everything for him,' Blackmoon replied. 'I maintained his moped, put away his rolls of cloth, ran errands for him. In return, he took care of me … It was good in the old days,' he said with a sigh. 'We had an easy life. We didn't ask for much. Actually, we didn't know if there was anything else …'

He bowed his head, saddened by the memory of that period of his life.

'What happened?' Bruno insisted.

'What?' Blackmoon, who had been lost in the past, said with a start. 'What happened? Something that's not going to stop now.' His voice had turned dark and hoarse. 'It was a mess. A bomb wiped out the market. We never understood why. Maybe because there was nothing to understand. Joma lost his workshop and his reason for living. He gave his sewing machines, his rolls of cloth and his scissors to his creditors and went off to war. I followed him …'

He was interrupted by Ewana who was back from the latrines. 'Don't listen to him,' Ewana said. 'He's a loser. He'd piss off a dead man in his grave just by praying for his soul.'

'Fuck you,' Blackmoon said.

'What would you fuck me with, scarecrow? You don't even have balls.' Ewana disappeared behind a ruined building.

Blackmoon started breathing heavily. His Adam's apple rose and fell in his throat like a piston. Slowly, his face stopped twitching and his eyes grew calm.

'What about you, don't you have any family either?' Bruno asked.

Blackmoon frowned, thought for a minute, then looked the Frenchman up and down. 'You aren't a shrink by any chance, are you? How do you always manage to get me to talk? You aren't stealing my soul like the griots?'

'I'm not a griot.'

'Then what's your trick?'

'I don't have a trick. We're talking, that's all. Man to man. Without any ulterior motive. I listen to you frankly and you open your heart to me.'

Blackmoon pondered Bruno's arguments and found

them admissible. 'Maybe you're right. It isn't that I don't trust you, but around here, if you trust people too much, you're a dead man. You never know when the lightning's going to strike … Joma doesn't believe in God or anyone. But he knows that with me, he can sleep easy. If he asked me to die for him, I'd do it … And even so, he doesn't trust me.'

'Have you ever killed for him?'

Blackmoon stiffened. The little grin that had been playing over his lips like a will o' the wisp now abruptly deepened the creases at the corners of his mouth. 'Were you ever a policeman?' he asked Bruno.

'No, never.'

'Then can you explain why your questions make me want to piss on you?' With that, he stood up, looked us up and down and grunted, 'They're all the same! You try to be nice, and they try to screw you over.'

And he went off to kick stones behind the rampart.

'I told you the boy was unstable,' I said sharply to Bruno as we went back to our straw mattresses in the jail. 'You upset him, and he won't forgive us in a hurry.'

'No, no,' Bruno reassured me, lying back on his mat. 'The boy is seriously disturbed, I don't deny that, but of all the sons of bitches who are keeping us in this hole, he's the least formidable and probably the only one who has a bit of a soul left. I've been watching him for weeks. He likes to let himself go without really dropping his guard, which complicates things with him … He's not as bad as he seems … He was the one who slipped me the miracle powder and the ointment. In these conditions, a gesture like that almost restores your faith in the human race …'

He rolled a cloth into a pillow and slipped it under his neck.

His excessive serenity exasperated me. I was seriously starting to doubt his 'great knowledge' of African matters.

'I think we should avoid getting too familiar with the boy.'

'Why's that?' he asked nonchalantly.

'These people are unpredictable.'

He gave a brief, dry laugh and dismissed my words with his hand. 'It's obvious you don't know much about Africa, Monsieur Krausmann.'

Bruno brought out this excuse every time I disapproved of his actions or his theories about the complexity of people and things. As far as he was concerned, I was merely a middle-class European who lived in a bubble, as indifferent to the bedlam of the world as a goldfish in its bowl; a conventional doctor with manicured nails, so narcissistic he could live in a mirror, who saw only a superficial exoticism where there were other mindsets and other truths to explore. He even showed contempt for the narrowness of my culture and my lack of curiosity when it came to looking a bit further than the end of my nose, and declared emphatically that a person who couldn't love one song from each folk tradition and one saint from each belief had only lived half a life. 'The African,' he said one night, 'is a code. Decipher it, and you'll achieve understanding.'

Bruno had told me the story of his life in Africa. In fact, that was all he had been doing in the time I'd been sharing the jail with him. He had fallen in love with the continent as a young man after reading *The Forgotten*

Trail, a novel about the Tuaregs by a French writer named Frison-Roche. Captivated by the Sahara and the peoples of the Hoggar, he had studied dozens of books dealing with the lives and customs of that part of the world, and had ended up hungrily devouring the work of the French naturalist Théodore André Monod, a great explorer of the desert regions as well as a scholar in many disciplines and an unequalled humanist, who had died at the beginning of the twenty-first century. At the age of nineteen Bruno had followed in his mentor's footsteps, setting off with a group of students from Bordeaux to search for the famous ancient route, buried beneath the *ergs* and *regs*, which, according to Frison-Roche, King Solomon had taken in order to establish trade relations with the black kingdoms. After a short expedition in the Ténéré, the group of students returned to Bordeaux empty-handed, but Bruno stayed, and was taken in, half dead with dehydration, by a Fulani family. He spent several weeks in a nameless village before resuming his investigations. He never returned to France. He was in his element in the desert, sometimes an anthropologist, sometimes an archaeologist, before deciding to follow the movements of the caravan people and nomadic shepherds, and it was they who really introduced him to what was most special and remarkable about Africa. His wanderings lasted fifteen extraordinary years, during which he discovered Niger, Upper Volta, from where he was displaced by a bloody coup, Ghana, Mali, Senegal and Mauritania. He returned to Upper Volta, now Burkina Faso, before being chased out by another coup, then went back up to Aguelhok in the north of Mali, where he taught French to surprisingly receptive kids in an open-air classroom. He knew all the tribes in the

and synthetic drugs; they soon became disillusioned with this absurd attempt at an idyll, and Souad, realising that happiness is impossible without money, didn't hesitate for one second before dumping her handsome but penniless lover when a club owner promised her the moon if she agreed to go with him to Cape Verde. Mad with grief and hunger, Bruno resumed his peregrinations, entrusting his fate to the whims of the unconsoling roads that took him from one country to another for six years. He ended up in Djibouti, where he got by on odd jobs and adulterated beer, and then, offering his services to the Western media, started venturing from time to time to Somalia for the purposes of a TV item or a journalistic investigation, until the day he was kidnapped by bandits near Mogadishu along with a star of Italian television to whom he had acted as both interpreter and guide.

'How can you still have faith in these people after what they've put you through?' I asked.

Lying there wrapped in his cloths, Bruno rested his left foot on his right knee and stared up at the rickety beams on the ceiling. Shafts of light filtered through the cracks in the sheet metal and scattered a multitude of golden coins on the sandy ground. An ash-coloured lizard held itself motionless on the wall, almost imperceptible against the cob. Above its head, a vast, tattered spider's web moved gently in the draught, like a hanging garden in a state of decay. In a corner, near the receptacle we used as a urinal, two beetles grappled in silence ... plus of course, searching for gaps in our mosquito nets, our very own pets, the flies!

'They didn't put me through anything, Monsieur Krausmann. I wanted to be one of them and I shared their depravity along with everything else. I did it of my own free will and I don't have any regrets. I have an almost religious veneration for Africa. I love its highs and lows, its pointless ordeals and its absurd dreams, its miseries as splendid as Greek tragedies and its frugality which is a doctrine in itself, its exaggerated effusions and its fatalism. I love everything about Africa, from the disappointments that punctuated my wanderings to the mirages that deceive those who are lost. Africa is a certain philosophy of redemption. Among these "wretched of the earth",' he went on, drawing inverted commas with his fingers, 'I've known happy moments, and I've also shared their worries to the full. These people have taught me truths about myself I would never have suspected in Paris or anywhere in the West. I was born in Bordeaux, in a pretty crib, but it's in Africa that I'll die, and it doesn't really matter if I end up in a mass grave or on some godforsaken dirt track, without a hearse or a gravestone.'

'Strange,' I said.

'I see a country where others see a continent, and in this country, I'm myself. As soon as this piracy business is over, I'll go off along the "forgotten trails" to catch up with the joys and sorrows I've missed because of my confinement.'

'I wish you courage, Monsieur Bruno.'

'Courage, Monsieur Krausmann, means believing in yourself.'

And already he was gone, a long, long way away, his eyes closed and his hands crossed over his chest. That was Bruno all over: whenever he praised Africa, he became a poet and guru at one and the same time, and an unbridled lyricism swept him away; without warning, his mind was no longer there, and in the suddenly silent jail, all that remained was his exhausted body, as stiff as a dead man's.

*

Three days later, Joma came rushing out of the captain's office, yelled for someone to fetch Chief Moussa, then, catching sight of Bruno and me in the yard of our prison, screamed, 'Hey, you two, get back in your quarters, and be quick about it!'

'It isn't time yet,' Bruno protested.

'There's no fixed time. Do as I say!'

'Do as I say!' Bruno aped him half-heartedly. 'We aren't your soldiers.'

Joma kicked over the barrier and rushed at us. I didn't even have time to stand up. Joma grabbed me by the neck and flung me into the cell. I got up and walked back to defy him. He raised his eyebrows, amused by my sudden burst of pride, brought his face close to mine and breathed his drunken breath in my face.

'Want to hit me, do you? ... Go on, then, show me what you're made of, pretty boy.'

Seeing that I held his gaze, he pushed me away with his hand, seized the grille and, with a single movement, lifted it and hung it from the hooks cemented into the doorway.

'What strength!' Bruno said ironically.

'Oh, yes,' Joma retorted, padlocking the door. 'That's life. There are those who have guns, and those who can only watch and weep.'

'For how long, Joma, for how long?'

'That'll depend on how brave you are, assuming you're brave at all,' Joma replied. '"If you wish to fight the gods,"' he quoted, '"Fight them and perish!"'

'Sophocles?' Bruno ventured, mockingly.

'Wrong ...'

129

'Shakespeare?'

'Why does it have to be a white man?'

'I'd be tempted to say Anta Diop, but he wasn't a poet.'

'Baba-Sy,' Joma said proudly.

'Who's he? I've never heard of him.'

A shudder ran through Joma. He put on the last padlock and rejoined his men, who were running in all directions. Orders rang out, the engine of the sidecar motorcycle roared, and the pirates rushed into their barracks and came out with weapons and baggage. Captain Gerima appeared in the doorway of the command post, his belly sticking out of his trousers and the American army belt around his neck. His eyes shone with a malevolent joy. His hands on his hips, he watched part of his flock getting into the back of a pick-up parked under a canopy. Chief Moussa appeared, spick and span in a made-to-measure paratrooper's uniform, his boots polished and his beret pulled down over his forehead. He saluted the captain, who returned the salute with lordly nonchalance. The two colleagues walked a little way together, as far as the well, conversing in low voices, then retraced their steps. Chief Moussa took leave of his superior with a click of his heels and ran to join the men crammed into the pick-up.

'Are they going on a raid?' I asked.

'I don't think so,' Bruno said. 'They don't usually have to lock us up.'

The pick-up manoeuvred round and headed for the infirmary. From the door of our jail, we couldn't follow it. I went to the window that looked out on the valley and waited for something that might tell me what was going on. Ten minutes later, I saw the sidecar motorcycle set off in front. When the pick-up reappeared on the other side of the rampart, my heart leapt in my chest: in the middle of the pirates crammed into the pick-up, I saw Hans, his hands tied behind his back, pinned to the bed of the truck.

The ground almost gave way beneath my feet.

The transfer of Hans plunged Bruno and me into a kind of daze. We had been half expecting it and, now that it had happened, we felt that we had been caught off guard. We were so upset we couldn't find words to comfort each other. Bruno retreated behind his mosquito net, and I was so dismayed I couldn't put my thoughts in order.

The sun had not yet set when two guards, rifles at the ready, disturbed our meditation. It was rare for food to be brought to us with firearms aimed at us. Blackmoon placed a tray in front of me with a metal plate on it, in which soup had congealed. He deliberately stepped on my toes and, having attracted my attention, made a sign with his eyes to indicate that the piece of bread that came with the soup had something in it for me.

The pirates left, padlocking the grille. I heard their steps shuffling in the yard before being lost in the noises of the fort. I bent over the slice of bread and tore it with my fingers; a piece of paper was hidden inside. I took it out, unfolded it very carefully and recognised Hans's feverish handwriting.

His little note was short: two sentences scribbled in pencil and set out on two lines:

Stand firm.
Every day is a miracle.

5

Against all expectations, it was Bruno who cracked first. His thick shell, formed through forty years' experience in Africa, shattered into pieces. With a kick, he sent his meal flying against the wall, threw himself on the grille, shook it angrily and then collapsed exhausted on his bundle of cloths. When the noises of the fort faded, he got up and started pacing up and down the cell, breathing harshly, like a wild beast looking for an opening in its cage.

The previous day, at nightfall, the pirates had lit a fire and danced like mad gods to music blaring from a huge radio cassette player. Laughing as he watched them writhing about, Bruno had found them brilliant. 'Do you realise what a sensation they'd be on the Paris stage?' he had cried, as enchanted as a groupie in the presence of his idol. I had asked him what our kidnappers were so happy about. 'The end of the civil war, probably,' he had replied. Actually, it was the transfer of Hans Makkenroth they were celebrating!

The sun had been up for some time when Bruno decided to show signs of life. He stared at the grille as if trying to blow it up with his eyes, then hoisted himself to his feet, shuffled over to the door, his legs like cotton wool, and grabbed hold of the grille in order not to collapse.

'Hey, Gerima!' he cried. 'Gerima, can you hear me? Come out of your lair, you son of a bitch!'

I ran to him and tried to calm him; he pushed me away and started yelling again.

'What are you waiting for to sell us on the black market, you bastard? You're an expert in that, aren't you? You did well for yourself when you filched rations from your unit. What's the difference between a hostage and a can of food? Can you hear me, Gerima?'

I put my hand over his mouth to stifle his cries; he bit me and, still clinging to the grille, screamed out all his rage and frustration. A guard hit his fingers with his rifle butt to make him let go; Bruno didn't even notice. He continued to pour out his anger at the captain, who emerged now from his command post, wiping his mouth with a handkerchief.

'Ah, there you are at last!' Bruno cried. 'I thought you were hibernating! I order you to let us go right now. This farce has lasted long enough. You're going to release us, you piece of shit. What right do you have to keep us in this hole?'

The captain signalled to two guards to fetch Bruno. I wanted to go with him, but I was pushed back inside the cell and the grille was banged shut.

Bruno was forced by the two guards to kneel at the captain's feet. He immediately got up again and resumed taunting the captain.

'Who do you think you are? Just because you're surrounded by a gang of nutcases, do you think you can lay down the law for the whole world? You're just a common highwayman, Gerima, a bastard of a deserter heading for ruin.'

The captain slapped Bruno.

'Didn't even hurt,' Bruno said.

A second, harder slap.

'Put a bit more strength into it, captain.'

A third slap.

Stunned, Bruno swayed a little. But then he regained his self-control and, driven by some kind of suicidal stubbornness, put his hands around his mouth like a funnel and cried, 'You're nothing but a loser, Gerima!'

Gerima threw his head back in a Homeric laugh, then, contorting his features into an expression of outraged hatred, grabbed Bruno by the throat. 'Now that you've made a spectacle of yourself, why don't you unplug your ears and listen to me for two seconds. I'm not a crook, I'm a soldier. You're not a can of rations, you're part of the spoils of war. You're going to go back to your fridge and be a well-behaved vegetable until the cook comes for you. And if you ever again bring out this pathetic Spartacus act of yours, I swear to God and all his saints that I'll hang you by the balls until you crumble to dust.'

'I'm not part of the spoils of war, and you're nothing but a trafficker of the worst kind.'

A guard made to hit Bruno, but the captain lifted his finger to stop him. He leant over Bruno and said, 'We're at war, and I wage mine as I see fit.'

'Rubbish! You pillage, rape, massacre poor defenceless devils, kidnap foreigners, blackmail governments that are in no way involved in the mess you've made …'

'That's war!' the captain exploded. 'What do *you* know about war? TV newsflashes that come on between the adverts while you're drinking aperitifs in your cosy living room, with your arms around your girlfriend? Newsflashes that you register briefly and then forget almost immediately?'

'Don't give me that!' Bruno retorted, totally un-impressed. 'We're following your pseudo-war in close-up, and in real time. We aren't in our living rooms, we're up to our necks in your shit, putting up with you morning, noon and night. You're nothing but a pack of bandits who don't believe in anything, scavenge on corpses and rob from the poor.'

'That's war, too.'

'I'll tell you what war is. War is a balance sheet. And yours is disastrous. Lots of murderers like you thought that a uniform would lessen their punishment. That doesn't work any more. Soldiers or not, the International Criminal Court is ready and waiting for them. You'll end up in front of it, too, and you'll be judged for your crimes.'

Mention of the International Criminal Court shook the captain: intoxicated as he was with the impunity he enjoyed in this territory where every abuse was allowed, he had probably not foreseen that eventuality.

He swallowed, then grunted with a flagrant lack of conviction, 'Your court can go to hell!'

'That's what genocidal tyrants cry out loud when they swagger around their village squares. Where are they now? In the dock, trying to make themselves very small. However many witnesses you get rid of, however hard you sweep around your mass graves to wipe out all trace of your crimes, your own accomplices will blab every last detail of your murders and rapes.'

Gerima was taken aback by Bruno's threats. He tried to

appear composed, but in vain. Sweat was pouring down his face, and his nostrils were quivering. Bruno realised that he had knocked him off balance, and that emboldened him to deliver the final blow.

'The world has changed, captain. There's nowhere you can escape punishment. The new laws reach far and wide. Wherever you go to ground, they'll find you …'

Gerima gave a bloodcurdling cry, threw Bruno to the ground and started beating him with his studded belt. Bruno covered his face with his arms and pulled his knees up to his chest to protect himself. In a frenzy now, the captain beat him and beat him, beat him with all his strength, again and again, extinguishing his moans and groans one by one. Bruno could neither get up nor hide behind his bruised limbs. Soon, his convulsions became less frequent and, after a few last jerks and shudders, eventually ceased altogether. The captain continued to strike Bruno's shattered body as if trying to reduce it to a pulp. It was the first time in my life I had witnessed such a violent, bestial scene. I was overcome, unable to resign myself to the idea that you could attack a defenceless person like that and still call yourself a man.

Bruno spent two nights in the infirmary.

When they brought him back to the cell, they had to drag him. Blackmoon was holding him by the armpit, and another pirate by the waist; Joma followed behind, a revolver in his belt. They laid him down very carefully on his cloths. Bruno asked for something to quench his thirst; they helped him to lift his head and drink from the neck of his flask. The water gushed over his cracked lips and onto his shirt. After three gulps, he choked and fell back on his straw mattress.

The two porters took off his shoes and prepared to leave.

'Thanks, Blackmoon,' I said.

From the way he suddenly clenched his jaws, I realised I had made a blunder. Blackmoon gave me a look that was a mixture of annoyance and fear. I had simply wanted to thank him for Hans's message; in my pressing need to resume my old habits in order to believe that I was still among human beings, I had forgotten to choose the right moment to express my gratitude. My fear grew all the greater when I noticed that Joma had also given a start.

Much to my relief, I realised that it wasn't the 'thanks' but the name 'Blackmoon' that had caught Joma's attention.

'What did he call you?' Joma asked his boy.

Blackmoon swallowed.

Joma gave him a shove. 'What have you been telling this white man?'

'I don't know what he's talking about,' Blackmoon said in a small voice.

'No kidding! So he can read your thoughts now, can he? You have a loose tongue, Chaolo. Make sure I don't tear it out.'

The three men went out, leaving the door of our jail open.

I went to Bruno. He was in a terrible mess. A clumsy bandage had been tied around his head. His face was battered; one eye was closed thanks to a nasty wound above it; his lips were bleeding in places ... He groaned when I touched him with my fingertips.

'What possessed you to provoke that monster?' I said.

He smiled at me through his wounds. His laughing eyes seemed to mock me. 'Undress me,' he said. 'My body's burning.'

'You fool!'

I took off his shirt as if tearing off his skin. He clenched his teeth, but couldn't stifle his groans. His chest was covered in marks and purplish scratches. His back had the same blue streaks, with darker patches on the shoulders and hips. I had to let him catch his breath before taking off his trousers. The skin of his knees was peeled, and his legs looked as if they had been attacked with a meat cleaver. There was a deep, suppurating cut on his left calf. The person working in the infirmary hadn't done much, merely putting poultices over the wounds without disinfecting them and smearing antiseptic over the bruises.

Bruno pointed with his chin at the bag containing the 'miracle powder'. 'Put that on the open wounds ... Then put the balm above my eye.'

Having nothing else to suggest, I did as I was told.

He watched me with a smile; every now and again, his smile turned to a grimace, then reappeared, enigmatic, absurd, disturbing.

'He gave me quite a thrashing,' he said with a hoarse laugh.

'Where did it get you?'

'It made a change from the general monotony, didn't it?'

'I don't understand you. You've been telling me to be detached and keep a clear head ever since I got here, and now you go off the rails like that. He could have killed you.'

'I did go a bit crazy,' he admitted. 'It happens to the toughest of us … Hans is the third hostage I've seen leave. It was as if a fuse blew inside me … I keep telling these sons of bitches that I'm not a hostage like the others, that I've been an African for forty years, that nobody in France knows what's become of me and so no government would ask for me back, but the bastards just won't listen to me. Even if anybody did ask for me back, I have no intention of leaving Africa. I'm an African, a wandering anchorite. I have no wife, no children, no money and no fixed abode, and my papers are years out of date … Who's going to bother spending a small fortune on a ghost?'

'That's no reason to put yourself in danger.'

'I've had enough,' he said, out of breath, his smile disappearing to be replaced by an immense weariness. 'I can't stand it any more, I've had it up to here … I want to go back to the dusty roads, and walk and walk without any particular destination, walk until I pass out. These walls are blinding me.' His voice was quivering now. 'They're stifling me, driving me crazy … I need wide open spaces and mirages and dromedaries. I want to stumble upon a hut in the middle of nowhere, share a shepherd's meal and take my leave of him early in the morning; I want to turn the corner of a cathedral-shaped rock and run into an old acquaintance, walk with him a little way and lose sight of him at nightfall. I want to see my pilgrim stars again, my Great Bear and Little Bear, and my shooting stars crossing my skies like signs of destiny. And when I'm so hungry I'd take a grasshopper for a turkey, and so thirsty I could drink the sea, I'll drop by a dive for reformed crooks and get as drunk as ten Poles, then, after spewing worse than a volcano, I'll wipe my mouth on the whores' petticoats and swear on their lives it won't happen again and set off through the deserts, barely capable of staying upright, to visit the ancient tombs buried in the sand; I'll bivouac at the foot of a rock and tell myself stories until I end up believing them more than anything in the world ... That's how it's always been, Monsieur Krausmann, in my life and in my mind. I'm a puff of smoke blown about by contrary winds, my eyes are hunters of horizons and my heels are cut out of flying carpets ...'

Broken, exhausted, moved by his own words, he huddled in his rags, brought his knees up to his stomach and made himself so small that his sobs almost drowned him.

Having wept all the tears he had in his body, he raised himself up on one elbow, turned to me and showed me his ruined teeth in a smile as tragic as a surrender.

'My God, a bit of self-pity does you a power of good every now and again!'

In the afternoon, Captain Gerima came into our prison yard. He began by yelling at a guard, just to announce himself, then appeared in the doorway and cleared his throat. His hand on the door, he looked into the corners of the cell, and his gaze came to rest on Bruno, who had retreated beneath his mosquito net.

'How is he?' he asked me.

'You almost blinded him in one eye,' I said in disgust. I would have preferred not to speak to him at all, but it just came out.

He scratched the top of his head, embarrassed. It was obvious he'd had a bad night: he had bags under his eyes and his jowls hung flabby and formless over his jaws. To make himself look perkier, he had buttoned up his tunic, which he usually left half open over his big belly – a mark, in his opinion, of the panache befitting a rebel chief. 'That's a real pity!' he said.

He was trying to be conciliatory, but as this was unusual in the life he had chosen for himself, the humility he was attempting to show struck me as pathetic and misplaced. There are people who are merely the expression of their misdeeds, vile because they have no scruples, ugly because their treachery makes them repulsive. Captain Gerima was one of them: if you held out a stick to help him up, he'd grab it to hit you with.

He shifted in the doorway, uncertain whether to come in or go on his way. He came in, his hands behind his back, his shoulders stooped like a general who has run out of tactics.

'I don't like people who stand up to me,' he said.

I didn't react.

He stopped, then said to the wall, 'This is the first time I've lost control like that. I usually handle the situation more tactfully … But the Frenchman really went too far.' He turned to me. 'Are the French all like that? Don't they know how to behave themselves?' He opened his arms and slapped them against his thighs. 'Is it any surprise I flipped? Has anybody bothered you since you've been here? You're being treated properly. You're given food and drink, and we let you sleep in peace. You won't find better-off hostages anywhere in the world. In other places, hostages are fed to the dogs, their throats are cut like sheep … I've never executed a hostage. And this Frenchman dares to mock my authority. How do you expect my men to respect me if I let my prisoners humiliate me?'

He wiped his face with his forearm.

'It's all a matter of discipline, doctor,' he went on. 'And without discipline, anything can happen. Some of my men are ready to flay you alive. They don't care about the money. What could they buy with it, where would they go? The whole country's ablaze. All they've ever known is war. And war has only one face: theirs! If it was up to them, they'd tear you to pieces just for the practice.'

He looked behind him, as if fearing to be overheard, and when he spoke again it was in a conspiratorial tone.

'Do you think I like rotting here, having to break camp purely on guesswork and constantly moving about to avoid ambushes? Do you think I enjoy it?'

He again looked over his shoulder.

'I'd be ready to swap my weapons, all my weapons, for your scalpel,' he continued. 'War's no picnic. I suffer from it just as much as a shepherd who steps on a landmine or a little girl cut down by a stray bullet. Nobody, and I mean nobody, is safe when tragedy is established as a dogma, when wrongdoing becomes logical. If you asked the greatest of fighters or the person who's amassed the most astonishing booty what he'd like most, he'd answer quick as a flash, "A moment's rest!" No people are made for war. Ours no more than yours. But we haven't been given the choice. I may be a brute, but I'd love to have a cushy job, and a little woman waiting for me in the evening, and maybe even a couple of kids who'd throw their arms around my neck when I got home from work. Just my luck, instead of a school exercise book they stuck a gun in my hand and said, "It's every man for himself." So I do what I can ...'

I simply stared at him, hoping that I wasn't letting him

see what I was thinking. My silence irritated him, but he could live with it. He must have realised that he had gone too far with Bruno and saw me as a witness for the prosecution whom he had to make an effort to win over. From the helpless look on his face, I didn't get the feeling I was successfully concealing the aversion I felt for him. His bestiality had shocked me, and I didn't think, whatever mitigating circumstances he put forward in his defence, that I could ever consider him as belonging to the human race.

He mopped himself with a handkerchief, wiped the corners of his mouth, where there was a kind of milky secretion, and put the handkerchief back in his pocket. His eyes searched for something on the ceiling, then came back to me, sizing me up. He took out a packet of Camels and offered me one, which I refused. I wanted him to go, to stop polluting the cell with his drunken breath, to leave me to the semi-darkness and the silence ... He wouldn't go. He stood there in the middle of the room, every inch a hypocrite, looking at a flaking patch of wall.

He stuck a cigarette between his lips, which were as thick and hard as wood, lit it and took a puff, putting on a show of nervousness.

'My mother died of old age at thirty-five. Our people didn't even have enough to buy an aspirin. In fact, we didn't even know what an aspirin looked like. When epidemics came, we weren't any better off than our sheep ... And they want us to believe that there's justice on earth and a God in heaven?'

He took a long drag, breathed it out through his nose, and stared at the burning tip of his cigarette, apparently finding something fascinating in it. He stood there for a while, lost in his memories, then turned to me again.

'There is no justice or mercy,' he said. 'There are those who live and those who survive, and in both scenarios, the unlucky ones suffer.'

He stubbed out his cigarette under his boot as if crushing the head of a snake. Before leaving, he stopped in the doorway and turned to face me.

'I didn't choose violence. It was violence that recruited me. It doesn't matter if it was of my own free will or without my knowing. We each make do as best we can. I don't hate anybody in particular and so I don't see why I shouldn't treat everyone the same. To me, black or white, innocent or guilty, victim or killer, it doesn't matter. I'm too colour blind to tell the wheat from the chaff. And besides, what's the wheat and what's the chaff? What's good for some people is bad for others. Everything depends on which side you're on. There's no point feeling regret or remorse. What difference does it make when the bad deed has already been done? I may have had a heart when I was little, today it's calcified. When I put my hand on my chest, all I feel in there is anger. I don't know how to feel sorry for people because nobody ever felt sorry for me. I'm only the hand that holds my rifle, and I don't know which of us, me or my rifle, gives the orders.'

He left the jail. Two of his henchmen came running in the bright sun, their rifles over their shoulders, and escorted him to his 'office'. Standing in one of the ruined buildings, Joma, who had been skinning a goat, stopped what he was doing and watched the captain and his praetorian guard cross the yard. When the three men disappeared into the command post, he perched on a low wall and kicked away a skeletal dog that had approached the animal carcass.

Bruno stirred in his corner. 'Has he gone?'

'Yes.'

He pushed back his mosquito net and sat up. 'What an actor! I hope you didn't take his little performance at face value, Monsieur Krausmann. The man's a crocodile, and you don't soften up a crocodile by wiping away his tears. That son of a bitch would praise the devil if it suited him. He doesn't believe a word he says. The fact is, he's scared. It's my mention of the International Criminal Court that's preying on his mind.'

I didn't reply. I admit the captain's words had thrown me. The human misery he embodied and his unexpected about-turn had made him less abstract to me.

That evening we were treated to better food: fresh meat, pancakes and a potato stew. In our famished state, this was a banquet.

'You see, Monsieur Krausmann?' Bruno said. 'No tyrant is above the law. You just have to remind him of the fact.'

6

Day broke. I knew that it wouldn't bring anything more than it had already taken from me. I didn't need to glance at the window to figure out what time it was. Here, in this anteroom to nervous breakdowns, time didn't matter: it was just a light replacing the dark, a dull, lustreless light that flashed unpleasantly across the mind and left no trace. Day broke, and then what? As far as I was concerned, it was merely a stranger passing through, who had nothing to do with me. *Before*, day had had a meaning, a purpose. It was the work that awaited me, or a train to catch. I recognised the morning instinctively. My hand would reach out mechanically to the alarm clock and switch it off. I didn't need it: I had a clock in my head, the alarm was merely for back-up. However sleepy I was, I would feel the dawn as a familiar presence, even in the dead of winter. I loved to sense it standing by my bedside, so tangible that I seemed to hear it breathe. That was *before*, at a time when every day had its commitments: patients to examine, fears to assuage, tasks to accomplish, plans to map out, prospects to establish. I had a status, a reputation, a schedule, lunches arranged long in advance, a watch on my wrist, a beautiful calendar on my desk; I had a mobile phone so that I could be reached anywhere, and voice mail in order not to miss news? One thing was sure, I never imagined for a moment that it could happen to me. The radio! It was an essential element of driving for me. Whenever I forgot to switch it on, a good part of my morning was out of kilter. But that was *before*, when everything that now seems fundamental was simply part of a well-worn routine. How could I have believed that some things didn't matter, that I was allowed not to care about them? ... What I would have given now to get back to those simple everyday gestures, those little pleasures and concerns that gave my life its particular pattern! What I would have given now to see my letterbox again, the bills that upset me, the circulars I threw in the bin without deigning to look at what they said! I missed the esplanades, I missed the banks of the Main, I missed the noisy restaurants, I missed everything: the placid flow of the crowds on the main streets, the queues outside the cinemas, the street vendors in the squares filled with tourists, my surgery, my patients, my neighbour, my neighbour's dog whose barking disturbed me when I was reading, my sofa that held so many wonderful memories, my can of beer sweating with coldness, my computer showing pending emails, even the constant spam I never managed to get rid of – all these fragments of life which, fitted together, made my existence an unexpected joy ... But now, the fact that day broke was a pure formality. For me, it was a blank page in the proofs of my captivity, a blank page that prolonged the blank pages of yesterday and the previous days; my jigsaw puzzle was made up of pieces so identical, so anonymous, that it was impossible for me to put them in the right place. My world resembled a botched watercolour that the painter had tried angrily to erase with his bare hands. There were times when I wondered if I wasn't already dead and buried, with a ton of dust over my body and a void in my head. I had stopped waiting, I had stopped holding on to things; my resolve had crumbled after so many fruitless vigils; I no longer felt able to keep the vow I had made the other night not to give in.

For his part, Bruno was brooding. It helped you see more clearly, apparently: you focused on your obsession and you blotted out everything around you. It was a matter of perspective. You just had to shift the context and your viewpoint changed. Bruno no longer saw things in the same way. He had shifted the context and was starting to reduce Africa to this gang of crooks with their pinhead pupils and animal instincts, who resisted all the rules of society.

As far as Bruno was concerned, the day was a diversion, a confidence trick, a pointless effort. So he had given up. I looked at him and saw only his motionless mosquito net. He hardly stirred. The spiders' webs displaying the corpses of midges as trophies, the lizard pretending to be a figurine pinned to the wall, the flies refusing to calm down: none of these things interested him. Bruno ignored even his wounds: he had stopped moaning with pain. I called him and he didn't hear me. I spoke to him and he didn't answer. *You are a goldfish in a bowl, Monsieur Krausmann,* he had said. *Your only company is a lead diver and a pirate chest opening and closing on bubbles of air.* And now he was the one shutting himself away in a bubble. Staring deep into space, Bruno was elsewhere, his face like a pale stain in the middle of his tramp's beard. The previous day, he had spat in his soup. Out of irritation. Out of disgust, perhaps. Then he must have forgotten and had meticulously scraped the bottom of his plate. I had thought he was over his crisis; he was only on the edge of it; an oath uttered outside, an order barked, and Bruno plunged back. I felt sad for him, and for me. We were together in the cell, but there was an ocean between us. I had loved hearing about his tribulations as a 'wandering anchorite', filled with humorous incidents and prophetic disappointments … What was he thinking about? His 'forgotten trails'? Aminata? Getting himself killed in order to have done with it? When you're brooding, you only think about one thing at a time, and from his hangdog look, he could have been thinking about anything. Renunciation is just as wearing as stubbornness. Bruno had had faith, now he had abjured it, and if he no longer knew which way to turn, it was because everything seemed to him like a trap: the danger wasn't in staying here, the danger was inside him.

There was a sense of tension in the fort. We felt it like a migraine. It was four days since Chief Moussa had left to haggle over Hans's head, and he hadn't been in contact since yesterday. Captain Gerima was in a foul mood again, constantly cursing his mobile phone and muttering, 'What the hell is he up to?' Chief Moussa had always kept him regularly updated and now, suddenly, he was impossible to reach. At first, the captain suspected it was a problem with the network; it wasn't. He had changed the battery several times before he realised that it wasn't a problem with the battery either. He again started fiddling with the keys of his mobile and let it ring endlessly at the other end of the line; nobody picked up.

This loss of contact was driving him mad. He called every half-hour: nothing. Then he would emerge from his lair, in a thunderous rage, and yell at his soldiers over trivial matters, kick the dust, swear at the top of his voice that he would beat to a pulp any bastard who dared to defy him. His men hid from him. As soon as he appeared in the doorway of his command post, they would vanish faster than ghosts. Even Joma was ill at ease whenever the captain flung his cap to the ground and stepped on it. I think our depression, Bruno's and mine, owed a great deal to the captain's anger. Gerima sensed that something was seriously wrong; things weren't going as planned, and his growing anxiety exacerbated our anxiety and made the air unbreathable. Sometimes, unable to bear the captain's cries of rage any longer, Bruno would put his hands over his ears and run to the padlocked door of our jail, intending to beg the officer to be quiet, but no sound would emerge from his lips.

At the end of the fourth day, Captain Gerima gave in to panic. He gathered his men, started up the beaten-up old lorry that had been gathering dust beneath a makeshift shelter, checked his troops' weapons and ammunition, ordered Joma to keep an eye on the fort until he returned, climbed into a pick-up and set off in a south-easterly direction. A strange silence fell on the region. Through the window, I saw the two vehicles head out across the valley at breakneck speed. When the dust had settled, I felt as if my heart were being squeezed like a lemon. Bruno hadn't moved from his corner. He had heard the captain's orders bouncing off the walls, the commotion in the yard, the clatter of rifles and the rumble of engines without paying any attention to them. Now that the captain had left, I walked up and down by the door, waiting for someone to come and tell us what was going on. Only Joma, Blackmoon and three or four disorientated pirates were left in the fort; they all looked distraught. They couldn't grasp the turn that events were taking and felt frustrated. In the general confusion, I realised that we hadn't been given anything to eat for twenty-four hours.

I went back to my mat and curled up.

Night arrived as abruptly as an uninvited guest, and then it was morning again. A static morning, empty and pointless. Bruno continued to hide under his mosquito net. I resented the way he had abandoned me to my solitude and the downward spiral that went with it. Having nobody to talk to any more, I feared that I too would sink into depression. There was no other way out in that kind of mental confinement. Sooner or later, you were bound to slump ...

And the endless waiting reducing my living space to an obsession ... Oh, the waiting, the void that sucks us in! And the incessant flies! They emerged from out of nowhere, buzzing, unbearable, invincible; they were like all the ordeals we were going through put together. I'd push them away and they'd attack again, intrepid and stubborn, like hundreds of insane leitmotivs. It was as if they had replaced the air, as if they were born from the boredom itself, as if they were the expression of the desert's measureless ignominy. They would survive erosion and apocalypse; they would still be there when everything else was gone.

The minutes stretched like shooting pains, trying to tear me apart. There is no worse torture than waiting, especially when there is no certainty as to where it will lead. I had the impression I was fermenting. I couldn't keep still. My bed was made of thorns. I no longer dared look through the window or go out in the yard. I was afraid of every

Someone worked the breech of a rifle; I sensed that I was in the line of fire, felt it on the back of my neck like a burn, and waited for the shot, which would be immediately followed by my flesh exploding; it would be sure to hurt, but I wouldn't cry out … 'The prisoner's getting away!' I also heard Bruno's voice: 'Don't be a fool, come back!' I was walking on shifting sands. The rampart was twenty metres away, ten metres … 'Let him go,' Joma ordered. 'Get back to work, I'll deal with him …' I went through the gap, tumbled down a steep path, and walked straight ahead, across the valley. The burning stones spurred the soles of my shoes. I walked. Without turning round. The sun beat down, cascaded over my shoulders like lava. The sweat steamed on my face, blinding me. I walked, walked … The soles of my shoes were nothing but molten lead; there was not a single tree to give me shade. The mouth of hell was breathing into my throat, setting my lungs on fire, turning my head into a brazier; I started to sway, but didn't stop. I tried to speed up, but my legs wouldn't follow me; I felt as if I were pulling a rock. After a few kilometres, my last strength abandoned me. I was a shadow swept along by its own laboured breathing. A jeep came up behind me and drew level. All I could see was its bonnet bumping along on my right. When I stumbled, it overtook me by a length and had to slow down to be level with me again. Joma was at the wheel. 'Where do you think you're going?' he said. 'You aren't in Trafalgar Square, you're in the desert. There are no tempting shop windows around here, no street performers in the square, no pigeons to come and eat out of your hand …' I dragged myself on, hallucinating, gasping for breath, but determined. 'You're not going anywhere, old man. In front of you, and behind you, there's only madness and death. Sooner or later you're going to pass out, and I'll be forced to tie you to the back of the jeep and take you back to the starting post.' Joma didn't try to bar my way; he drove slowly by my side, amused and curious to see just how long I could stay upright.

I didn't know how long I'd been walking. I could no longer feel the ground beneath my feet. My skull was rattling. I felt like throwing up. My eyes were like a broken mirror, a kaleidoscope; in front of me, the valley fragmented before darkening and sinking into a sea of soot.

I emerged from the fog, groped around me. Was I still alive? Thin filaments of light fell from the ceiling, revealing part of the place. I was confined in a space some two metres square, with a hatch above me perforated with lots of little air holes. My shoes, my trousers and my shirt had all been removed. I was stark naked and lying in my own vomit. I vaguely heard voices, sporadic noises which sounded over the thumping of my heart in amplified staccato. I tried to get up but not a single one of my muscles responded; my whole body was one horrendous pain.

The heat was unbearable. Unable to sit up, I lay there on the floor, hoping to conserve the little energy I needed to hold on. Soon, the filaments of light faded; I no longer knew if it was night or if I had fainted.

The hatch lit up and darkened again twice. Nobody came to see how I was. There was a ghastly taste of modelling clay in my mouth. I imagined nauseating food, and found myself chewing it. In the silence of my hole, the sound of my jaws was like that of two stones being rubbed together. I thought of my mother, saw her silhouette on the wall. She had close-cropped hair, which was not the way I remembered her, a face like a convict's and a stoical look in her eyes. Smells from time immemorial came back to me: the smell of the soap my mother used to wash me; the smell of the maple syrup pancakes that I loved. Then the smell of my childhood was drowned out by others, the smells of analgesics and chloral hydrate and damp sheets and grim wards at the end of interminable corridors. Outside, the noises and the voices faded again with the holes in the hatch. I wanted to cry out, but I didn't have enough breath to raise my voice, which stuck in my throat like a blood clot. I was hungry and thirsty … I caught a glimpse of Jessica's smile. I think it was that smile that had once given me the strength to overcome my shyness. I had never been good at expressing my private emotions to the people I loved. My mother would have appreciated it; she had felt alone ever since, one evening after a big argument, my father had gone out to buy cigarettes and hadn't come back. Maybe because my mother didn't know how to smile. Otherwise, I would have told her of all the love I had for her. Just as I had managed to tell Jessica, in that lovely little restaurant in the fifteenth arrondissement in Paris called La Chaumière. We were sitting at a window table looking out at Avenue Félix Faure. Jessica was holding her translucent hands up to her cheeks. I found it hard to meet her intimidating gaze. We had only known each other for two days. It was the first time we had been alone together. She had finished her seminar that morning, and my conference was due to end the following day. I had left her a note at the hotel reception: *I would be delighted if you would agree to have dinner with me.* And she had. There are opportunities you don't miss; if you don't grab them, you can spend the rest of your life regretting them in vain. *True* luck only comes along once in a lifetime; other pieces of good luck are merely combinations of circumstances. I don't remember what we ate that evening. I was feasting on Jessica's smile, which was better than any banquet. 'Did you know I was going to accept your invitation?' she had asked me. 'I wouldn't have dared leave you that note if I hadn't,' I had replied boldly. 'Can you read thoughts, Dr Krausmann?' 'Only eyes, Fräulein Brodersen. Everything goes through the eyes.' 'And what do you see in my eyes, Dr Krausmann?' 'My happiness …' At the time, I had found my declaration pathetically innocent and pretentious, but Jessica hadn't laughed. I think she had appreciated it. Sincerity has no talent or refinement; and if it doesn't have the elegance of flattery, it has at least the merit of its convictions. She put her hand on my wrist, and I immediately knew that Jessica was meant for me.

It was night again. I recognised it by its silence. A wild, sleepless night, full of self-disgust, which fled at the first glimmer of dawn. I felt myself leaving with it, piece by piece, my body jolted by muscular contractions. My nerves had become blunted; the moorings that had held me were coming loose. How many days had I been kept in this pit? Hunger and thirst made my delirium a premonition: I was dying … A funnel was sucking me into a swirling aurora borealis. I passed through a succession of rings of fire at dizzying speed. *'Wake up, Kurt,'* said a voice from beyond the grave. *'I don't want to wake up.' 'Why don't you want to wake up, Kurt?' 'Because I'm having a dream.' 'And what are you dreaming about, Kurt?' 'I'm dreaming of a world where joys and sorrows are forbidden, where a stone doesn't mind being trodden on because it can't defend itself or move away; a world so deeply silent that prayers subside, and a night so gentle that the day does not dare dawn ... I'm dreaming of a motionless journey in space and time where I am safe from anxiety, where no temptation has any effect on me; a world where God himself looks away so that I can sleep until time stops turning.' 'What is this motionless world, Kurt?' 'My eternal kingdom in which I will be earth and worm, then earth and earth, and then infinitesimal dust on the breath of nothingness.' 'That's not yet a place for you, Kurt. Go back to your fears, they are better than this sidereal chill. And wake up, wake up now before it's too late.'* I woke with a start, like a drowning man thrusting his head out of the water at the last moment. I was in Essen, the town where I was born. In short trousers. Buried in the skirts of my mother who was taking me to mass. We were walking together along a narrow, colourless street. The church stood out against a gloomy sky. Inside, it was freezing cold. The rough vaults weighed heavily on the shadows, making the place of meditation as cold as a refrigerator. The penitent sat on rustic pews, praying. The pastor was preaching a sermon. I couldn't remember his face, but his voice was clear in my memory. I was only six – I couldn't remember or understand what he was saying and yet his voice emerged from deep down in my subconscious with amazing clarity and precision: *'It is true that we are insignificant. But in this perfect body which age breaks down as the seasons pass and which the smallest germ can lay low, there is a magical territory where it is possible for us to take our lives back. It is in this hidden place that our true strength lies; in other words, our faith in what we believe to be good for us.*

If we can only believe, we can overcome any disappointment. For nothing, no power, no fate can stop us lifting ourselves up and fulfilling ourselves if we truly believe in our dreams. Of course, we will be called upon to go through terrible trials, to fight titanic battles that could easily discourage us. But if we don't surrender, if we continue to believe, we will overcome any obstacle. For we are worthy only of what we deserve, and our salvation draws its inspiration from this elementary logic: "When two opposing forces meet, the less motivated of the two will fail." So if we want to accomplish what we set out to do, let us make sure that our beliefs are stronger than our doubts, stronger than adversity.'

For a fraction of a second, the pastor's face appeared to me, and Hans's voice shook me like an electric shock: *Stand firm. Every day is a miracle.*

The hatch was raised. I covered my eyes with my hands to shield them from the sudden light and waited to recover my sight. Slowly, the configuration of the stones became clearer, then that of the walls. Something fell to the ground and rolled between my legs. It was an orange. A soft, battered orange, not much bigger than a prune. I picked it up greedily – I was aware that my gesture wasn't exactly decent, but I didn't care – and bit into it as if biting into life. Without peeling it. Without wiping it. When I heard it tearing beneath my teeth, when the acidity of the very first squirt of juice hit my palate, when the taste reconciled me with my senses – for all at once I recovered taste and smell and hearing – I realised that I was intact. I closed my eyes to savour every morsel. I think I took a good ten minutes, maybe a little more, to slowly chew the orange, without swallowing anything, to make the pleasure last as long as possible: a pleasure that was exaggerated of course, but which, at that moment, had the violence of an orgasm. I chewed it into little pieces, turning each piece over and over several times on my tongue until I had transformed it into a spongy paste that I began sucking again with delight; I had the feeling I was tasting a fruit that was like no other. When all that was left of it in my mouth was the distant taste of bitter pulp, Joma's laughter brought me abruptly down to earth.

'Stand up in there! The convalescence is over. Get out of there, and be quick about it, you wimp.'

Arms gathered me up, pulled me out of my hole, and dragged me across the burning ground. My clothes were thrown in my face and I was forced to get dressed. My lack of coordination made this latter operation an acrobatic feat. The sun burnt my eyes. I couldn't tell my shirt from my trousers, and had to rely on my sense of touch. All the same, I somehow managed to put on my pants, and then my trousers. At the end of this bizarre gymnastic exercise, I presented myself to Joma, who, very proud of the state he had reduced me to, declared, 'Now, Dr Krausmann, you have some small idea of what it means to be an African.'

Bruno let out a curse when Joma threw me into the jail. I fell face down, my nose in the dust. Joma turned me over with his foot, bent over me like the angel of death gathering up a lost soul, grabbed me by my shirt collar, and finally let go of me, exhausted by his own abuses.

Bruno was shocked. 'I suppose you're pleased with

yourself, Sergeant-Major Joma.'

Joma cracked his neck joints and retorted, 'I never wear stripes or medals. I leave those accessories to clowns and veterans.'

'Where do you think you are? Abu Ghraib?'

'We can't afford that kind of luxury hotel.'

Bruno got up on his knees and cried, 'You're nothing but a monster.'

'Thanks to you, Mr Civilised Westerner. We learnt everything from you people. And when it comes to such skills, I don't think the pupil can ever surpass the master.'

With a gesture of his head, he ordered his men to follow him outside.

As soon as the door was closed, Bruno ran to me and lifted my head. From the distressed, incredulous way he looked at me, I realised what a sight I must be.

'Good Lord, you look like a zombie.'

He dragged me to my mat, wedged a cloth behind my back, and helped me to sit against the wall. I wanted to get up and walk about to relieve the aching of my stiff muscles, but I had all the energy of a dehydrated old slug. My bruised body didn't have a single tendon that worked. Like someone who has been exorcised, I had the impression that the demonic entity that had possessed me was my own soul and that all that remained of me now was an empty shell.

'Give me something to eat ...'

Bruno ran to fetch me a piece of meat. I tore it from his hands and bit into it with the feeling that I was fighting over every mouthful with my hunger, that my hunger and I were Siamese twins, that I was the mouth and it was the belly, that it was robbing me of the taste of flesh, and I was robbing it of the meat's nutritional strength. Bruno had to calm me down. He advised me to go easy and take my time chewing. When I finished gnawing at the bone, he ran to fetch me a piece of bread and what remained of some gelatinous soup. I gulped them both down in one go.

'Bloody hell, where have you been?' sighed Bruno with pity.

He handed me his flask. I knocked back the entire contents and immediately fell asleep.

7

Loud voices rang out in the yard. Bruno, who was standing by the door, motioned to me to come closer. Gathered in the doorway of the command post, the pirates were squabbling, all making a noise at the same time like farmyard animals, each one shouting louder than the others to make himself heard. Some were within an inch of coming to blows. On one side, there was Joma, who was trying to handle the situation, and Blackmoon, sitting on the steps, his hands on the handle of his sabre and his chin on his hands; on the other, the four remaining pirates, all in an excited state. The tallest, who was almost white-skinned, had a falsetto voice that cut through his comrades' protests. He was waving his arms about in all directions, calling the sky, the fort, the barracks, the valley, to be his witnesses. I couldn't understand what he was saying in his cabbalistic jargon. Bruno translated the most forceful statements for me: things were getting nasty, he said. A very thin man in a tracksuit tried to get a word in edgewise and was immediately taken to task by a boorish fellow with a talismanic necklace and a mouth big enough to gobble an ostrich egg. He was so furious that he was dribbling from the corners of his mouth. He stood up on tiptoe to dominate the others and pointed to a wing of the fort, a gesture that the thin man dismissed with his hand, provoking even more bedlam than before.

'It's three weeks since the captain left to join Moussa!' the thin man cried. 'And we haven't heard anything from him! That isn't normal.'

'So what?' Joma retorted, his fists on his hips.

'We don't have any more provisions,' said a stiff teenager with unusually broad shoulders.

'It isn't only that,' the thin man went on. 'The captain was very clear. If we didn't hear from him, we should evacuate the fort and fall back to Point D-15.'

'How did he tell you that?' Joma cried. 'By telepathy? We don't even have radio contact with him. If we're forced to leave here, it'll be for Station 28.'

'That makes no sense,' the tall man with the falsetto voice said. 'The captain went to Point D-15, in the south. That's where it's happening. There's nothing for us at Station 28. It's two days further north, and we don't have enough fuel. Plus, it's a high-risk area, and there are only six of us. How will we fight if we're ambushed?'

'That's enough!' Joma roared. 'We already talked about that yesterday. We'll only leave this fort for Station 28. I'm in charge here. And I warn you I won't hesitate to execute on the spot any joker who dares disobey my orders. The situation's shambolic enough, and no form of insubordination can be tolerated.'

'What do you think we are?' the man with the necklace protested. 'Cattle? Who are you to threaten us with death? We tell you we haven't any more provisions, and we haven't heard from the captain. How long are we going to stay here? Until a rival gang attacks us?'

'We have to join the rest of the squad at Point D-15,' the

four 'mutineers' insisted. 'That's where it's happening.'

Bruno took advantage of a moment's hesitation to intervene. 'Haven't you figured it out yet? Your comrades aren't coming back. They've run off with the money.'

The pirates turned as one towards our jail, thrown by Bruno's allegations. For a few seconds, not a muscle moved on their sweat-streaked faces.

'It's perfectly obvious,' Bruno went on, becoming bolder now. 'You've been tricked, for heaven's sake! I bet the captain and Moussa were in cahoots, that they plotted the whole thing between them. Who knows, maybe they dumped your friends in the wild and are off in some land of milk and honey right now while you're here rotting in the sun.'

'Shut up,' Joma ordered him.

But Bruno wouldn't let it go. 'Just think about it for one second.'

Joma raised his pistol and fired twice at Bruno, who flattened himself against the wall. The shots cast a chill over the fort.

'We don't only slaughter cattle!' Joma said to the rebels. 'The first person who thinks it's amusing to defy me, I'll blow his brains out. While the captain's away, I make the decisions. Now get back to work, and tomorrow at dawn we leave for Station 28.'

The pirates dispersed, throwing each other grim looks.

Late in the night, Bruno woke me. He put his hand over my mouth and motioned me to follow him to the window. In the pockmarked sky, the moon was reduced to a nail clipping. The fort was plunged in darkness.

Bruno pointed with his finger. I had to concentrate to make out four figures moving furtively around the jeep; one of them climbed in and took the wheel, the other three leant on the bonnet and started pushing the vehicle towards the gate. The jeep slid gently over the sandy yard, manoeuvred carefully to get around the well, edged its way between the water tank and a heap of loose stones and noiselessly left the enclosure. It disappeared behind the embankment, and reappeared further on, still pushed by the three figures. When it reached the track leading to the valley, two or three hundred metres from the fort, its engine roared, and it set off at top speed, with the lights off. Alerted by the noise, Joma came running out of the command post in his underpants, an automatic rifle in his arms. He called his men; when nobody appeared, apart from a sleepy Blackmoon, he realised it wasn't an attack: the four 'mutineers' from the previous day had just parted company with him. Cursing, he ran to the gap, peered into the valley, which was still shrouded in darkness, and started firing wildly like a maniac.

Joma remained on guard on the rampart until sunrise, clicking the breech of his rifle and every now and again letting out cries of rage that seemed to perplex the night. He took his subordinates' defection as a personal affront. Whenever Blackmoon tried to comfort him, Joma threatened to tear his heart out with his bare hands if he didn't shut up. Several times, he looked in our direction and, despite the distance between us and the dim light, Bruno and I felt our hair stand on end.

Having waited in vain for a sign on the horizon, Joma went back to his room to dress. He put on a hunting vest, combat trousers and new hiking boots, hung two cartridge belts around his neck and across his chest, wrapped his head in a red scarf and came back out into the yard, his big pistol stuck in his belt and a Kalashnikov in his hand. His milky eyes sought to bury all they surveyed.

Towards eight o'clock, he got us out of our jail and told Blackmoon to tie our wrists behind our backs.

Joma finished hanging jerry cans of fuel on either side of the pick-up. Into the back of the vehicle, he threw a full duffle bag, a satchel with straps, two rucksacks, a box of canned food, slices of dried meat rolled in brown paper, a crate of ammunition and two goatskin canteens filled with drinking water. Bruno and I were on our knees in the dust, wondering what fate our kidnapper had in store for us as he prepared to leave the fort. Was he going to kill us? Leave us there? Take us with him? Joma was giving nothing away. He grunted orders which Blackmoon begrudgingly followed for his own protection, but without any undue haste.

'What are you planning to do with us?' Bruno asked.

Joma carefully checked that the ropes were tight and the jerry cans well balanced. The way he was tightening the knots betrayed a growing inner anger, which Bruno's words only served to stoke.

'You say you've read lots of books,' Bruno went on, 'that you know the works of the great poets by heart. You must have learnt something from them ... Let us go. Or else come with us. We'll say you saved our lives.'

Joma said nothing.

'It's pointless now, Joma. Actually, it's always been pointless. If only you stepped back a bit, you'd see that what you're doing is absurd. Why are you keeping us so far from our homes, so far from your home? What do you blame us for? Crossing your path? We've never done you any harm. I'm an African by adoption, and Dr Krausmann does humanitarian work. Imagine that! Humanitarian work! ... Joma, for heaven's sake, let us go. Captain Gerima is nothing but a crook, and you know it. Soldiers like him don't fight, they just line their pockets. They don't have any ideals or principles. They'd walk over their mother's body for the smallest coin ... Gerima is using your frustrations. He's manipulating you. I'm certain he dumped his men in the wild and ran off with the money. Your comrades realised that. That's why they left.'

Joma turned on his heel, charged at Bruno and gave him a kick in the stomach that knocked the breath out of him and bent him double. Bruno fell on his side, his eyes bulging with pain.

'My comrades left because of you, you son of a bitch!' Joma said, spitting at him.

I was horrified by this character. However many times he lashed out, I'd be just as disgusted and indignant. Things with Joma had become personal. I hated him, I hated him for what he represented: a monster in the raw, straight out of the primeval slime, with the instinctive violence of the very first fears and the very first hostilities; a big devil carved out of a block of granite with no other facet to him but his own brutality; his pumped-up body, his gestures, his voice, his megalomania, his quickness to fly off the handle, everything about him stank of murder. I hated him because he was an outrage to common sense, and because he had injected gall into my veins like poison so that I had the feeling I might end up being like him. I realised, to my immense sorrow – I was a doctor, after all – that there wasn't room on this earth for the two of us, that the world couldn't contain, at the same time and in the same place, two people who had nothing in common and whom nothing seemed able to reconcile.

Joma read my thoughts. My animosity towards him appealed in some obscure way to his vanity, as if he got most satisfaction from the disgust he inspired in me.

'Do you want my photo?' he cried.

I didn't reply.

He snorted with disdain, pushed me away with his foot and grunted, 'Humanitarian work? That was all we needed. You blond, blue-eyed idiot with your pretty face and your Rolex watches and your Porsche, you're in humanitarian work? You hypochondriac, racist mother's boy who'd disinfect the pavement if you found out that a black man had been walking along it before you, you want me to believe you're so upset by world poverty that you'd give up your creature comforts to share the sufferings of niggers with bloated stomachs?'

'You don't really believe what you're saying,' I said.

'I stopped believing in anything the day I realised that bullets speak louder than words.'

'Maybe that's your problem.'

'Oh, yes?'

'Definitely … I'm not a racist, I'm a doctor. When I examine a patient, I don't have time to dwell on the colour of his skin.'

'Stop, you're breaking my heart … People like you disinfect their eyes the minute a beggar crosses their path. You're just a fucking racist come to sniff our mass graves in the name of a sacrosanct Christian charity which has no more the odour of sanctity than an arsehole.'

'You have no right to call me a racist. I won't allow it.'

'You see?' he retorted. 'Even when you're under my control, you think you can give me orders. You're at my mercy, completely at my mercy, and you expect me to ask YOUR permission to shoot you down like a dog ...' He shook his head. 'These damned whites! Always drunk on their own importance. Even if you put holy water in their wine, they wouldn't sober up.'

He went back to his room to make sure he hadn't forgotten anything.

The valley sloped gently for some thirty kilometres before it reached a chain of rocky mountains whittled away by erosion. They weren't really mountains: given the traumatic flatness of the surroundings, the smallest hill took on a significance ten times greater than its actual measurements, as if in this tomblike landscape, every milestone needed to exaggerate its size in order not to disappear for ever. For four hours now, Joma had been taking us across a mineral, almost lunar universe, and not for a moment had I had the feeling that we were going to get out of it. The same trails led to the same rocks, the same thirsty soil lay in the same dried-up river beds, and always that blazing sun poured its molten lava down on our heads. The motionless dust lent something both vain and definitive to the horizon – a kind of still image of the end of the world.

With my back against the duffle bag, my legs sticking to the bed of the pick-up, I watched this merry-go-round of decay turn and turn and realised that I had lost interest in everything. I didn't even feel the need to imagine what awaited me. I was starting to understand why, in some war films, heroes who've repelled enemy attacks and fought valiantly for days and nights on end, emerge suddenly from their shelters and brave their attackers' guns ... In any case, I had no idea what went on in our kidnappers' heads. I didn't know their mindset or their conception of human relations. However hard I tried to penetrate the way Joma's mind worked, for example, it was as if I were trying to decipher the cryptograms in an esoteric book. 'These people are alive now, but they come from another time,' Hans had said. I had refused to believe it at first. My upbringing and culture had taught me that as long as you kept a clear head, you could overcome any misunderstanding. But these maniacs didn't have clear heads, and I could see no way to reason with them.

Bruno's nose was bleeding. A bump in the road had thrown him against the side of the pick-up and almost knocked him senseless. I'd yelled to Joma to drive more carefully, and Joma had deliberately driven even more recklessly to show me how little he cared about what was happening to us in the back. Beside him, Blackmoon was silent. He hadn't said a word since we had left the fort. He was looking but without interest, listening without hearing. Something was bothering him. He was mired in his own thoughts. Whenever Blackmoon kept a low profile, you knew he was collecting himself before bouncing back. His silence was subversive; it was the calm before the storm. There was a striking contrast between the unstable boy of those first weeks and the one now sitting in the cab, and I wasn't convinced it was a change for the better.

About midday, we halted amid a tangle of disembowelled hillsides and scrawny shrubs. I was relieved to sit on the soft sand after the metal bed of the pick-up. Bruno, who couldn't clean himself because his wrists were tied behind his back, had blood on his beard and half of his shirt. He slumped by my side while Joma stood at the top of a ridge and searched the surroundings with his binoculars. Crouching not far from the pick-up, Blackmoon, his sabre stuck in the sand, laboriously wiped his lensless glasses with his *cheche*.

Joma came down the hill and walked around the vehicle, his chin between his thumb and index finger, thinking. When he noticed that we were watching him, he gave us a V-sign and climbed back up onto the ridge.

'I think our Goliath is lost,' Bruno said to me.

'I think so, too. We've been this way already. See that rock over there that looks like a jar with handles? I'm sure I saw it less than two hours ago.'

'That's right. We came past here in the opposite direction.'

Joma came down from the ridge again, spread an old map on the bonnet of the pick-up and started looking for points of reference. After this fruitless exercise, he hit the bonnet in annoyance.

We drove back the way we had come for dozens of kilometres until we reached a massive cliff looking down on a plain bordered by scrub. In the distance, a herd of antelopes was fleeing from a predator. Joma went and stood at the edge of the precipice, took out his map and again started looking for landmarks. An anthracite foothill to the south was bothering him. Joma checked the coordinates on the map, compared them with the landscape in front of him, and orientated himself with the help of a compass. His features relaxed, and we realised that he knew where he was now.

We stopped in the shade of a solitary acacia. The sun was starting to set. Blackmoon untied us so that we could eat the slices of dried meat he gave us in brown paper and went and sat down halfway between the pick-up, where Joma was, and us.

'Playing hard to get or what?' Joma shouted to him. 'Come over here.'

Blackmoon stood up reluctantly and joined his chief, who handed him a can of food and a metal canteen.

'What's the matter?'

Blackmoon shrugged.

'You usually ramble on even when you have nothing to say.'

Blackmoon lifted the canteen to his mouth in order not to reply. Joma took out a large knife, cut a piece from his slice of dried meat and bit into it without taking his eyes off his subordinate. He started talking to him in a patois that Bruno translated for me simultaneously.

'Why don't you say anything?'

'Do I have to?'

'I don't like your silence, Chaolo. Should I take it that you're angry with me about something but you don't dare lance the boil?'

'What boil?'

'Precisely. What's the problem?'

'I don't know what you're talking about.'

'No kidding!'

Blackmoon turned away in order not to have to suffer Joma's inquisitive gaze. But he knew that Joma was waiting for an explanation and that he wouldn't give up until he got it.

'Well?' Joma insisted.

'You won't listen to me anyway.'

'I'm not deaf.'

'No, I don't want to get into an argument with you.'

'So it's as bad as that, is it?'

'Please, Joma, just drop it. I'm not in the mood.'

'Just try. I'm not going to eat you.'

Blackmoon shook his head. 'You're going to get upset, and then you'll make my head spin with your theories.'

'Are you going to come out with it, or what?' Joma roared, spattering saliva from his mouth.

'You see? I haven't said anything yet, and you're already making a fuss.'

Joma put his meal down on the ground and looked his subordinate up and down, his cheekbones throbbing with anger. 'I'm listening …'

Blackmoon hunched his shoulders and breathed in and out like a boxer on his stool after a tough round. He raised his eyes to his chief, lowered them again, then lifted them as if lifting a burden. Having summoned both his breath and his courage, he said, 'You're the teacher I always dreamt of having, Joma. I wasn't your boy, I was your pupil. But I don't like the teaching you've forced on me.'

'Can't you be a bit more precise?'

'I've never refused you anything, Joma. I love you more than my father and my mother. I left my family for you, my village, everything …'

'Get to the point, please.'

'Let them go!'

The blade of a guillotine couldn't have cut short the debate with such startling abruptness. Joma almost choked. Stunned by Blackmoon's words, he blinked several times to make sure he had heard correctly. Throwing a rapid

174

glance in our direction, he realised that we had also heard the boy's suggestion; he grabbed Blackmoon by the neck and pulled him close.

'What are you talking about?'

Blackmoon started by loosening the fingers around his neck. Calmly. Then he mopped his forehead with his *cheche* and returned Joma's fiery gaze.

'I don't want to raise my hand to anybody any more, Joma. I've had enough. I want to go home. All this talk of revolution and justice and God knows what else doesn't grab me any more. I don't believe in any of it. For years now, we've been running all over the place, and I still don't see the end of the tunnel. What's changed since we started playing at being rebels? Not a damned thing. And you know why? Because there's nothing to change. The world is what it is, and none of us can change it because we aren't God.'

Joma was dumbfounded. After a long silence, he said, 'You're right, boy. You should have kept your mouth shut ...'

We set off again as soon as the meal was over. It was Joma himself who tied our hands behind our backs, as if he didn't trust Blackmoon. Of course, he had not lingered too long over his subordinate's remarks. As far as he was concerned, they were just idle words spoken by a young boy overwhelmed by the turn that events were taking. All the same, it had made him slightly ill at ease. During the ride, he didn't say another word to Blackmoon, but kept looking at him out of the corner of his eye.

*

Late that afternoon, a puncture almost catapulted us into a rock. The pick-up skidded, and Joma's aggressive attempt to control it sent it flying over several metres. Bruno and I were almost thrown out.

Joma made us get down and ordered Blackmoon to bring him the spare wheel and the jack. After taking off his hunting vest, he crouched to loosen the wheel nuts. He removed the flat tyre, replaced it, and worked the jack. Just as he was putting the nuts back on, Blackmoon took his sabre and cut through the ropes tying Bruno and me. This gesture both surprised and terrified us. It was obvious that things were about to go downhill. Blackmoon, though, looked calm and implacable. He didn't seem to realise the significance of his act, nor did he appear to care about the consequences.

'It isn't meal time yet,' Joma yelled. 'Tie these idiots up again, and be quick about it.'

Blackmoon interposed himself between Joma and us, impassive. 'Let them go and let's go home,' he said.

Joma threw the damaged tyre in the back of the pick-up, lifted the jack and put it away in an iron case soldered to the running board, wiped his grease-stained hands on a cloth and put on his vest. In all this time, he hadn't looked at us once.

'Stop this nonsense, Chaolo.'

'Why won't you listen to me?'

'Chaolo, you're going too far this time,' Joma said slowly, as if telling off a naughty child.

'These men haven't done anything to us.'

'Chaolo …'

Blackmoon signalled to us to leave. Neither Bruno nor I

moved. Leave where? Leave how? We were in the middle of nowhere, our two kidnappers had fallen out, and it looked as though the situation could only end badly for us. A cold shiver went down my back. Bruno was ashen. His eyes shone with terror.

'You taught me a whole lot of theories,' Blackmoon said in a flat tone. 'You told me why some things were right, and others weren't, and I drank in your words like holy water. But you're doing the exact opposite of what you told me, Joma. You had a good head on your shoulders when I met you, and you've turned bad. You lash out and you yell, and you drive me a little crazier every day. I thought war was crap, and that was what made people such pains in the arse. And I said it would all sort itself out in the end, and that one of these days when we'd dealt with the things that bothered us, we'd go home. Except that you don't seem to want to go back to the village or become a reasonable person again, the way you were before. Do you remember? We were all right before. We didn't ask for the moon, and we were content with simple things. Don't you see? I miss those simple things now.'

'Chaolo!'

'You were unlucky, and I understand. I understand it isn't easy to stay good after what happened to you, but we've gone too far. And I don't want to follow you any more, Joma. Because I don't know where you're taking me. When I look behind me, I don't see any trace of what we were, you and I. I'm not proud of the path we've taken. Even your books don't smell good any more ... I've listened to you all my life. Now you have to listen to me. I don't have big words to persuade you, I don't have your

177

education, but I want you to know that my affection for you is the same as ever and it's because I still have it that I no longer agree with you.'

'That's enough now.'

'What happened to Fatamou wasn't because of these two men.'

Joma let out an unusually savage cry and charged at the boy. Not expecting such a lightning reaction, Blackmoon took the full force of his chief's fist in the face. The force of the blow sent him flying; he fell on his back, then half raised himself, grimacing in terrible pain, unable to breathe. In a fraction of a second, his face crumpled and became waxen. Dazed, he groped for his glasses, found them broken in half, picked them up unsteadily and showed them to Joma with sad eyes.

'Look what you did to my glasses, Joma.'

'I forbid you to talk about my private life.'

Blackmoon stared at his glasses as if contemplating a catastrophe.

'Get up!' Joma screamed. 'And tie these dogs up for me!'

Blackmoon tried to raise himself, but none of his muscles responded. The expression on his face was abnormal. It was as if his features had melted, as if the light in his eyes were going out. His mouth filled with blood, which began dangling from his chin in long strands. Suddenly, a red patch appeared beneath his side and started to spread over the ground. Only then did Joma realise the gravity of the situation. He ran to Blackmoon. No sooner had he touched him than the boy let out an inhuman groan. Turning him over on his side, Joma realised that, in falling back, his protégé had impaled himself on his sabre.

178

'Oh, Lord,' he cried out, 'what is all this?'

He clasped the boy to him, talked to him to keep him awake, begged him to hold on. But he soon realised that it was pointless. Overcome with remorse and grief, Joma turned to the sky and implored it, all the while shaking the frail body, which was draining of its blood in wild spasms … and there, before our very eyes, the brute who had tried to be as devoid of compassion as a crushing machine sank heavily to the ground and began sobbing like a little child.

Blackmoon stared at us over his chief's shoulder then, slowly, his eyes rolled back and his neck went limp. He had given up the ghost.

Joma continued to clasp the boy to him, cradling him. His sobs spread across the plain, bounced off the rocks, whirled in the air …

Bruno ran to the pick-up and came back with the rifle that had been hanging inside the cab. 'I'm sorry,' he said, 'but this is where we part company.'

Tears streaming down his cheeks, Joma laid the boy with infinite care on the ground and turned to us.

'Please don't force me to shoot,' Bruno went on. 'Take what you need from the truck and let us go.'

Joma stood up, wiping his eyes with his wrist. He had never seemed so huge to me. His nostrils were quivering with a hatred that had reached its peak. Bruno took a step back. He was afraid, but refused to panic.

'Go on, shoot!' Joma said. 'What are you waiting for? Show me what you have in your belly, you worm. Show some guts, damn it! Shoot!'

'I've never hurt anyone, Joma. Let us go.'

'What's stopping you? The arms are on your side now.'

179

He put his hand on his belt, took out his pistol and threw it on the ground. Then he opened his arms wide and stood directly in front of Bruno.

'But make sure you don't miss, because I certainly wouldn't.'

He took one step forward, two steps, three ... Bruno tried to retreat, but Joma soon caught up with him. I stood there, petrified, completely overwhelmed. Although Bruno was in an agony of indecision, I could neither help him nor join him. Joma passed right by me, but didn't even see me: he had eyes only for the Frenchman. Bruno was paralysed; Joma was only two metres from him, and no shot rang out. Suddenly, in a flash, Joma swept the rifle away with one hand and with the other grabbed Bruno by the throat. Hanging at the end of Joma's arm, Bruno began pedalling desperately in the air. He was pushed to the ground. Joma squeezed with all his might, pressed with all his weight on Bruno's neck. The Frenchman struggled, twisted, struck out, his heels scrabbling in the dust. For a moment, his eyes met mine, and in them I saw horror in its purest form. Soon, his fists folded over his chest, defeated, and a damp patch appeared on his trousers. Bruno was dying; Joma knew it and was waiting to gather his soul like fruit ... A shot rang out! A thunderbolt from heaven couldn't have unleashed such a noise. It shook me from head to foot. For several seconds, I stood there in a daze. Joma was knocked sideways by the impact. Incredulous at first, he let go of Bruno's throat and lifted his hand to his own neck. When he saw the blood spurting between his fingers, he turned to me, looked me up and down with a strange kind of joy and, as his mouth filled with blood, said, 'I'm proud of you. Now, you're a real African.'

He collapsed onto his side, his eyes glazed and his features frozen for ever.

It was only then that I discovered a pistol in my hand.

I don't remember what happened next.

All I know is that Bruno and I got in the pick-up and drove and drove until the night absorbed us like blotting paper.

8

Day dawned. Like a pointless prayer over a deaf, wretched
and naked desert. A few rocks lay crumbling in the dust,
like flotsam washed up by a sea that had vanished thousands
of years ago. Here and there, garlanded with poisonous
colocynths, thin strips of undergrowth indicated the
outlines of what had once been river banks, where now
solitary acacias stood like crosses. And that was all. There
was nothing else you might hope to see: no caravans,
no huts, not the slightest trace of a bivouac ... There's
something so perverse about the desert. It's a code, a trap
set for you, a treacherous maze where even the boldest are
doomed to failure, where the faint-hearted lose themselves
among the mirages, where no patron saint would respond
to your call for fear of appearing ridiculous. It's a place of
prayers that go unheard, a *Via Dolorosa* that never stops
expanding, where stubbornness turns to obsession and
faith to madness. *Here lies the vanity of all things in this
world*, the bare stones and endless vistas seem to say. For
here, everything turns back to dust, the taciturn mountains
and the luxuriant forests, the lost paradises and the failed
empires, even the noisy reign of men ... Here, in this
godforsaken vastness, tornados come to abdicate and the
winds die empty-handed like waves on remote beaches,

since only the inexorable course of ages is certain and invincible. Far, far in the distance, where the earth slopes into roundness, the horizon is pale and motionless, as if the night has kept it spellbound until morning ... I too hadn't slept a wink all night. Sitting paralysed on my seat in the cab. My head reverberating with gunshots. As wretched as the desert. How could I lay claim to a modicum of sleep when I hadn't yet grasped what I had done? I had tried to reconstruct mentally what had happened and I had managed only to become even more confused. How had Joma's pistol ended up in my hand? I hadn't the faintest idea. My subconscious had quite simply blocked out the period of time between Bruno on the verge of dying and the shot; a blank had descended in the middle of my memories and remained suspended above the abyss into which my being had rushed. I, Dr Kurt Krausmann, who had never touched a gun in my life, had killed a man! What had driven me to such an extreme didn't matter. The only thing that mattered was that I had killed a man, and I would have to live with it for the rest of my life. Bruno had tried to reason with me for much of the night. His words hadn't reached me; I couldn't assimilate them. He had shown me the blackish bruises on his neck and sworn that if I hadn't intervened, he would be dead, and so would I. But that damned shot resonated endlessly in me like a wrecking ball smashing into a wall! I saw only Joma's bulging eyes and the blood trickling from his mouth. How many times had I got out of the pick-up to throw up? My throat was sore from the vomit, and my stomach felt as if it had been turned inside out. Bruno swore he would have done the same, that there was nothing else I could have done. Of course there was nothing else I could have done, but I had

hadn't the slightest idea where we were, he suggested we stay here to give us time to think about what to do with this sudden, unexpected freedom of ours. The site we were occupying gave us a clear 360-degree view of the plain. If a vehicle or a camel driver appeared anywhere in the vicinity, we'd be able to identify it or him with the help of the binoculars and thus avoid unpleasant encounters. Someone might just come along who could lead us out of this labyrinth of rocks and sand.

I had no objection to Bruno's suggestion. To be honest, I was in far too confused a state to think of anything better.

Bruno began by making an inventory of the things we were carrying in the back of the pick-up. In the duffle bag, we found two military uniforms, a pair of shoes, some vests, a *cheche*, half a dozen full Kalashnikov magazines tied together in pairs with sticking plaster, some wide-ranging books on European poetry, a brand-new pair of boxer shorts, sports socks and a pile of red scarves in their original wrapping. In the rucksacks, Joma had thrown canned food, pans, packets of bread and rusks, dried meat, cases of ammunition, defensive grenades, candles, boxes of matches, an oil stove, a sachet of coffee, some powdered sugar and a pocket torch. I looked for my watch, my ring and the other objects taken from me on the boat, but didn't find them. Bruno grabbed the satchel and opened it by forcing a small padlock. Inside, along with all kinds of papers, including several sheets in tortuous handwriting with lots of crossings out, we found a passport belonging to Joma, an indecipherable identity card, press cuttings carefully sorted into plastic wallets, a small bundle of banknotes, a blurry wedding photograph … and a book that left us stunned. It was a slim volume of poems, the cover of which would have been utterly unremarkable if Joma's face hadn't been plastered all over it.

The title of the book and the name of the author were underlined in red:

Black Moon
by Joma Baba-Sy

'Wow!' Bruno said.

I grabbed the book from him. The back cover blurb read: *A tailor by profession, Joma Baba-Sy is also a maker of verses and a tormented soul whose impassioned tirades call on Africa to awaken.* Black Moon *is his first book, but it already establishes him as a genuine poet who is sure to make his mark on the literature of our continent. Joma Baba-Sy has been awarded the National Prize for Letters, the Léopold Senghor Prize and the Trophy for Best Committed Poetry.*

'That brute was a poet,' Bruno said, almost breathlessly.

Again, my limbs froze. I pulled my sheet around me and went and lay down on the dune, facing the sun. I wanted to look at the desert without seeing it, to be silent and think of nothing.

The sun had chased away the mist, and you could see to infinity. The few sticky clouds that had ventured into the sky had disintegrated, leaving in their wake only a stringy, fragile shroud. We had worn our eyes out looking through the binoculars, searching for the smallest gleam; sometimes, we thought we saw a convoy or a group of nomads, but they were only mirages. Late in the morning, we had witnessed a terrible attack by three jackals on a stray dog. The poor, solitary beast had fought with real valour, but its attackers, more cunning than hungry, had torn it to pieces in the end. Once their dirty work was over, they had gone off along a river bed and disappeared.

We ate, drank coffee, and went back to our observation posts. Laying siege to the desert is a monotonous task … By late afternoon, I was starting to feel restless. Bruno admitted that waiting for a miracle wasn't such a good idea after all, and we set out in a northerly direction. What a relief when, after an hour's drive, we spotted a collection of huts! All at once, there was light at the end of our tunnel. Almost ecstatic with excitement, Bruno pulled up. He rubbed his eyes and only got out of the truck once he was sure he wasn't hallucinating. I joined him on a hillock, impatient to get the binoculars from him.

'There's someone there,' he exclaimed, stretching his arm out towards the village.

A figure was walking up and down the village square, a dog at its heels, going from one hut to another and bending to pick things up. It was a man. He was alone. The village seemed uninhabited. Bruno took back the binoculars and swept every corner, alert to a trap. But there was nothing to alarm us. The man was calmly going about his business. We decided to try our luck.

As we approached the huts, we noticed forms lying on the ground. The man didn't seem to notice the roar of the truck, and continued to pick things up without paying any attention to us. The doors of the huts were wide open, but nothing moved inside. No women or children. The forms lying in the dust were animals, and they didn't move. There were two donkeys in the square, some goats in the middle of an enclosure, a dromedary lying in its trough, and here and there some dogs with twisted bodies. All of these animals were dead.

'Something bad happened here,' Bruno said.

The man was gathering branches and leaves in the square. His arms were laden with bundles of sticks. He hadn't yet noticed us, in spite of the noise of our vehicle; maybe he was deliberately ignoring us. His dog, which had run away when it heard us arrive, started back towards its master, although without going too close, ready to scuttle away again. It made a curious impression on me, with its ears down and its tail between its hind legs: it seemed to be in a state of shock.

We parked the pick-up at the entrance to the village and got out, our senses on the alert. The animals were lying in pools of blood. There were bloodstains everywhere, some indicating where bodies had been dragged. Bullet cartridges glittered amid the stones. As slowly as a sleepwalker, the man went over to one of the huts, laid his burden down and came back to get the pieces of wood that marked off the enclosure where the goats had been killed. Bruno said something to him in an African dialect, but the man didn't hear him. He was a doddery old fellow with a stooped back and white hair, as thin and dry as a nail. His face was chiselled, with hollow cheeks that made the bones stand out. His absent gaze seemed to be swallowed up by the curdled white of his shaded eyes.

A terrible buzzing came from the hut. Human corpses lay inside it, besieged by thousands of frenzied flies. You could see arms and legs, the bodies of women and children heaped one on top of the other, some naked and displaying open wounds. Paralysed by the sight, we were immediately overcome by the terrible stench of putrefaction, a stench the scarves over our faces were unable to keep at bay.

'I've seen lots of massacres in my life,' Bruno said with a mixture of sorrow and disgust, 'and every time it's made me sick.'

'Do you think it was Gerima's men?'

'I don't see any tyre marks on the ground.' He pointed to horse droppings and countless hoof prints in the sand. 'These poor devils were attacked by horsemen. There are all kinds of criminal gangs operating like this. They decimate isolated families who are unfortunate enough to be in their path.'

'I don't understand what goes on in these monsters' minds.'

'A goldfish can't bring the complexity of the ocean back to the tranquillity of its bowl, Dr Krausmann,' Bruno said with a hint of reproach.

'I don't live on another planet,' I retorted, exasperated that he could still come out with these insinuations after all I had been through.

'Neither does a goldfish. But what does it know about storms? The world has become colour blind. On both sides, everything is either black or white, and nobody cares to put things into perspective. Good and evil are ancient history. These days, it's a matter of predators and prey. The predators are obsessed with extending their living space, the prey with their survival.'

'You've been too long in Africa, Bruno.'

'What is Africa, or Asia or America?' he said in disgust. 'It's all the same. Whether you call it a brothel or a whorehouse, it's the soul that's in it that determines its vocation. Whether you say "it smells bad" or "it stinks" doesn't change the air around you. The South Pole is only the North Pole lying flat on its back, and the West is only the East on the other side of the street. And do you know why, Monsieur Krausmann? Because there are no more shades of grey. And when there are no more shades of grey, anybody can rationalise anything, even the worst atrocity.'

Evening was starting to fall. The old man had finished his wood gathering, still walking back and forth in front of us, still ignoring us. Only once had he raised his hand, stopping Bruno dead in his tracks as he went to help him, and waited for the Frenchman to step back before continuing to gather branches; not once did he so much as glance at us. We had now been waiting there for half an hour, hoping he would pay us a moment's attention. We needed to know where we were, if there was a town not too far from here, or a barracks, or anybody who could take charge of us. Bruno had tried to talk to the old man, taking care not to upset him, but it was as if he had been addressing a djinn, as if they walked right through each other like shadows. Was the old man blind and deaf? No, he could see and hear, he was simply refusing to talk to us. He stood there, dignified, outside the hut. From the way his lips were moving, we realised he was praying. Next, he grabbed a can of petrol that stood at his feet, poured its contents over the lifeless bodies, sprinkled the branches and the walls, struck a match and threw it into the hut. A blue flame spread over the bundles of wood, making first the foliage, then the straw flare up, and becoming thicker as it reached the walls. Soon, acrid smoke was escaping through the cracks in the roof while the crackling grew louder. The old man watched the fire spread its greedy tentacles, twist the branches in its flames, then, like a whirlwind, engulf the bodies and the few pieces of makeshift furniture surrounding them.

'Let's go,' Bruno said.

'What about him?'

'He won't tell us anything and he won't follow us.'

'At least ask him. He might point us in the right direction.'

'Monsieur Krausmann,' Bruno cried irritably, 'that man is just as dead as his family.'

We got back in the pick-up. Bruno noisily engaged the gear stick, did a U-turn and set off into the gathering night. Turning, I saw the old man standing outside the blazing hut like a condemned soul at the gates of hell.

We had chosen to bivouac near a cave.

The stale smell of the *regs* spread through the coolness of the evening. A jackal barked somewhere. The night had returned to relieve the day of its mirages and give the darkness back its emptiness. Bruno and I hadn't exchanged a word for more than an hour. We were each too busy putting our thoughts in order. We had lit a fire in the shelter of the cave, eaten dried meat, emptied a few cans of food and drunk a bitter coffee that hurt my palate, then, exhausted by all the driving, we got ready to sleep.

Bruno threw a handful of sand over the fire to extinguish it and, unable to hold on any longer, went and urinated on a dune. Relieved, he spread a blanket over the ground, wiped the dust off his backside and lay down. I heard him moving about in search of a comfortable position. After a great deal of twisting and turning, he at last moaned with contentment, curled up and stopped moving. I knew he wouldn't close his eyes until he had relived his old wanderings and reviewed, one by one, the people who had meant something to him. Every night until now, he had told me an episode of his African adventures, his encounters and his setbacks, his lost loves, his little deaths and his redemptions … I hoped against hope that he wouldn't make an exception tonight. I needed him to talk to me, to make me drunk on his tribulations, to tell me about the women he hadn't been able to hold on to, the opportunities he hadn't been able to seize. His inspired voice might perhaps allow me to shrug off the guilty conscience that was infiltrating the furthest corners of my mind. Bruno was extraordinarily gifted at giving any disaster its dignity and finding a meaning in the unlikeliest things.

'You haven't uttered a single woman's name since we've known each other,' he said all at once.

The wind began to whistle through the cave while the shadows cast their spell over the nocturnal beasts you sensed in the darkness, far from their lairs, raking over a hunting field as dry as a bone. All the same, I was pleased to hear his voice. I would have liked him to talk about himself, and about Africa – his romanticism and his optimism would have been good therapy for me – but he had chosen to focus on me and, not expecting it, I didn't know what to say.

'I can't remember you ever having talked about women, Monsieur Krausmann. Is there someone in your life?'

'I'm a widower,' I said, hoping that he would change the subject.

'I'm sorry,' he said after a moment's embarrassment. 'Illness?'

'An accident.'

'A road accident?'

'No.'

'Work-related?'

'In a way.'

He lifted himself on one elbow and looked at me, his cheek resting in the palm of his hand. 'Curiosity is an African flaw,' he admitted. 'Nobody here knows where curiosity ends and impoliteness begins. But you're not obliged to answer me.'

'Actually, I don't have anything very interesting to say about the subject,' I assured him.

'Then I shan't insist.'

'It's more complicated than that.'

'I assume it is ...'

He lay back down, crossed his hands over his stomach, and gazed up at the myriad of stars in the sky.

'I often think about Aminata,' he said. 'I wonder what's become of her, if she's happy with her cousin, if she has children, if she still remembers the two of us ... She seemed happy with me. I made her laugh a lot. I think she liked me. Maybe not as a lover, but at least as a friend ... I'd picked her out among the girls in her tribe. She was very beautiful. A bit on the plump side, but really attractive. Eyes that sparkled like diamonds. And a smell like a meadow in springtime ... I asked for her hand without consulting her, and the elder gave his permission. It's a common practice among the Azawed ... She could have refused. Nobody would have forced her. The elder informed her of my intentions, and she didn't object ... I don't understand why she left. I try to find excuses for her, but I can't. I can't remember ever depriving her of anything. I was no thunderbolt in bed, but I performed my conjugal duties decently ... Her cousin didn't visit us often, and never alone or outside a religious or family celebration. Never once did I catch him and Aminata looking at each other in a suspicious way. Then suddenly, away they flew like turtle doves. Without any warning, without a word of explanation. I was devastated.'

'Are you still angry with her?'

'I've often been angry with myself, but never with her ... There are things we can't really explain. They come down on our heads like tiles off a roof, and that's it ... Do I miss her? I'm not sure. She was a good girl, a generous girl. I don't have the feeling she betrayed me. She simply made a choice. Did she realise how much she was hurting me? Not for a second. Aminata didn't have a bad thought in her head. She was sweet-natured, and quite innocent.'

'You still love her.'

'Mmm ... I don't think so.'

'Oh, yes, you still love her.'

'No, I assure you. It's ancient history ... Aminata, for me, remains a vague regret. A misunderstanding of the flesh ... Anyway, that's life: it only takes from us what it's given us. Neither more nor less.'

In the sky, the stars were trying to outshine each other.

Now Bruno was waiting for me to speak, to tell him something. I think he really wanted to hear what I had to say. Just as he was turning his back on me to sleep, convinced that I wasn't going to tell him any secrets, my voice anticipated my thoughts and I heard myself say, 'She killed herself.'

'I beg your pardon?'

'My wife ... She committed suicide.'

'Oh, my God!'

He didn't add another word.

I stared at the stars until they merged together. I was stiff and cold, barely aware of the hard stones I was lying on. When, hours later, Bruno started snoring, I turned on my side and, with wild eyes, waited patiently for dawn to restore to the day what night had stolen from it.

9

It took us four hours of hard driving over stones as sharp as shards of glass to go a mere seventy kilometres. The ground was terraced over an interminable succession of natural paving stones, all white-hot. The pick-up swayed over the cracks, jolting and settling in an unbearable clanking of old iron. The abrupt twists of the steering wheel were grinding my wrists to a pulp. I was on the brink of a nervous breakdown. I found it hard to believe that you could cross vast swathes of land without seeing any people or coming upon a village. That pirates should choose little-used roads was understandable, but that you could drive for hundreds of kilometres without glimpsing the merest hut with a semblance of life around it was driving me mad. Every time we thought we were on the verge of getting out of trouble, we found ourselves back at square one, in the middle of nowhere, facing the same inhospitable horizon and surrounded by hills crushed beneath an outrageously sovereign sun, which, after forcing the earth to its knees, was trying to subjugate the sky and its Olympians. Destiny was starting to wear the mask of farce: what was the point of going on, I wondered, since our fate was sealed? Seized with suicidal frustration,

I felt like pressing down hard on the accelerator, closing my eyes and tearing straight ahead at breakneck speed ...

Bruno was in no better a state than me. He had stopped peering through his binoculars at our surroundings, or suggesting which way we should go. He sat in the passenger seat, his shoulder against the door, and dozed, even though disturbed by the discordant jolts of the truck. I was angry at him for not being more insistent with the old man the previous day. He might have pointed us in the right direction; he might even have agreed to come with us. But Bruno claimed to know Africans better than anybody, to know exactly when you should make demands on them and when not. I asked him how come, after three days' driving, he had no idea where we were. After all, he claimed to have been a guide to Western journalists and scientific expeditions. He replied in a condescending tone that in this part of the world a guide was basically someone who kept strictly to the routes he knew by heart, since you just had to deviate one millimetre from the beaten track to put yourself in as much danger as any fool ...

We decided to rest in the shade of a monumental acacia whose branches were adorned with offerings to marabouts and ancestors: scarves, rag dolls, pieces of jewellery, combs tangled with hair, tiny terracotta pots at the bottom of which animal blood had dried. The area was strewn with dromedary droppings and traces of bivouacs. Near the revered tree, Bruno discovered a well without a coping, along with a rudimentary drinking trough. We washed ourselves from head to foot, cleaned our clothes and spread them over the burning stones to dry. Bruno dug out a pair of boxer shorts for me from the bottom of the duffle bag, but they were too big for me; I made do with a pair of Y-fronts and a vest, both still in their cellophane. I had lost a lot of weight. My body was covered in spots, some turning grey; I had a boil under my right armpit, with two others in my groin; my thighs had deep furrows in them and there was a thick whitish crust on my knees. Bruno preferred to stay naked. With his unkempt beard and reptilian hair, he looked like a guru. He performed a series of gymnastic moves, opened his arms wide and crossed them, crouched down and stood up again, twisted his neck so that the vertebrae cracked, then, in order to draw a smile from me, he turned his back to me and bent over to touch his toes, thus offering me the hairy indentation of his backside, which he began to wiggle in a coarse manner. He continued this clownish exhibition until I burst out laughing. Pleased with his success, he waved his arms about in a burlesque choreography and, now an angry witch doctor, now a ballerina, went from a mystic dance to a classical ballet with staggering ease. Dazzled by his sense of improvisation and his comic gifts, which I would never have suspected he possessed, I laughed until the tears ran down my face, and it was as if I were expelling all the filth polluting my body and mind.

We ate in the shade of the acacia and slept, cradled by the cool breeze.

When I woke up, I found Bruno absorbed in the book by Joma Baba-Sy. When he closed it, he made an admiring pout. He lingered over the photo on the cover and admitted to me that he couldn't believe a mass of rage and bestiality like Joma could harbour so much sensitivity … He reopened the book, skipped several pages, stopped at a particular poem and read it out loud:

Africa,
Death's head,
Bathing in the troubled waters
Of your horizonless seas,
What have your sunstruck bastards
Made of your memory?
On your ravaged shores
Your ballads lie rotting
Like flotsam
And in your godless sky
Your most pious wishes
Chase their own echoes.
Africa, my Africa
What has become of your tom-toms
In the silence of charnel houses?
What has become of your griots
In the blasphemy of weapons?
What has become of your tribes
In the deception of nations?
I have questioned your rivers
And your lost villages
Looked for your trophies
In the trances of your women
Nowhere have I found
Your age-old legends.
Your kings are deposed
Like your statues of wood
The voice of your traditions
Has faded and died
Your stories are told
In praise of tyrants
Your destiny denies you

Like a rejected mother
And none of my prayers
Find an echo in you.
Africa, my Africa
You have put death in one of my hands
And wrongdoing in the other
And you have stolen my masters,
My saints, prophets and apostles
Leaving me only my eyes
To weep over the insult
Your children inflict on you
Every day that God makes.
What will become of me
In the shadow of your ravens?
What can I hope
When I can no longer dream?
Perhaps to end up
Where everything began
Between a tombstone
And a cancelled vow.

'Incredible, isn't it?'

I shrugged my shoulders.

Bruno put the book down, rummaged in the satchel, and pulled out a wedding photograph. It showed a party taking place on a large patio hung with Chinese lanterns. Surrounded by tipsy guests, Joma posed solemnly beside his bride. Curiously, even though for two days and two nights I had been trying to shake off the crime I had committed, I found myself wanting to know a little more about my victim. Deep inside, I knew the idea was senseless, but driven by a morbid curiosity, like a murderer returning to the scene of his crime, I took the photograph from Bruno. The low quality of the image made it hard to distinguish much about Joma, who was barely recognisable among the guests. We then turned to a number of articles cut out of a poorly produced local newspaper. The texts were full of misprints; all of them praised in fulsome style 'the force of an exceptional poet'. A somewhat more sober article included an interview in which Joma told how he had gone from being a penniless village tailor to becoming a bard. In the same interview, he expressed the opinion that 'with the Word we can overcome adversity'. In another cutting, there was a photograph, stuck between a crossword puzzle and a game of spot the difference, showing Joma receiving a trophy from the hands of an African lady in traditional costume, with a few lines by way of caption relating the ceremony. Next, we came across a small item reporting a bomb attack which had left two children wounded and a woman dead, the woman being 'the young wife of the poet Joma Baba-Sy who received the Léopold Senghor Prize two weeks ago'. This last sentence was underlined in red. The article had been carefully preserved in a plastic wallet.

'Life is strange,' Bruno sighed, putting things back in the satchel.

I went to look for my clothes.

We loaded up the pick-up. Bruno wasn't too keen on resuming the journey. He looked at the drinking trough, the marabout tree, the offerings hanging from the branches, the tranquillity of the place, and suggested we spend the night here, arguing that since it was a sacred site, there was no risk of being attacked and that with a little bit of luck someone might turn up. The dromedary droppings weren't fresh, but the well looked as if it was often used. I would have been happy to agree to his suggestion, and was about to do so when we heard a whistling sound. 'What's that?' I asked. Bruno frowned. A quick glance around revealed nothing suspicious. Immediately, there was a swirl of dust close to us, followed by another soon after. Bruno shoved me inside the cab, started the engine, engaged the gear stick and set off at top speed. The pick-up's rear window exploded. 'Get down!' Bruno screamed at me as he accelerated. There was a sharp noise, and the windscreen cracked into a spider's web pattern. Somebody was shooting at us! The pick-up wove in and out among the stones and the wild grass to avoid the bullets, leapfrogged on the uneven track, jumped several metres into the air, before falling again in a din of mistreated metal. The engine was being pushed to its limit. In our wild flight, we crashed straight into something; the pick-up skidded, almost overturned, but somehow righted itself. The impact had been unusually violent, and my head had hit the ceiling light. Now I clung to my seat and the dashboard. After a dizzying race, Bruno realised that the steering was going awry. A strange noise, like the grinding of defective gears, was coming from the right-hand side of the bonnet and getting louder with every bend. Stopping was out of the question. We had to get out of the sniper's range as quickly as possible. A few kilometres further on, the vehicle became uncontrollable. The wheel that had been hit was becoming gradually looser, making it virtually impossible to steer. Bruno parked on the side of the track to assess the damage. He peered under the bonnet while I kept a lookout, my legs trembling and my heart pounding fit to burst. Apart from the dust that was settling in our wake, there was no threat in sight. Bruno joined me. His downcast expression told me that the damage was catastrophic. He informed me that the ball joint and the shock absorber had taken a major hit and that the shaft drive wouldn't last much longer. Not having the right tools or any spare parts to do an emergency repair, we got back in the cab and set off again, very slowly, and very aware of how much the vehicle was swaying. Bruno drove extremely cautiously, concentrating on the road, dodging the stones and ruts as if he were carrying nitroglycerine. Sweat dripped from his chin. We managed to cross a river bed but when we reached the opposite embankment the vehicle suddenly tipped forward and stopped. There was nothing more we could do. The shaft drive had broken and the wheel had come away from its stump ... We were stuck.

Cursing, I climbed a hillock. When I reached the top, my heart almost failed: in front of us stretched the same labyrinth that had been driving us mad for days. My legs gave way and I fell to the ground. My elbows planted on my knees, my face in my hands, I looked left and right, and saw nothing but perdition. Something told me that the desert was aware of our desperate state and that when it had squeezed the last drop out of us, it would close its fist over us and reduce us to dust which the winds would then disperse among the mirages.

'What are you looking at?' Bruno asked, flopping to the ground beside me.

I pointed to the dereliction around us. 'I'm looking at the loneliest place on earth.'

'There are two of us,' he said. 'And we're still alive. All is not lost. We just have to take the drama out of the situation.'

'I don't have the formula for doing that.'

'The formula is in here,' he said, tapping with his finger on my temple.

His gesture annoyed me.

Bruno let his gaze wander over the rocky ridges in the distance, then picked up a stone and weighed it in his hand. 'Have you ever been face-to-face with your own death, Monsieur Krausmann?'

I didn't reply, considering the question ridiculous and inappropriate.

'The loneliest place on earth,' he went on, 'is when you're facing a firing squad. You don't know what it's like. It's then that you realise how long eternity lasts. It lasts the space of time between two commands: "Aim!" and "Fire!" What came before and what will come after don't matter.'

'You're not going to tell me that happened to you.'

'But it did. I was twenty-four. With a rucksack on my back and a compass in my hand, I thought I was Monod. I'd crossed the Tassili, the Hoggar, the Tanezrouft, the Ténéré. Not even Rimbaud travelled as much as I did. It was a wonderful time. Nothing like the mess things are in now.'

He put the stone down and let his memories flood back.

'What happened?'

He smiled and opened his eyes wide. 'A military patrol picked me up on the shores of Lake Chad. The sergeant immediately accused me of spying. That's the mindset around here. If you aren't a hostage, you're either a mercenary or a spy. After some pretty rough questioning,

I was court-martialled and sentenced to death the same day I was arrested. The trial was held in the refectory, surrounded by soldiers having their meal and the clatter of knives and forks. The judges were a sergeant and two corporals. I found the procedure a bit hasty and the solemnity of the court somewhat grotesque, but I was young, and in Africa the grotesque is commonplace.'

He started tracing little circles in the sand with a distracted finger. His face became blank.

'They came for me early in the morning. They had to drag me because I couldn't stay upright. I wanted to scream, to struggle, but I just couldn't react. I was shaking like a leaf when they tied me to the post. It was only when I finally looked up and saw the firing squad that I realised how alone I was in the world. The whole universe had been reduced to the barrel of a rifle. The horror of it! My blood was beating louder than war drums in my temples. And it was so silent in that shooting gallery you could have heard a match being struck anywhere for miles around ...'

'I can imagine.'

'You can't. It's beyond imagination. When the sergeant cried, "Take aim!" I ejaculated. Without an erection. And when he cried "Fire!" I shit myself. I didn't hear the shots, but I really felt the bullets go through me, pulverising my ribcage, bursting open my innards. I collapsed in slow motion. I think it took me an eternity to reach the ground. I lay there in the dust, shattered, looking up at the pale sky. I didn't feel any pain. It was as if I was gently drifting away like a puff of smoke. And just as I was about to give up the ghost, the sergeant burst out laughing. Then the firing squad also started laughing. Next, the rest of the platoon came out from behind the embankment, splitting their sides and slapping their thighs ... The sergeant helped me to my feet. He told me he'd never laughed so much in his life.'

'It was a fake execution.'

'That's right, a fake execution! Just a bit of fun for soldiers stuck in the middle of nowhere with nothing to do and bored out of their minds. "No hard feelings," the sergeant said, patting me on the back. He gave me a packet of smuggled cigarettes by way of compensation and a kick up the backside to make sure I got out of his sight as quickly as possible ...'

'I hope you took legal action.'

'Oh, of course,' he said, ironically, getting to his feet. 'Let's go!'

'No way.'

'What do you mean?'

'I'm not moving from here. I don't know where we are and I'm fed up with it. You can go if you like. But I'm staying here until fate has pity on me. One way or another.'

My decision was stupid, but I stood by it. What I said, I felt and demanded. I was at the end of my tether. It was like being on the edge of a precipice; in front was only the abyss, a sheer drop and the dreadful feeling that I was giving up. What mattered and what didn't? The neurotic search for an unlikely salvation, or renunciation? I could no longer stand blaming myself. Bruno understood that I was going through a bad patch and was in no mood to be dissuaded. He didn't insist, but went back to the pick-up to sort through the bags. He filled the two rucksacks with the bare essentials, placed them on a clump of grass along with the two canteens of drinking water and the automatic rifle, crouched in the shade of a shrub and took his head in both hands.

Evening found us still in our separate spaces: I at my improvised lookout post watching the sun bleed itself dry, Bruno leaning back against his shrub. When the darkness reached my thoughts, I went back to the pick-up, grabbed the jerry cans, poured petrol over the vehicle, struck a match and threw it on the bodywork. A swift flame spread through the cab and surged over the bonnet. Bruno shook his head sadly. He thought I'd gone mad. I hadn't gone mad. I was aware how stupid my gesture must seem, but it was an act I'd thought through: I wanted to attract someone's attention to us, and I didn't care if that someone was a nomad or a bandit. I wasn't afraid of being taken hostage again; the only thing I knew for sure was that I had no desire to wander in that damned desert until I died of thirst and exhaustion; I refused to end up a heap of anonymous bones surrounded by the carcasses of long-dead animals polished clean by successive sandstorms.

Day dawned. All that was left of the pick-up was a heap of charred, smoking scrap iron licked in places by the odd flickering flame. We hadn't slept a wink, on the alert for a figure or a shadow or a noise. Nobody had come, no military patrol, no marauding gang, no camel driver, no djinn. Bruno asked me if I was pleased with my little performance and if I had recovered enough to follow him. I put one of the rucksacks on my back, draped a canteen across my shoulder and set off after him.

*

We walked all morning in the fierce sun, spent the afternoon in the shade of a rock, and in the evening resumed our trek until late in the night. When I took off my shoes, scraps of skin remained stuck to them. I slept until midday.

After two days of wandering, we collapsed in the middle of a stretch of scrub. We had used up half our reserves of water and our blistered shoulders could no longer bear any load. Bruno, who seemed to be holding out better than I was, suggested that I let him go off on his own to look for help. The state of my feet had slowed our progress, and the blisters were likely to become infected if left untreated. I promised him I'd be much better after a good night's sleep.

We had dinner and sank into the arms of Morpheus without even realising it.

A baby was crying as day dawned. I thought I was dreaming, but Bruno had heard it too. He was sitting up, eyes wide, trying to see where the wailing was coming from. He put a finger to his lips, ordering me to keep quiet, and grabbed his rifle. The crying was coming from a *thalweg*. We walked around a low wall of undergrowth and slid along a slope, unleashing tiny avalanches of stones as we passed. A woman was crouching in a copse, cradling a baby that lay snuggled against her chest. Suddenly, she turned and saw us just above her. At the sight of the rifle, she hugged her child so tightly to her she could easily have suffocated it. Bruno made a gesture with his hand to reassure her, but she was so terrified by the weapon she didn't even see it. He said something to her in a local language. She didn't seem to understand. I told

Bruno to lower his rifle. At that moment, ragged, ghostlike figures began appearing. Within a few minutes, we were surrounded by about forty women, children and men who had been sleeping in the long grass; our intrusion had woken them and, one after the other, they emerged from their hiding place, unsure whether they should surrender or run. Bruno put his rifle down on the ground and raised his arm in a gesture of appeasement. 'We don't wish you any harm,' he said. They stared at us, more concerned by our physical degradation than by the weapon on the ground. Taking us for devils, the children hid behind their mothers' ragged skirts. There was a movement at the back of the group, and they stood aside to let a white woman through. She was a sturdy woman in her fifties, as blonde as a haystack, and it was as if providence, with a click of its fingers, had restored my people to me. I would gladly have thrown myself into her arms if it hadn't been for the fact that the expression on her face was one of suspicion and hostility.

'Who are you?' she asked in English, with a strong Scandinavian accent. 'And what do you want with us?'

'We're lost,' Bruno said. 'We've been drifting across the desert for days now.'

'If that's the case, why are you armed?'

'We were taken hostage, and we escaped. We have no idea where we are and we don't know where to go.' He held out his hand and let it hang in mid-air. 'My name's Bruno, I'm an anthropologist, and this is Dr Krausmann.'

The woman looked us up and down, then said through clenched teeth, 'Lotta Pedersen, gynaecologist.'

She told her companions to go back to their places and motioned with her head for us to follow her. She led us over to where another, younger white woman was sleeping beneath a vault of branches. This woman, who seemed to be in charge of the group, greeted us with a degree of respect. 'I'm Dr Elena Juárez,' she said, shaking our hands. Three Africans joined us, two of them in white coats with red crosses on the breast pockets. She introduced them. The youngest was Dr Orfane. He was slim and rather handsome; his tin-framed glasses made him look like a matinee idol. The other two, Omar and Samuel, both in their early thirties, were nurses.

Bruno briefly told them about our captivity, and about the way we had evaded our kidnappers before our stolen pick-up gave out on us. He omitted the tragic episode of Joma. In her turn, Dr Elena Juárez told us how, while her group was conducting a vaccination campaign, she had found herself at the head of an army of refugees. Having dropped Lotta Pedersen and Dr Orfane in a tribal village, she had left with the two male nurses to make a list of the patients in a neighbouring hamlet. On the way, their Land Rover had been put out of action by an antipersonnel mine. Then they had been pursued by armed men across the scrub and only owed their salvation to the fact that night had fallen and their driver, Jibreel, had such a good sense of direction. When they got back to the tribal village, they had found the families in a state of shock. A rebel attack was believed imminent. They had to leave quickly. So it was that the medical group now found itself, after almost a week on the road, stuck with forty fugitives. I asked Dr Juárez if they at least knew where they were going; she assured me that the group had an excellent guide, in the person of the driver, and that in three or four days, barring any unforeseen incidents, they would reach their camp, a reception centre run by the Red Cross.

'There were twenty-eight of us at first,' Dr Juárez said. 'Other fleeing families have joined us on the way. Unfortunately, two old women died of exhaustion yesterday.'

A man whose eyes had rolled back jumped out in front of us. He was wearing a city suit that had seen better days, the jacket open to reveal a bare, hollow stomach. Wagging his finger, he called heaven to be his witness and declaimed in a sepulchral voice, 'They came at dawn. They burnt down our huts, killed our goats, our donkeys and our dogs, then rounded us up in the square and started killing us, the fathers in front of their children, the babies in their mothers' arms. If the devil had been there that day, he would have taken to his heels.'

'It's all right, Mr Obeid,' Dr Juárez said, signalling to one of the nurses.

The nurse took the man to one side, put an arm around his shoulders and walked him away, talking to him softly. Dr Juárez explained that the man was a teacher, the only survivor of a massacre that had wiped out his family, and that he intoned his complaint from morning to night, blaming the shrubs and the stones.

'We have other survivors among us, and I'm afraid their traumas are irreversible,' Dr Orfane said. 'What's your speciality, Dr Krausmann?'

'General medicine.'

'Well, that's something,' Dr Juárez said, and ordered the group to break camp.

Bruno and I went back to look for our rucksacks, which

we had left on the other side of the *thalweg*. When we returned, Lotta asked us to hand over the rifle to Jibreel, a tall, well-built man in a turban. Relieved, Bruno did as he was told. We set off, Dr Juárez and the guide in front, Lotta and Dr Orfane in the middle, and the two nurses bringing up the rear. Bruno and I trotted behind a ragged young man dragging a cart on which an old, weary-eyed woman lay – it wasn't exactly a cart, more a clever assembly of wooden planks fitted with arms from a barrow and mounted on two moped wheels. The rims of the wheels scraped on the stones, making the cart sway. The old woman was very slight, like a mummy removed from its sarcophagus. Her wasted body shuddered each time there was a jolt. It was a pitiful, tragic sight. The young man was pulling his cart with unflinching energy, at an even pace, as heedless of the effort he was making as an automaton.

'Is she your grandmother?' Bruno asked him.

'My mother,' the young man said.

'Oh, I'm sorry! … Is she sick?'

'Can't hide anything from you, can we?'

The young man's tone was sharp. Bruno offered to relieve him, and received a respectful but categorical refusal.

'My friend here is a doctor,' Bruno said. 'If you like, he can examine her.'

'There's no need, sir.'

'What she has may be serious,' Bruno insisted.

'There is nothing serious in life, except the harm we do.'

The young man had started walking faster, to make it clear to us that he wanted to be left alone.

Ahead of us, the line of survivors dragged themselves along as best they could, bundles on their heads, babies

212

on their backs, giving me an overarching image of a terrible world whose infamy I barely grasped and for which nothing in my life had prepared me. A world whose merciless gods had lost all the skin from their fingers, so often had they washed their hands of it. A Sisyphean world abandoned to the cowardice of men and the ravages of epidemics, a world of torture and violence, where contingents of the living dead wandered from place to place through a thousand torments, hope crucified on their foreheads and their shoulders collapsing beneath the weight of a nameless curse.

At the first stop, I took Bruno to task. I pointed out to him that I was old enough to offer my services without needing an intermediary. He was taken aback. In point of fact, I was scared to approach these people myself. Their misfortune both overwhelmed and horrified me. I could find a whole heap of unanswerable excuses for myself, justifying my attitude by the fact that I had been through an incredible ordeal and pretending that having not washed for so long I had developed a kind of hypochondria. Yes, I could invent all kinds of get-out clauses, but I wouldn't be able to hide my face. Never having had to deal with this kind of patient, and having neither gloves nor masks nor any other kind of protection at my disposal, I was afraid of being contaminated by some tropical microbe. I wasn't proud of myself, but I couldn't help it.

Bruno unwound his scarf and ran to give a hand to Lotta, who was busy calming the delirious teacher. Even though he had refrained from judging me, I was convinced he was disappointed in me.

An hour later, I found myself with a child in my arms – his mother had fainted and could no longer carry him. He was a puny boy, his skin withering on his bones. Dressed in something resembling a vest, his belly bloated and his skull bald, he stared at me with his empty eyes. I took his fingers out of his mouth; he kept them on his chin for a moment then stuffed them between his lips again. I took them out once more; understanding that I didn't want him to put them back in his mouth, he turned away and flopped onto my shoulder. Without thinking, I put my hand out and hugged his sparrow-like body. I felt his little heart beating against mine. Something in me was falling back into place. I was becoming a human being again.

10

In the evening, at the time when the earth turns upside down like an hour glass, I took my seat on a pile of loose stones and watched the sun dying on the horizon. The heat had abated, and a hypothetical silence, like that of a truce, hung over the plain. A line of ragged trees wound through hills as polished as shells reflecting the light of the sunset. Under less inclement skies, such a fresco would have filled me with contentment. But my heart had learnt to resist such spells. What had once fascinated me now saddened me, because I fear that I could no longer revive my old joys, no longer look at things in the same way. My passions had broken free of their moorings, and the happy, indulgent observer I had once been could not forgive talent its imperfections. No magic spoke to me now, no Rembrandtesque tableau or idealised image. The only light I cared about was the one at the end of my tunnel. When would it appear? I wanted time to speed up, I wanted the sun to disappear and reappear the next minute, I wanted some conjuring trick to make tomorrow arrive faster than tonight. Ever since the guide had promised us the end of our wandering, I had been unable to keep still. Urged on by some feverish drive, I often found myself going ahead of the convoy until Bruno called me back. The day before, noticing that I was wearing shoes unsuitable for a forced march, the father of a family had offered me his son's espadrilles. 'He won't need them where he is now,' he had said. My feet were still bleeding, but the pain had eased. Anyway, it wasn't my legs that were carrying me, but the hope of an imminent end to all this; I felt almost like praising the saints in whom I had never believed.

Dr Juárez brought me coffee. She sat down beside me and gazed at the sunset. She was a very pretty woman, with the profile of a goddess and large dark eyes, which, when they came to rest on you, enveloped you entirely. She must have been in her thirties, in spite of her dimpled face and youthful figure. Her long chestnut hair cascaded down to her hips, when she didn't gather it in a bun. During the two days' walking we had done together, not once had I heard her complain. Of course, whenever she got the chance she slept like a log, but as soon as she was on her feet she pushed herself onwards. The previous day, she had come to see me; my limp worried her and she wanted to take a look at the state of my feet. Her voice was so soft I hadn't paid any attention to what she was saying. While she spoke, I couldn't take my eyes off her crimson lips, which had made her uncomfortable. It had taken me a good five minutes to realise that she had left.

'It feels like a sandstorm is coming,' she said now.

'Oh, no!'

'Yes. We're going to have to get our *cheches* out and pray it isn't a big one.'

She placed her lips on the rim of the glass and took a small sip. She had pretty hands with slender fingers, but no ring or any other adornment, except for an old watch with a leather strap and a crucifix around her slender neck.

'We lost another old woman,' she said.

'I know.'

She shook her head, and a loose lock of hair fell over her eye. She again lifted her glass to her mouth, which was round and full, and squinted at the sunset. I wondered how shoulders as frail as hers could bear such heavy and unpredictable responsibility, how a woman her age managed to live with danger, what motivated her to that extent when the mere fact of going to the aid of some poor devil automatically exposed her to major risks? I tried to imagine her fleeing across the scrub, a pack of fanatical killers at her heels, or held captive in a sordid hideout at the mercy of depraved kidnappers, and her devotion seemed to me as inhuman as the conditions faced by these tribes she was trying to save.

She gave a start. 'I'm sorry. What was it you said?'

'What?'

'Excuse me, I thought you said something.'

'No, no ... Maybe I was thinking aloud.'

She tensed her wonderful mouth with its dazzlingly white teeth. The way she had of biting her lip was a joy in itself.

'And how are your feet?'

'Getting better ... How come your camp hasn't sent anyone out to look for you? They haven't heard from you for days. It would only be natural for them to worry and send out patrols or helicopters to find you.'

'They don't know our situation at the camp. Our radio was destroyed in the Land Rover.'

'All the same ... You left on a mission. They know your

route. You weren't going on holiday. This is a dangerous area. I'm amazed that you've been left to your own devices.'

'There's nothing to say they aren't searching for us. But I don't think we can expect an armada of helicopters. We're in Africa, after all. We don't have such means at our disposal.'

'And you agree to work in such conditions?'

'Gladly. Imagine this country cut off from the world, these people without aid ... Fortunately there are NGOs, Dr Krausmann.'

'Where are we exactly?'

'In Darfur.'

My Adam's apple jumped in my throat. 'What? I thought we were in Sudan!'

'Darfur is a region of Sudan. Sudan's the largest country in Africa. More than two and a half million square kilometres. Five times the size of Spain.'

Darfur ... I was in Darfur, that land of atrocities, endlessly talked about in news items to which I'd listened with only half an ear between a slug of beer and the phone ringing. Darfur, that bloodstained Atlantis patrolled by elusive ogres, where the darkness was as red as sacrificial altars and the mass graves as vast as landfills! So it really existed, and I was in the middle of it. I had been through so much, overcome so many ordeals, only to end up in Darfur! I didn't know whether to laugh or cry. Those brief news reports that had once flashed past on my TV screen now all came back to me, clear and explicit this time, with their daily massacres and movements of population, their crows perching on the corpses of children and the surreal testimonies of those who made it out alive. How to survive in a snake pit, in an open-air gladiatorial arena where everything was allowed and where death might cut you down at any moment without warning? Was the end of the tunnel, as promised by the guide Jibreel, merely wishful thinking, a mirage? It was a huge blow to my morale. I felt faint. I didn't recognise my voice when I heard myself swallow and say, 'You're joking!'

'What do you mean?'

'Are you sure we're in Darfur?'

'I've been working here for two years.'

'Do people live that long around here? This country's generally thought of as the antechamber of hell.'

She threw her head back in a throaty little laugh that made her shoulders shake. 'There is no hell on earth, Dr Krausmann, only devils, and they aren't invincible. It hasn't been easy to make this territory fit to live in, but we've fought tooth and nail to defend it. We've had to stand up to the government and their henchmen, to legions of fanatics and death squads that have tried to chase us out of here. Some of our doctors have been kidnapped, others murdered, but that's only strengthened our determination. We're gaining ground every day.'

I wished I could share her enthusiasm, only I wasn't sure it would have quelled my doubts. The naivety of what she was saying saddened me more than it reassured me.

Dr Juárez noticed that her glass was empty; I offered her mine, which I hadn't touched. She gently refused, put her arms round her legs and placed her chin on her knees. Her shirt gaped open in a place where a button had come undone, revealing the silky swelling of her breasts. The sun had just sunk beneath a mass of blood-red splashes and the first stars were starting to appear in the sky.

'You say you were kidnapped in the Gulf of Aden, Dr Krausmann?'

'In those waters. Why?'

'The pirates usually operate in Somalia. Negotiations are easier there. I don't see what your kidnappers hoped to find around here. The rules and the stakes differ from one country to another. Being so lawless, the Somali coast offers more room for manoeuvre. Opting for Sudan strikes me as strange.'

'Isn't that this continent all over?'

'What do you mean?'

'Everything's strange in Africa. People kill, steal, ransom, hold life cheap ... So whether it happens in Somalia or Sudan, what's the difference basically?'

'Not much, in a way. But—'

'But what, Dr Juárez? As far as I'm concerned, nothing justifies what happened to me. No instability, no revolutions. None of that is any of my business. It isn't my story and it isn't my future. I don't know these people from Adam and I have nothing in common with them. We were just passing by, my friend Hans and I. We were sailing in international waters. We were on our way to the Comoros. The worst of it is that it was for a good cause. Where is Hans Makkenroth now? On what market stall is he being displayed? That's *my* problem. Whether it happens here or next door is of no concern to me. I just want to know what happened to my friend and if there's any chance I'll see my city and my country again.'

'Right,' she said, taken aback by my sudden anger.

Someone started moaning behind a copse. 'Duty calls,' Dr Juárez said, getting quickly to her feet – saved by the bell. She hadn't been expecting my outpouring of bitterness and she felt sorry she had provoked it. I didn't blame her. I was even furious with myself for being so rude to a woman who had come to comfort me. Didn't she have enough worries with her horde of survivors without me unloading all my resentment on her? Giving me a disappointed look, she ran down the slope. When she had gone, I realised that I should at least have offered her my help and taken the chance to clear up the misunderstanding.

Bruno joined me on the ridge. We both watched the shadowy, half-starved figures moving about in the river bed, some looking for a place to sleep, others fussing over their exhausted families. I saw only human debris, trailing behind them the twist of fate that had spared them, and clinging to a strange conviction that resembled neither their prayers nor a destiny and which seemed to connect them to life like a thread. What purpose lay behind their martyrdom? I tried to see a meaning in their survival and couldn't find a single one. These people had nothing; they were at the end of their tether, their tomorrows were minefields, and yet, through some sad phenomenon, they clung to anything to keep going. Where did they find the strength to hold on, the faith to believe in the rising day, a day as poor and wretched as them? They knew that what they had been through the day before was ready and waiting for them the next day, that the cycle of their suffering was never-ending, that where men raged, the gods refused to intervene; they knew all these things and acted as if none of it mattered, refusing to face facts and looking beyond good and evil for an illusion to latch on to, no matter if it was all ash and smoke.

'That's Africa, Monsieur Krausmann,' Bruno said as if he had read my thoughts.

'That doesn't explain such doggedness.'

'That's where you're wrong, my friend. These people want to live.'

'But what do they have to live for?'

'That's not the question. They want to live, that's all, live life to the end … I've been knocking about this continent for decades. I know its vices, its disasters, its brutality, but nothing alters its desire to live. I've seen people who were nothing but skin and bones, others who had lost the taste for food, and others who were thrown to the dogs and the scoundrels, not one was ready to give up. They die at night, and in the morning they come back to life, not at all put off by the troubles that await them.'

'And you think that's wonderful?'

'Isn't it obvious I do?'

'Strange, I see only an unspeakable tragedy and none of the good things you see in it.'

'Africa isn't something to be seen, Monsieur Krausmann, it's to be felt, experienced, smelt.'

'Well, it certainly has a strong smell!'

I had upset him. He was so sensitive that any disagreement struck him as a declaration of war, which was why he was so ready to take my reply at face value. But I had no intention of correcting what I'd said. I was convinced he knew what I was referring to. Africa did have a strong smell. Its air was polluted by the stench of dungeons and mass graves and massacres. It was a fact he couldn't deny or question, because if you turn away from horror you have no chance of eradicating it. Bruno had to admit that his certainties were not truths, that his viewpoint was biased. That was what I couldn't stand about him: that blissful squint which distorted his relationship with Africa and which saw virtue in suffering and contours where there was only flatness. We had often argued about that. Before, I had thrown in the towel, tired of having to keep the debate on track while Bruno went off at tangents and saw hidden doors, finding a kind of panache even in decay. But that wasn't the case any more. The centaurs he had idealised while we had been rotting in Gerima's jail were there, before our eyes, and I saw nothing of the myths they were supposed to embody.

'You disappoint me, Monsieur Krausmann.'

'It isn't me, it's Africa.'

'You don't know anything about Africa.'

'Which Africa? The one you see or the one you smell?' I looked him in the eyes. 'In concrete terms, what fascinates you about it?'

'Exactly what just struck you: the hunger for life. An African knows that life is his most precious possession. Sorrow, joy, illness are simply part of a person's education. An African takes things as they come without granting them more credit than they deserve. And although he may be convinced that miracles exist, he doesn't demand them. He's self-sufficient, don't you see? His wisdom cushions his disappointments.'

'Did you say wisdom?'

'You heard me correctly, Monsieur Krausmann,' he said, more and more angrily. 'He's a splendid creature, the African. Whether he's sitting in the doorway of his hut, or under a carob tree, or on the banks of a crocodile-infested river, he's himself. His heart is his kingdom. Nobody in the world knows better than him how to share and forgive.

If I had to give generosity a face, it would be the face of an African. If I had to give brotherhood a sound, it would be that of an African laugh.'

'And what if you had to give death a face? Stop this, Bruno. What kingdom are you talking about? What brotherhood? Are you blind? You don't have to raise poverty to the rank of prophecy to make the wretched of the earth into the just. You're talking nonsense, Bruno. I don't know Africa as well as you do, but what I see with my eyes is irredeemable. And I don't see any of the things you're trying to show me ... It's through protest that we lay claim to hope. And these people don't protest. They flee when they should resist. They quickly gather their kids and their bundles and run blindly. The least sign of a tornado in the distance makes them panic ... You want to know what I really think? These people don't live, they exist, and that's all.'

'You've got it all wrong, Monsieur Krausmann. Here, when life loses meaning, it still keeps its substance intact, in other words, that absolute determination that Africans have, never to give up on any single minute of the time that nature grants them.'

'Even a griot would laugh at your oracle, Bruno. And do you know why? Because it gives him nothing to get his teeth into. When you're dying of starvation, you don't give a damn about eulogies and orations because nothing in the eyes of the starving person is worth the illusion of a meal.'

'We aren't looking at the same things.'

'Yes, we are. Except that where you paint a fairy tale, I see a disaster.'

'Africa is more than the sum of its famines, wars and epidemics.'

'Then what else is it, in your opinion?'

'The refusal to—'

'The refusal to what?' I cut in. 'To transcend misfortune, is that it? You can't turn vomit into a banquet, Bruno. This continent has a serious problem with bad governance, corruption, lack of discipline, lawlessness. Violence is practised here like a priestly vocation. That's the truth, and there aren't any others. We're dealing with a human catastrophe. The people I see here are doomed. As long as they have such irresponsible leaders, they'll continue to suffer ... There's a rational explanation for bankruptcy. And Africa is bankrupt, my friend. Making it believe the scars on its body are beautiful tattoos is to make it an innocent. Painting an innocent with gold and releasing him into the wild is a recipe for chaos. And chaos is right here, in front of our eyes ... Look at them: they're scared, they've lost everything, they're running without knowing where they're going, and every day they die of hunger and exhaustion. That's Africa, Bruno. A foul wound. A mess and a madness. And you don't gild the image of someone who's wearing a straitjacket. I'm outraged to hear you praise a scorched land where not even a hint of promise remains. You have to look things in the face and ask yourself the right questions. What's become of the schools, the training centres, the institutions, the jobs? What's become of order, justice, democracy, dignity? All I see is flights and raids and rapes, a people without gods or virtues forced out of their homes, at the mercy of thieves and genocidal tyrants, and that's worse than death.'

'I don't think we're on the same wavelength, Monsieur Krausmann,' Bruno said, getting to his feet, offended by my diatribe.

'We aren't even on the same planet.'

The following morning, the convoy did not leave at the appointed time. A slight sandstorm had blown up, but the real reason for the delay was the young man with the cart. He was on his knees beside his mother, his fist in his mouth. His mother was resting on a mound of sand. Her swarthy complexion had darkened. She seemed to be dying. Dr Juárez, Lotta Pedersen and the two nurses were by her side, with a first-aid box containing a few meagre drugs. Dr Juárez took her blood pressure; the face she made as she put away her stethoscope wasn't encouraging. The old woman's breathing was a barely audible hiss. The emergency care she had been given had not woken her. In expectation of a death, the refugees appeared one after the other. A few sympathetic hands came to rest on the shoulders of the young man, who did not even notice. Dr Juárez said something to him in a local dialect. The young man shook his head and bit his fist, no doubt to suppress a sob. When he realised that everyone was hanging on his words, he cleared his throat and declared that for him and his mother the adventure was over. He explained to Dr Orfane that the old woman could no longer bear the jolts of the cart, that the planks of wood had eaten into her flesh and bones, and that there was no point prolonging her ordeal. Dr Juárez tried to persuade him to carry on. She suggested putting a blanket under the old woman's body in order to absorb the knocks, while the two nurses offered to take turns pulling the cart. The young man refused categorically. Bruno also intervened. His great, oft-vaunted knowledge of the African factor had led him to think that he could succeed where others had failed. The young man didn't even listen to him. In fact, he wouldn't listen to anyone. A family of refugees volunteered to stay with him, but to no avail. He wanted to be alone with his mother and not owe anything to anybody; his torn bundle, his canteen of water and his remaining items of food would be enough for him. 'Go,' he said. 'Don't waste time because of us.' After half an hour's discussion, Dr Juárez gave up, convinced that the young man wouldn't follow us. After weighing up the pros and cons, the three doctors opted to continue the march without further delay, as the sandstorm looked as if it was likely to get worse.

We limped along for the rest of the day, choosing subsided areas and river beds in order to avoid being spotted. Despite the poor visibility, the guide Jibreel gave the impression that he knew where he was taking us, which helped us overcome our fatigue. Our progress was slowed by the dizziness of the old people. We were aware of the need to keep going because every delay was a danger. Towards evening, the wind died down and the curtain of dust started to disperse. Dr Juárez chose a bare basin for the night.

Since our altercation, Bruno had been avoiding me. The few times our eyes met, he turned away before I had time to give him a sign. I realised how much I had hurt him and I was sorry I hadn't kept my opinions to myself.

Two boys and a little girl, who seemed to be from the

same family, approached me as I was laying my sleeping bag on a bed of sand. They were dressed in faded vests that hung down over their grazed knees and threadbare shorts. The older of the two boys, who must have been about eight or nine, wore amulets on his arms that were identical to Joma's. The little girl and the other boy had puffy faces, rheumy eyes and runny noses. They sat down next to me, in silence. I took a can of food from my rucksack. The older boy shook his head and with his chin indicated the torch sticking out of my pocket.

'Do you want it?'

He nodded.

I held out the torch. He took it in his calloused hands with their grazed knuckles, looked at it with joy, showed it to his brother and sister. From the way he pressed it to him, I understood that he was asking me if he could keep it. I nodded. The three children let out squeals and ran off immediately, for fear I might change my mind. Subsequently, the younger boy came back to collect the can of food and ran to catch up with the two others without turning round. Dr Juárez, who had witnessed our little game, emerged from the shadows and crouched opposite me, two cups of coffee in her hands.

'I hope I'm not disturbing you.'

'On the contrary.'

'Thanks …'

'I really must apologise for my behaviour yesterday.'

'Oh, it doesn't matter. We're all a bit on edge, and it's good to get things off your chest from time to time.'

'I'm not in the habit of being so impolite.'

'I don't doubt it for a moment.'

'Sometimes, I can't believe what I'm becoming. It's as if

I get a kick out of being unpleasant. But that's not what I'm like. I'm usually the kind of person who backs off when arguments get too heated. After you left, I behaved very badly towards Bruno. That's why he's upset with me.'

'It's odd, he has the feeling he was the one who behaved badly towards you. He told me about your little row.'

'No, it's my fault. Bruno is a good person. I'm the one who was out of control. I admit I'm finding it harder and harder to see things clearly.'

She offered me a cigarette. I told her I had quit when I left university. She thought I had made the right decision. She herself had tried many times, but after two or three months of abstinence she always ended up having one. She took out a lighter, lit her cigarette, puffed at it insistently. I let her smoke in peace, even enjoyed smelling the intoxicating odour of burnt tobacco.

'We aren't too far from the camp now,' she said.

'I was starting to despair. I've hardly slept since I found out we are in Darfur.'

'You can sleep soundly tonight. We're no longer in any danger. The area is more or less secured.'

'More or less?'

'I mean that the rebels and bandits have stopped operating in this part of Darfur since the African Union sent military units.'

'Pleased to hear it.'

'As soon as we get to the camp, we'll inform the authorities that you're safe and sound. If all goes well, you'll be back home in less than a week.'

'Let's get to the camp first. This country has made me superstitious.'

She laughed, and her dimples showed, emphasising the fineness of her features.

'What town are you from, Dr Krausmann?'

'Frankfurt ... You can call me Kurt.'

'Only if you agree to call me Elena.'

'All right, Elena. It's a nice name ... Are you from Madrid?'

'Seville.'

'I love Seville. I've been there several times. It's a wonderful town, and the people are very welcoming.'

'I haven't been back for years. My parents moved to Valencia. They run a little restaurant on the coast ... Do you have children?'

'My wife didn't want any. Or rather, she was in no hurry. Her work wouldn't allow it.'

'Is she also a doctor?'

'She was in marketing ... What about you? Do you have children?'

'My patients are jealous. They don't like unfair competition.'

Her eyes came back to me, shining like jewels. I let her sip her coffee and puff on her cigarette before asking her if her patients were excessively possessive. She considered my question, seemed to guess what I meant by 'excessively possessive', lifted a ravishing eyebrow, but didn't have time to answer. One of the nurses arrived, looking embarrassed. He didn't need to say what had brought him. Elena had understood. Once again, duty called, and our conversation was interrupted just as it was getting interesting. She gave me a little wave and stood up. I offered to assist her, but she advised me to get some rest: the last stage, she said, was often the roughest. Her hand brushed against my shoulder. I almost put my cheek against it. Out of pure reflex. That didn't escape her. She hastened to follow the nurse. I contented myself with watching her walk away.

I couldn't get to sleep after that. And not because of the danger.

3
Homecomings

1

We reached the Red Cross camp at nightfall, completely exhausted and in a very sorry state. The old people collapsed as soon as they were through the gate, and had to be picked up. The women and children staggered in the dust, mere scraps of flesh wrapped in rags, their mouths drooping with hunger and thirst. We had lost two more of the group on the way and taken turns pulling the sickest. Male nurses came running to meet us. Stretchers were unfolded. Nobody in the camp had been expecting so many people to arrive. Nothing had been prepared for them. Elena tried to see that things were done in the right order, but she soon ran out of energy and had to step aside. A tall, lanky man joined us in the main yard. He was the director of the centre. In his sixties, with stooped shoulders and a large nose, he was a full head taller than any of us. In marked contrast to his affable, gentle manner, his stentorian voice rang out like a whip. He began by issuing instructions to his staff, told the stretcher-bearers to take care of the old people and children first, ordered hot meals and two tents to be got ready, then, once the families had been dispatched and calm restored, he turned to Elena and her team, who, no longer able to stand, had sat down on the ground, their heads bowed and their arms around their knees. Bruno and I didn't know if we should go straight to the two tents or wait where we were for our fate to be decided. The director hadn't taken any particular notice of us. To be honest, there was nothing to distinguish us from the other refugees. Filthy, with our legs as thin as wading birds' and our downcast expressions, we looked like two scarecrows dumped in a field. The director crouched by Elena, patted her on the wrist in support and helped her to her feet. While Elena, Lotta and Orfane were delivering their report in the director's office, the two nurses took their leave of us and headed to a wing of the camp. Slowly, the bustle of the families settling into the tents died down and gave way to the hum of a generator. The camp was lit by floodlights as well as a number of anaemic-looking street lamps. You could see the rows of tents around the administrative block, a water tank mounted on metal scaffolding, a second block with lighted windows that looked like an infirmary, a third block with a chimney on top – presumably the kitchens – a glazed hut at the entrance to the camp which served as a guard post, and, somewhat further back, a huge canvas shed with a red cross on it. There was a car park on the south side of the camp, where two ambulances and two Land Rovers stood beneath corrugated-iron canopies. It was like being in a military fort, and nothing like the refugee camps you usually saw on television. No crowds, no rioting, no campfires, no disturbances. Everything seemed scrupulously laid out.

A few minutes later, Lotta Pedersen came to fetch us. She led us to the director's office, a prefab equipped with cupboards, a computer, padded chairs and shelves filled with medical books and pamphlets, registers, numbered files arranged in chronological order, hard-cover encyclopedias and a neat pile of paperwork. Elena was sitting slouched on an old sprung sofa, a glass of water in her hand. She looked exhausted, her dimpled face was drawn and her eyelids were drooping. Orfane was perched on the arm of the sofa, his hands crossed over his knee. Having by now been informed who we were, the director received us with great respect, offered us a small carafe of filtered water and waited while we drank. He told us his name was Christophe Pfer, that he was Belgian and that he had been working for the Red Cross for seventeen years. He had the scars to show for it – one on his chin, a souvenir from the war in the Balkans, and a bad knee, the result of an ambush in a forest in El Salvador. He was a genial man – a wise man, too, after two decades spent dealing at close quarters with human stupidity and the problems it caused all over the world. With his curly grey hair, thick moustache and nonchalant demeanour, he reminded me of Lee Marvin in *Cat Ballou*. Like anyone with a radio or access to the internet, he knew about the kidnapping of two Germans by pirates off the coast of Somalia, but had never expected to be welcoming one of them on his own premises. He informed me that the international press was still talking about our kidnapping and that a large-scale search had been launched to find us. I asked him if there was any news of Hans Makkenroth. He had none. Actually, he had difficulty believing it was really me, because he too found it strange that the kidnappers had chosen Sudan instead of Somalia in which to barter our release. Bruno asked if giant posters with his face on them had been displayed on the front of every town hall in France, provoking marches on the Champs-Élysées demanding his release. Pfer had to admit that nobody knew about his disappearance. Bruno pretended to be shocked, before pointing out that he was no common tourist, but an African in every fibre of his being, that his misadventure was strictly an African affair and that it had absolutely nothing to do with the Western media. Then, aware of the bewilderment he had caused, he made a whole series of self-mocking gestures as if to make up for it. Pfer scratched behind his ear: since humour was inappropriate in these painful circumstances, he must have been wondering if this Frenchman was entirely of sound mind. Nevertheless, he promised to contact our respective embassies as soon as radio contact was established and advised us to have a good bath and a hot meal and go to bed. Bruno asked permission to join 'his African brothers' in the tent. He was subtly staking a kind of claim by his request. I winked at him, just to let him know that I understood him and approved. He turned on his heel like a soldier and headed for the tents.

Orfane offered to take care of me for the night. He invited me to his airy, restful quarters, a cabin complete with air conditioning, two padded benches, a small desk, a fitted wardrobe and a narrow but shiny tiled bathroom. I almost fell over backwards when I looked in the mirror above the washbasin. After what I had been through physically and morally, I had been expecting it, except that instead of a castaway, I discovered a shipwreck. I looked like a zombie, with my wild beard, dirty, dishevelled hair, dusty eyes, furrowed cheeks and skin the colour of papier mâché. My shirt was nothing but a filthy rag and my crumpled trousers resembled a floor cloth. I supposed I must smell like a dead rat. Orfane pointed to a bar of Aleppo soap and a bottle of shampoo on a stainless-steel stand next to the shower head. I quickly undressed and got in the shower. While I washed, my host switched on a mini stereo. The Afro-American music that started up made me quiver from head to foot. It had been so long since I had listened to anything other than coarse insults and moaning. In the old days, I hadn't been able to start my car without switching on the radio or the CD player. Now I realised how much I had missed music and how its absence had impoverished me. A stream of pure air rushed into my lungs. I had the feeling I could hear my soul being rebuilt. My heart was pounding so hard I feared a heart attack. My whole being demanded music, demanded it as a hymn to life. The foamy water flowing over my body reconciled me with myself. As the voice of the singer filled me with intoxication, I rubbed and soaped myself aggressively to expel the dirt from my flesh and from my mind. The water at my feet was almost black with it.

Orfane threw me a dressing gown and suggested I take the bench near the window. A waxed cardboard tray was waiting for me on the bedside table: steaming hot soup, a plate of salad, white bread and a slice of smoked fish. I threw myself greedily on the food. Orfane took a can of beer from a mini refrigerator, handed it to me and went into the bathroom to wash. When he came out again, wrapped in a thick white loincloth, he went to fetch a bottle of soda from the fridge and opened it with his thumb.

'Would you like another beer?'

'No, thanks … Is that your wife?' I asked, pointing to the photograph of a black woman on the desk, next to another photo in which three black men were posing with a white man.

He gave a broad smile. 'That's my mother when she was thirty.'

I looked at the photograph in its wooden frame. The woman appeared lost in thought. There was something graceful and proud about her. Bruno had told me that Africans worshipped their mothers, convinced that no prayer would be granted without Mama's blessing.

'She's very beautiful,' I said.

'Of course, my father was the village chief.'

He drank from the bottle, put it down on the bedside table and lowered the volume a little on the stereo.

'Nina Simone, "Don't Let Me Be Misunderstood" ... That's my sedative. That and Marvin Gaye. When Marvin sings, the black clouds dissolve and summer floods my thoughts ...'

'I like him,' I said. 'He's magical.'

'Isn't he?'

The bench creaked beneath his athletic body. He reached out his arm and picked up the photo of the four men. There was something very tender in that movement of the hand. He showed me the photo. The men were standing in a crowded, smoky bar. One of the black men, a stocky man in a docker's cap and a coat that was too big for him, was visibly delighted to be having his photograph taken with the other three.

'That's my father, the white man's Joe Messina, that's Robert White, and that one's Eddie Willis ... There's an incredible story behind this photo.' He put it back down on the edge of the desk. 'It was my father who taught me about music. He was the village chief, like I said, and very spoilt. He always asked for records for his birthday, and he celebrated his birthday every time a hit song came out. He loved black American music. Our house almost collapsed under the weight of all the records: Otis Redding, Louis Armstrong, Jimi Hendrix, Aretha Franklin, Dee Dee Bridgewater, Abbey Lincoln … We had to move whole boxes of them to see where to put our feet. It drove my mother crazy. My father was the only one who knew his way around. He knew exactly where to find such and such a track. My father had a particular weakness for the Funk Brothers. One morning, he left his rosewood throne, his ostrich feather headdress and his sceptre cut from a baobab tree and disappeared. We thought he'd been kidnapped or murdered, but we never found his body or any trace of him. He'd vanished into thin air, just like that.' He clicked his fingers. 'One evening, three years later, he came back to the village. Without warning … He'd gone to the United States, on a "pilgrimage" to Detroit. He'd crossed whole countries with no money and no papers, done whatever pitiful little jobs he could find to pay for a train or bus ticket, worked for months in ports waiting for the right boat and the right moment, and managed to stow away as far as Detroit. And why did he do all that? To be photographed with his idols, Joe Messina, Robert White and Eddie Willis. Just to be in a photo with those three guys. No more, no less. The next day, with his trophy in the bag, he set off on the return journey.'

'You're exaggerating …'

'I swear it's the truth, the whole truth, and nothing but the truth,' he laughed, raising his right hand. 'My father used to say: "Nations can't survive without myths and young people can't bloom without idols." When those two points of reference are missing, things are a mess. African rulers refuse to admit that. That's why they're sending their people back into the Stone Age.'

I refrained from hazarding the slightest opinion on that subject.

'Would you mind if I took everything off?' he asked. 'It's hot, and I like to sleep naked.'

'Put the air conditioning on.'

'The electricity is supplied by a generator. It's strictly rationed, and is switched off at ten o'clock, in other words, in the next fifteen minutes.'

Without waiting for my permission, he took off his loincloth, and his ebony body made a sharp contrast with the white sheets.

'What's your favourite kind of music, Dr Krausmann?'

'Classical, obviously.'

'I suspected as much. Of course, that's quite natural for a descendant of Beethoven ... I like everything. From Mozart to Alpha Blondy. I don't discriminate on grounds of race or morality. It was when man detected a sound and a rhythm in noise that he discovered himself. And that made him superior to the other creatures. I love musicians. I love singers, from sopranos to choirboys, from baritones to rappers. Do you see, Dr Krausmann? Music is the only talent that God envies men.'

'I agree with you, Dr Orfane.'

He increased the volume of the stereo and closed his eyes. 'Are your parents still alive?'

'My mother died years ago,' I said.

'Oh, I'm sorry. And your father?'

'Do you mind turning off the light?'

'Of course not. What about the music?'

'No, leave it on, please.'

'You're lucky. The stereo's connected to a car battery. Generator or not, at Orfane's place, it's always party time.'

'Good night, Dr Orfane.'

'Good night, Dr Krausmann. I put a pair of trousers, a shirt and clean underwear out for you on the chair. We're pretty much the same size, so they should fit you.'

'Thanks.'

'You have quite a few boils and your complexion's a bit off. We'll have to take a look at all that tomorrow morning.'

He switched off the light.

Despite my tiredness and the softness of the sheets, I couldn't get to sleep. My brain was whirring. I wasn't thinking about anything specific, but every image, however vague, kept me in suspense as it spread through the maze of my insomnia. I thought of the most absurd things, only dismissing those connected with the ordeal I had been through. I had no desire to twist the knife in the wound. I didn't have the strength. I wanted to fall into a sleep so deep that I would achieve oblivion. But my twisted muscles prevented me from unwinding. I lay on my right side, my left side, on my back, on my stomach, my head under the pillow, on my forearm, but it was impossible to get to sleep. I imagined myself at home, in my scented bed; the absence of Jessica stoked my obsessions. I thought about Frankfurt, my surgery, my patients. There was no way to loosen the hold my anxieties had over me. In desperation, I stared up at the ceiling and listened to the damp, bloodless night ponder its nostalgia in the shelter of darkness. Orfane started snoring and muttering in his sleep. I got out of bed, went outside and sat down on the steps of the cabin. There was a big golden moon in the middle of the sky, so close that you could clearly see the outlines of its craters. Some shadowy figures were moving about near the tents. I felt like a beer but didn't dare go and look for one in the fridge. The sickly-sweet breath of the desert blew on my naked torso. I sat there until my eyes began to blur with dizziness. I groped my way back to my bed in the dark. I think I fell asleep before my head hit the pillow.

The sun was at its height when I woke up. I put on the clothes Orfane had lent me and went to the office. Pfer offered me coffee and told me the fax had been sent and that our embassies would soon respond. I went back out to stretch my legs, but was intercepted by Orfane who marched me to the infirmary, gave me a thorough examination, and tended to my blisters and boils. On my way out of the treatment room, I came across Elena, who was tying up her laces next to her cabin. She looked rested and relaxed. Her face lit up when she saw me. She stood up and asked me from a distance if I had slept well. I told her I'd slept like a log. She threw her head back with a delightful laugh and confessed that, in her case, they'd had to send for a deep-sea diver to bring her up out of her coma. Elena was sublime, with her hair hanging loose down to her hips and her bronzed, finely featured Andalusian face. She was wearing faded jeans, an open-necked shirt that revealed the pendant around her neck, and bright-yellow espadrilles. 'It's my day off,' she said, to justify her casual dress. 'As there's nothing in the way of entertainment, at least I dress relaxed.' Jessica would never have tolerated jeans on her body, let alone canvas shoes on her feet. Jessica was strict about the way she dressed; everything had to be impeccably cut, her made-to-measure suits had not a fold or a thread out of place. She would spend more time trying on a dress in a high-end shop than a surgeon operating on a seriously ill patient. I had often suggested she dress less formally, but to no avail. Both at home and in the city, she was inflexible on the matter. True, the clothes she chose perfectly matched her diaphanous skin and gave her platinum-blonde hair the lustre of sunlight. Jessica, my God! Jessica … When I was small, on my way home from school, I would deliberately make a wide detour in order to walk past a magnificent house with a garden as beautiful as a dream. In short trousers, my satchel on my back, I would slow down to sneak a look at this residence, which compensated all by itself for the dullness of our suburb. I loved the glittering tiles on its roof, the sophisticated lines of its façade, the marble columns standing guard on either side of the flowery front steps, the monumental oak door. I wondered what the people who lived inside were like, what luxury and opulence they must be familiar with, and if, once night had fallen and the lights were out, their sleep gave them as much joy as the comfort with which they were surrounded. One day, coming back from school, I saw an ambulance outside the front door of the beautiful residence and neighbours on the pavement watching stretcher-bearers bring out a corpse. I learnt later that the wealthy old woman who had lived alone in that dream house had been dead for many days without anybody noticing … Thinking of Jessica, it was that splendid residence that came spontaneously to only one freighter aircraft to serve all the camps, it was rotated in a random way, and sometimes they lacked basic foodstuffs for weeks, which was why the director insisted on a severely restricted diet. I assured her that after the disgusting stuff the pirates had given me out of rotten cans, it would be ridiculous of me to turn my nose up. Her hand came to rest on mine. 'Oh, I can imagine,' she sighed. The touch of her fingers and the musky smell of her skin were strangely comforting, and I hoped deep in my heart that she would not take her hand away immediately.

After the meal, Elena showed me around the camp. Then we walked to the other side of the fence and looked around a huge building site some hundreds of metres away. Elena told me that this was a pilot village intended for refugees who had been forced to leave their lands. A broad avenue cut the site in two. On either side, buildings were going up, some still at the foundation stage, others almost finished. Woodwork and roofs were still missing, but the work seemed to be advancing, given the dozens of workers bustling about and the profusion of wheelbarrows and hacksaws.

'The refugees don't only need food and medical care,' Elena said. 'They need to regain their dignity, too. They're building this village themselves. Of course, architects and supervisors came from Europe to get things going, but the refugees are doing the actual construction. They're happy to have the work and plans for the future. A little further south, we've built farms and laid out orchards. The farms are run by widows so that they can provide for their families. The orchards have been entrusted to shepherds who've turned into farmers. And they seem to like it. Soon, the first houses will be ready and this village will be born. Initially, we'll be able to house forty-three families. By the end of the year, we'll have room for another sixty-five. Isn't that wonderful? When we set up the camp two years ago, there wasn't a single hut left within a radius of a hundred kilometres. It was like the valley of shadows. And now look what we're doing. I'm so proud.'

'So you should be, it's quite an achievement. Congratulations.'

'The village will be called Hodna City. In Arabic, it means something like "reassurance".'

'It's a pretty name. It sounds good.'

Elena was delighted. She was full of an almost childlike enthusiasm, and her shining eyes danced with light.

'Over there, we have a school. Three classes of forty pupils each, and six native teachers, all survivors of atrocities. Plus a football pitch, with wooden goalposts. You'll see, after classes all the kids rush to watch the match … We're trying to give these people a normal life. And they're ready for it. They've already forgiven.'

She paused here for a moment or two before resuming as volubly as before. She told me there was also going to be a big assembly hall, a library, perhaps a cinema, a traditional market in the square, stalls and cafés in the avenue, and lots of other facilities.

'Do you have a barber anywhere around here?' I asked. 'I have to get rid of this fleece on my face.'

'Yes, we do. A really good one.'

Twenty minutes later, I found myself sitting on a stool in the open air, a towel around my neck and foam on my face, at the mercy of Lotta Pedersen's razor and scissors. The Scandinavian gynaecologist was magnificent in her role as an occasional hairdresser. And as she rehabilitated my image, a swarm of kids stood around us and laughed uproariously at the sight of a woman shaving a man.

A gaudy turban around his head, Bruno sat twiddling his thumbs in the doorway of the administrative block. He had washed and spruced himself up, made friends among the storekeepers – which explained the brand-new *kamis* and Saharan flip-flops that he was wearing – but he hadn't touched a hair of his Rasputin-like beard. With prayer beads around his finger and kohl on his eyelids, he looked like a sheikh about to address the masses. But he wasn't happy: he was grim-faced and his nostrils were quivering. He had tried several times to get through to Djibouti by phone, and each time he had heard ringing at the other end, the line had been cut off. Bruno suspected the switchboard operator of stopping him from contacting the outside world. It was quite likely, he said, that the director of the camp had received instructions from the government to keep our situation secret. How else to account for the fact that neither the French nor the German embassy had reacted to the fax they had been sent early that morning?

Pfer assured us that the fax had indeed reached its destination and that his supervisors in Khartoum were making the necessary arrangements with the relevant authorities.

The next day, there was still no news from Khartoum. Bruno and I spent the whole morning in Pfer's office, waiting for the fax to screech or the phone to ring. About midday, the switchboard operator managed to make contact with Djibouti and Bruno burst into sobs on recognising his partner's voice at the end of the line.

Then his laughter burst out through his tears. I didn't understand what he was saying in Arabic, but it was clear that the line was vibrating with the overflow of emotion. Bruno wiped himself with his turban, hiccuped, grinned, struck his forehead with the palm of his hand, jumped up and down on his seat, and every now and again let out shrill cries. His partner passed the phone, one by one, to family members, neighbours, the shopkeeper opposite, an old friend, whoever, and I imagined all these people hearing the news, stopping whatever they were doing and rushing to the phone to say how happy they were to learn that their dear Frenchman was still alive and how they couldn't wait to see him again in the flesh. The conversations went on. Sometimes, Bruno was forced to wait while the next speaker was fetched from the other end of the street or a bedridden old acquaintance who absolutely had to talk to him was helped from his bed and dragged to the phone. Silences were followed by euphoric yells, and again tears and laughter mingled. By the time he hung up, Bruno was transformed. He was in seventh heaven, and his eyes sparkled. He gave me a big hug, then grabbed Pfer and danced like an orphan who'd been given his family back.

Pfer suggested we go to the canteen to celebrate. As we left the office, we saw two male nurses running across the yard towards the main gate of the camp. Children were standing outside their tents, pointing at something. Shielding my eyes from the sun, I saw a figure swaying in the distance, a burden on its back. Pfer, who had immediately realised what was happening, sent his secretary to alert the infirmary. We gave up on the canteen and hurried to catch up with the two nurses. The figure didn't stop on seeing help arrive. It kept on staggering towards the camp. The two nurses tried to relieve it of its burden, but it refused and carried on its way, like an automaton. Bruno was the first to identify the figure: it was the young man with the cart who had been abandoned with his mother in the desert! There he was, before our very eyes, tottering but still upright, his mother on his back. He entered the camp, barely able to stand, empty-eyed, deaf to the words of the male nurses who tried to take the old woman from him. It was as if he wanted to see his exploit through to the end, jealously guarding his trek and rejecting any help he judged premature. The children, who had recognised him, ran towards him, incredulous. They didn't cry out, didn't go too close to him, simply escorted him to the infirmary, where a doctor and two of his assistants were waiting. The old woman was immediately laid on a stretcher and taken into the treatment room.

His lips white and his eyes on the verge of rolling back, the prodigal son collapsed exhausted against the wall, his arms dangling, his calves covered with cuts, his back steaming, half dead but valiant, incredibly valiant, supremely valiant.

Bruno turned to me and said, proudly and vengefully, '*That's* Africa, Monsieur Krausmann!'

2

That afternoon, Pfer summoned Bruno and me and informed us that representatives of our respective embassies would be arriving the following day. There would probably be journalists in the delegation, and maybe also Sudanese military. He gave an outline of that kind of encounter, which he had witnessed before, and its emotional impact, which could be quite severe. Bruno merely nodded, but once Pfer had finished his briefing, he announced that he had no intention of going back to Bordeaux, but preferred to return to Djibouti. Pfer promised to see what he could do and let us go.

Bruno took me to see an old man lying in a tent. He wasn't sick, just too old to stand. His face had collapsed and his gestures were sparing, and all he could do was smile in a dazed kind of way. Bruno told me he was a marabout and warrior, as well as an incomparable diviner able to sense water over a wide radius and locate it without needing a rod or a pendulum. According to Bruno, the old man, who was Ethiopian in origin, was an emblematic figure in the Horn of Africa. His reputation extended from the Yemeni Bedouin to the fabled Masai of Kenya. He had been the instigator and one of the leaders of the armed revolt against the Italian invasion in 1935 – Mussolini was said to have put a fabulous price on his head. After the national liberation at the beginning of the 1940s, he had been much feted by Emperor Haile Selassie. Then the coming of Communism to Ethiopia had turned the traditional structures upside down, and the old man had spent a decade rotting in the Marxist regime's dungeons, while Mengistu's henchmen murdered, 'disappeared' and forced into exile the most influential members of his tribe. Still hounded, he had ended up joining the swarm of refugees and had wandered from one country to another until age had caught up with him. Taken into the camp, he was waiting to die the way legends die in those lands where memories grow dim with the generations. I wondered why Bruno was telling me all this, then realised that there was no ulterior motive, that he was simply proud of 'his people's' charisma. As he spoke, the old man kept his eyes fixed on me. He must have been over a hundred and reminded me of an Apache chief on his catafalque of feathers. He wore a talismanic necklace and an amber rosary by way of a bracelet. A ring bearing the effigy of some ancient deity looked like a large wart on his finger. Bruno assured me it had belonged to Haile Selassie himself, who had given it to the marabout as a mark of friendship. The old man muttered something; his words emerged from his toothless mouth as if from an abyss, sepulchral and disjointed, and faded in the air like plumes of steam. He reached out his arm to me and placed his open hand on my forehead. A wave of energy went through my brain, and a strange sensation, as if I were levitating, forced me to take a step back. He said something in his dialect, which Bruno translated: 'Why are you sad?

253

yesterday, and the day before that. Your eyes were full of
her.'

'Please, Bruno. Now is not the time.'

'Love doesn't care about time. When it arrives, the world
can wait, and everything else pales into insignificance.'

He plunged his spoon into his soup, fished out the
piece of bread and lifted it to his mouth, his eyes already
withdrawing far away. We ate in silence, taking no further
interest in each other, then parted company. I went back to
Orfane's cabin, took a shower and lay down on the padded
bench. I tried to think of nothing, but that was impossible.
I was a whirl of thoughts. Jessica's ghost on one side,
Joma's on the other, and me caught in the crossfire. I
switched off the light to make myself invisible. Orfane
came back late. I pretended I was asleep, praying that he
wouldn't put the light on. He didn't. He undressed in the
dark, slipped beneath the sheets, and immediately started
snoring. I dressed again and went out into the night. The
generator was off. The moon cast an anaemic light over the
camp. Over by the tents, somebody was still up. I thought
I recognised Bruno's voice, but wasn't sure. I walked along
the fence, my arms crossed over my chest, my head bowed.
Two puppies came and sniffed my calves. I crouched down
to stroke them. They moaned contentedly and ran off
towards the gate, where a night watchman was dozing,
a tiny transistor radio against his ear ... A cigarette end
gleamed intermittently in the darkness. It was Elena. She
was sitting on the steps of her cabin, in vest and shorts,
smoking and staring down at her feet. As I was about to
turn and walk back the way I had come, she noticed me and
gave me a little sign with her hand.

255

'I can't get to sleep,' I said by way of excuse.

'Neither can I.'

'Worried?'

'Not really.'

She shifted on the steps to make room for me. I sat down next to her. The touch of her body unsettled me. I felt the heat of her skin against mine, smelt her subtle perfume. I had the impression she was shaking, or perhaps it was me.

'You should quit smoking,' I said to fight back the wave of emotion overwhelming me.

She smiled and tapped on the cigarette to get rid of the ash. 'One or two cigarettes a day isn't so bad.'

'If you aren't hooked, why not give up altogether?'

'I like one in the evening before going to bed. It relaxes me a little. And it also keeps me company.'

'Do you feel lonely?'

'Sometimes. But I don't make a fuss about it. I do a lot of thinking, and that does isolate me a bit. So when I'm alone and I light a cigarette, it's like having someone else between my thoughts and me. Someone who supports me, if you see what I mean.'

I didn't press her. She looked at me and I looked at her. The moonlight gently illuminated her. She was very beautiful: I'll never stop saying that. Her vest clung to her voluptuous torso, her silky arms were long and magnificent, and her eyes were like two rubies wrapped in velvet. Her musky smell intoxicated me.

'I haven't seen you all day.'

'I was with the old woman,' she said, referring to the mother of the young man with the cart.

'How is she?'

'She'll recover.' She flicked her cigarette away and turned to face me. 'Are you religious, Dr Krausmann?'

'Kurt.'

'Are you religious, Kurt?'

'My mother was religious enough for the whole family. She took everything on herself ... Why?'

'I was thinking of the old woman. We left her for dead, didn't we? We all thought she was dying. The only reason we gave in to her son's demands was because we thought he wanted to be left alone to bury her. I can't believe she's still alive. I've been in Africa for six years now. I was in the Congo and Rwanda before this. And there are things I've seen that go beyond human understanding. There are phenomena in these countries that I can't grasp or explain. It's extraordinary.'

'What's extraordinary?'

'The miracles,' she said, looking in my eyes in search of something. 'I've witnessed quite a few supernatural events. I've seen people come through terrible ordeals, sick and dying people get up out of their beds, and things so unlikely I can't talk about them without sounding ridiculous.'

Her hand grasped mine, a gesture she had whenever she felt she was losing her way. It was much more a question of clinging to something than a considered move.

'This continent is a holy land, Kurt. I don't know how to say it. The people are ... I can't find the words.'

'Strange?'

'Not in the conventional sense of the word. They carry a kind of allegory inside them, or rather a truth that's beyond me. And it comes home to me with such strength that it makes me shiver. There's a biblical inspiration in these people. Something that strengthens my faith, even though I don't exactly know what it is.'

'Maybe because you give too much of yourself.'

'It has nothing to do with that. In the Red Cross, we don't have any respite. There are so many priorities that everything becomes urgent. But this is another dimension, don't you see? When the old woman opened her eyes this morning, I saw a kind of revelation in them that bowled me over. As if a dead person had come back to life. I … I'm still in a state of shock.'

Holy land, I thought. My whole culture being incompatible with what I considered some kind of surreal folklore, that kind of statement disturbed me. Ever since the misunderstanding that had almost compromised my friendship with Bruno, any reference to an idealised Africa had made me uncomfortable. I hated to argue about subjects that led nowhere. I'd even say that I endured them with a patience I disliked. My embarrassment wasn't lost on Elena, who frowned and asked me if she was tiring me.

'Why do you say that?'

'I have the impression I'm boring you with my ramblings …'

'No, no, I'm listening. I don't know much about Africa. I come from a continent where miracles are simply remarkable coincidences.'

She turned up her nose in mild annoyance and sighed. 'You're right. I suppose it's very difficult to connect with that kind of story when you don't have faith … Can I get you a beer?'

I gladly accepted. She went into her cabin, leaving the door open so that I could follow her inside. I hesitated, and she came back to fetch me. She apologised for the mess. Her cabin was an exact copy of Orfane's, with the same padded benches, fitted wardrobe and tiled bathroom. I sat down on a chair next to the desk and crossed my legs. Elena brought me a can and a glass.

'Who's that?' I asked, pointing to a signed photograph pinned to the wall showing a black woman surrounded by a happy gang of kids.

'Marguerite Barankitse.'

'An African singer?'

'An icon in the aid field.'

'She's beautiful.'

'In her heart and mind, too. She's an exceptional lady and a great fighter. She rescued tens of thousands of orphans and child soldiers and built a hospital, a school, and farms to help the widows and their offspring. I'd give anything to do in Darfur what she managed to do in Burundi.'

'You've already done a lot.'

'We can do better. We don't have enough medical staff.'

She sat down cross-legged on one of the padded benches. Polite as I was, I couldn't help admiring the curves of her legs, barely covered by her shorts.

'I don't see any other photos,' I observed.

She burst out laughing, with that spontaneous singsong laughter of hers that was like the chirping of birds. 'I don't have a boyfriend, if that's what you're trying to find out.'

'I wouldn't dream of it.'

She raised a sceptical eyebrow and let me sip my beer. 'I married when I was twenty,' she said. 'A handsome Andalusian, intelligent, generous. But he was possessive, and I was independent. He wanted me for himself alone and forgot that he was only my husband. We'd loved each other since high school. We continued to love each other at university and got married as soon as he graduated. Two years after our honeymoon in Cape Town, we broke up.'

'These things happen,' I stupidly stammered.

'I love my work, Dr Krausmann,' she went on, brushing her hair back.

'Kurt.'

'I'm sorry ... When I was a teenager, I had two idols. Robert Redford for my girlish fantasies. And Mother Teresa. My husband took the place of the first and tried to overshadow the second. We can't have everything we want in life, can we, Kurt?'

'That depends on what we want.'

'I wanted to help people. Ever since I was very young, that's all I've dreamed about. In my fairy stories, I didn't see myself as a princess or Cinderella, but as a nurse devoted to the destitute. I imagined myself tending to the wounded on the battlefield. And when I saw what Mother Teresa was doing among the "untouchables" and the lepers, I was certain. It was exactly what suited me. It was quite natural for me to choose the Red Cross ... What hospital do you work at in Frankfurt?'

'I'm in private practice.'

'What about your wife?'

My breathing accelerated when I told her that my wife was dead. I expected her to apologise profusely, as people usually do when they've been indiscreet, but she didn't. She looked at me with sympathy and said nothing. I assumed that her long experience of death had hardened her and that she approached this kind of situation philosophically. Her eyes searched mine, shifted to my lips, then, in an almost mystic movement, she took my hand in hers and held it for a long time.

'I have to go,' I said reluctantly.

Lotta came to fetch me early the next morning. Three military vehicles bearing the insignia of the African Union were parked outside the camp's administrative block. Soldiers rigged out like draught horses, their rifles at rest, were sitting in the back seats, stiff and silent. A light-skinned young officer in a multicoloured parka stood to one side, conversing with Pfer, who merely nodded his head, his hands behind his back. Bruno was already there, in his disguise as a Muslim dignitary, cooling his heels outside Pfer's office.

The officer saluted me, then held out his hand. 'Captain Wadi,' he said. 'I command the Omega detachment, stationed thirty kilometres to the south of here. I have orders to ensure your safety and that of the delegation which will be arriving by plane in two hours' time.'

'Dr Kurt Krausmann, pleased to meet you.'

'I'm glad to know that you're safe and sound, Dr Krausmann. The director has told me about your misadventure.'

'Misadventure? Is that what you call it?'

He took no notice of my reservations about his definition and invited me to follow him into the office. Bruno sat down on the sofa, looking morose. Not once did he look up at the captain. He seemed to have an aversion to soldiers, and the proximity of this young officer made him ill at ease. I took a seat while Pfer went behind his desk. The captain preferred to remain standing, to feel in control, I suppose. He was somewhat sickly-looking with a thin, clean-shaven face, crew-cut hair and glittering green eyes that were in marked contrast to his bronzed complexion. He could well have been an Arab or a Berber.

'According to the captain, the plane has taken off from Khartoum,' Pfer said to relax the atmosphere, given that an inexplicable sense of embarrassment had fallen over the room.

Bruno shrugged. He addressed Pfer in order to avoid speaking to the captain. 'In that case, why summon us now?'

'I need some information,' the captain said.

'What information?' Bruno grunted, still looking at Pfer. 'We don't owe anybody anything. Representatives of our embassies will be here soon, and as far as my friend and I are concerned, they are the only people we should speak to.'

'Sir—' the captain began.

'Monsieur Pfer,' Bruno interrupted, standing up, 'we ask permission to leave immediately. We aren't criminals or illegal immigrants. And we have nothing to say to strangers. Kurt and I will return to our quarters until our officials arrive.'

The captain placed a file stuffed with papers on Pfer's desk and folded his arms across his chest, his nostrils dilated with anger. 'We're not talking about an interrogation, sir, but a normal procedure which is within my rights. I'm responsible for security in this area and any information that can improve living conditions in my sector of operations—'

'Can we go?' Bruno asked Pfer, deaf to the captain's injunctions.

Pfer was embarrassed. He took his head in both hands and stared at the calendar in front of him. Bruno ordered me to follow him. Disconcerted by Pfer's reaction, I decided to fall in with Bruno's plan. The captain made no attempt to stop us. He opened his arms wide and brought them down against his sides in an irritable slap.

Bruno gave me no explanation for his refusal to cooperate with the young officer. We crossed the yard, he at a furious pace, I hobbling along behind. He had to stop to let me catch up. Elena and the others being busy with their patients, he took me to see his 'brothers', who occupied the tent near the infirmary. There were half a dozen of them, all convalescents: an old veteran with mocking eyes, two teenagers and three battered-looking men, including the thirty-year-old in plaster who had been telling naughty jokes in the canteen two days earlier. They were laughing like mad and our arrival didn't put them off.

'I won't set foot in a souk again in a hurry,' a boy with a bandaged hip was saying.

'I'm sure the shopkeepers will be really upset,' one of the wounded men said ironically.

'It's my right,' the boy said. 'I'm the one who chooses where to spend my money, aren't I?'

'Let him speak!' said a man with a burnt face. 'Otherwise he'll lose the thread of his story.'

The others fell silent.

The narrator coughed into his fist, delighted to be the centre of attention. He resumed his story. 'I'd just been paid, and with my wages and savings, I was hoping to buy some nice fashionable trainers, with a label on the tongue and wonderful white laces. All my life, I've only worn old flip-flops with holes in them. I wanted to get myself something awesome to show off to the girl next door, who was always cutting me dead. I went to all the bazaars, and it took me all day. Finally, by chance, I came across a street peddler who took some Nikes out of a box that really took my breath away. I tried them on and they fitted me like a glove. They cost an arm and a leg, but I didn't haggle. When you want to treat yourself, you don't scrimp, isn't that right, Uncle Mambo?'

'You're absolutely right, son,' the veteran said in a learned tone. 'Personally, when I want to give myself a treat, I never think of the price of the soap.'

Roars of laughter shook the tent. The boy waited for the others to calm down before continuing, not at all disturbed by the lingering guffaws around him. 'I took the Nikes and checked them from every angle. They looked so good my mouth was watering. I could already imagine myself strutting past the girl next door's window. But just as I was putting my hand in the back pocket of my trousers to pay, I realised that someone had robbed me of half my money.'

'Damn!' exclaimed a young boy, entranced by his comrade's story.

'I hope you managed to get your hands on the thief,' said the thirty-year-old in plaster.

'How could I find him in that crowd? There were loads of people in the market that day.'

'Easy,' the veteran said. 'You just had to look for a one-eyed man. Only a one-eyed man would have left the job half done.'

Laughter rang out again. Bruno laughed for form's sake.

His mind was elsewhere. Later, he would admit to me that, not having papers, he was dreading the possibility that the Sudanese authorities would send him back to France, which was why he had no desire to talk to the officer in charge of our security.

We stayed with the convalescents until midday, long enough for me to realise how amazing these people were. Had these survivors forgotten the misfortunes that had befallen them or had they discovered an antidote? As I observed them, I wondered from what ashes they had been reborn. They had an astonishing ability to downplay adversity. Their strength lay in their mindset, a unique, ancient mindset forged in the very magma of this good old earth of men. A mindset that had come into being with the first cry of life and would survive hard times and the downward spiral of the modern world with undimmed vigour. Bruno hadn't been completely wrong. Deep inside these people, there resided an enduring flame that brightened and revived them every time the darkness tried to overwhelm them. Evidently, they had instinctively assimilated what I would not be able to grasp without wading through endless and often pointless mathematical probabilities. These people were an education. They laughed at their disappointments as if at an unsuccessful farce. Here they were, happy to be together, in total sympathy with each other, and if they laughed at their own naivety, it was in order to underline the fragility of things so that they could handle it better. I envied them, envied the maturity they had gained from so much suffering and so many nightmarish ordeals, their philosophical distance which allowed them to rise above traumas and disasters,

of crazy theories that betrayed just how low he was feeling.

'It could be,' he said, 'that the Sudanese authorities intercepted the fax announcing our arrival here and held on to it. Our embassies haven't been informed. The presence of the soldiers doesn't bode well. It stinks of conspiracy.'

'That makes no sense.'

'We're in Africa, Monsieur Krausmann. How do we know the pirates who kidnapped us aren't in league with the government? Have our embassies been in touch with us? Like hell they have! Nobody's contacted us. Don't you find that strange? Just out of politeness, an official should have phoned to reassure us and ask if we were being well treated. But there seems to be a complete blackout.'

Bruno was getting carried away. I guess he was really disturbed by the possibility of being taken to the border and sent back to France. At about three the following afternoon, a small propeller plane landed without incident on a stretch of wasteland not far from the camp. On board were the first secretaries of our respective embassies, a German secret service man, a correspondent from a major television channel and his cameraman, two newspaper reporters and three Sudanese army officers. A technical problem, we were told, had forced the pilot to return to base and the delegation had had to charter a second plane to accomplish its mission, which allayed Bruno's mad suspicions. Pfer let us use his office, the narrowness of which obliged the cameraman to twist in all directions in order to film the event. After the handshakes and the introductions, the German first secretary, Gerd Bechter, informed me that arrangements had been made for my repatriation and that I could go home whenever it suited me. I asked him if there was any news of Hans Makkenroth. He told me, much to my dismay, that the search had so far yielded no results.

'How can that be?' Bruno cried. 'They were holding him to ransom.'

'We've never received any ransom demand,' Gerd Bechter said. 'We know the boat was hijacked between Djibouti and Somalia. But after that, we lost all trace of you, Herr Makkenroth and your Filipino companion.'

'Tao was thrown overboard by the pirates,' I said.

The journalists nervously scribbled that information in their notebooks.

'Who reported the attack on the boat?' Bruno asked suspiciously.

'Herr Makkenroth's Cyprus office. Herr Makkenroth had been calling them twice a day, at nine in the morning and ten at night, to report his position and the weather conditions. Then they lost radio contact. No faxes or emails either. They kept trying to get in touch with the boat, but without success. Forty-eight hours after contact was lost, Herr Makkenroth's family in Frankfurt alerted the embassy and we immediately launched a search. The boat was spotted in a creek on the northern coast of Somalia and recovered by French special units dispatched from Djibouti. No arrests have been made, and we're still in the dark, without any leads or witnesses.'

'I'm not going back to Germany without Hans Makkenroth,' I said.

'Dr Krausmann, you're expected in Khartoum today.'

'It's out of the question. My friend is somewhere in the region, and I refuse to abandon him to his fate.'

'The search is ongoing.'

'Then I'll wait for it to lead somewhere.'

'Your presence here will be of no help to us. Let's go back to Khartoum and then we can see where we are.'

'Please don't insist. I'm not moving from this camp until I know what happened to my friend.'

Bechter asked the others to leave us alone. Everyone left the office. The French first secretary took advantage of the situation to talk in private with Bruno.

Bechter's awkwardness annoyed me. He walked up and down the room, went and stood by the window to get a grip on himself, then came back towards me and implored me to follow him to Khartoum. Nothing he said would make me change my mind. In desperation, he took out his mobile phone and called the ambassador. When he had him on the line, he held the phone out to me, but I categorically refused to take it.

'You can't stay here, doctor,' he said, after apologising to the ambassador.

'Is there something I don't know?'

'We have no proof that Herr Makkenroth is still alive,' he said bitterly.

It was a blow, and my forehead and back suddenly broke out in a sweat.

'Could you be more explicit?'

He went to fetch one of the Sudanese officers, a colonel with greying temples, and asked him to explain the situation to me. The colonel told me that the information he had suggested that Hans Makkenroth was probably dead. One night, about four weeks earlier, an isolated shepherd had received a visit from a group of armed men in flight. They had a number of wounded men with them, including a bearded European whose description corresponded to that of Hans. He was in a critical state.

'There's nothing to prove it's him,' I said. 'Hostages with a beard are two a penny. I had one myself when I arrived in this camp. We weren't in a health spa, colonel.'

'When the armed men pointed at their prisoner, they mentioned he was German,' Bechter said. 'There are no other German nationals reported missing in this region.'

'Hans got a sabre blow in the back during the attack on the boat. He recovered from it before he was transferred.'

'This wasn't a sabre blow, doctor,' said the colonel. 'The hostage had been hit in the head and chest and had lost a lot of blood. The shepherd was sure about that. They were gunshot wounds.'

I felt as if the ceiling were collapsing on my head. Shaking all over, I made an effort to steady my breathing. I was in a state of weightlessness, unable to preserve even a semblance of self-assurance. The colonel tried to put his hand on my shoulder, but I recoiled. I hate to be touched when things get too much for me.

'No,' I stammered after a long silence, 'there must be some mistake. Hans was sold to a criminal group for money. The reason they haven't asked for a ransom yet is because my friend is being auctioned. His last buyer will soon put in an appearance. This shepherd's talking nonsense. Or maybe he's an accomplice of the kidnappers and is lying to divert suspicion from himself and allow his associates to gain time. They're hoping you'll call off the search.'

'Doctor—'

'I won't allow you to manipulate me, colonel. I refuse

to listen to you and I refuse to go with you to Khartoum. I'm not moving from here until I get an answer to my question: where is Hans Makkenroth?'

'I understand how you feel,' Bechter said, 'but I can't approve your decision. I assure you you'd be more useful to us elsewhere.'

'We have to go back today,' the colonel said to me. 'We chartered the plane for the day, and it'll be dark soon.'

'I'm sorry, colonel. Your priorities are not the same as mine.'

As far as I was concerned, it was inconceivable that I should go back to Germany without Hans. I wanted to get out of Africa without leaving anything behind and without taking anything away with me. I wanted to dismiss anything that might mar my return to a normal life. It would be hard, very hard, but I intended to succeed because it was the only way for a survivor to learn to live again. I would be able to turn my back on the hateful memories that were dogging my heels and shake off the invective-laden voices and terrible gunshots that still echoed in my head. I would manage to convince myself that my stay in Africa had been nothing but a bad dream, and every morning that the world still had in store for me I would wake up to the sounds that were dear to me.

The delegation failed to persuade me to leave the camp. Bruno was on my side. He refused to abandon me, convinced that Hans was still alive and was being moved from one buyer to another somewhere in the desert. As the sun was going down, the two first secretaries resigned themselves and granted us a few days to think it over, on condition that we cooperate with an officer who would remain in the camp and keep in close contact with the African Union forces deployed in the sector.

When the plane took off, I was overcome with a mixture of dread and loneliness. What if the shepherd was telling the truth? What if Hans had succumbed to his wounds? That possibility was the final blow. My knees gave way and pain gripped my body and my mind.

In the canteen, I stared at my plate without touching it. I couldn't even have swallowed my own saliva. The rattle of knives and forks sounded to me like hailstones, crushing my thoughts into thousands of shards. Bruno noticed how badly affected I was. He took my hand, but the gesture felt like a bite. I asked him to excuse me and went outside to get some air.

I walked in the darkness without knowing where I was going. Images of Hans went round and round in my head. I saw him again at the controls of his boat, limping through a *thalweg* with his shirt clinging to his wound, not finding words to say at Jessica's funeral, fanning himself with his hat in the sun at Sharm el-Sheikh. I had the impression that a whole chunk of my universe was missing, that the absence of Hans had created an impossible gulf between me and the world. However hard I tried to dismiss the idea he might be dead, it kept coming back, as fierce as a hornet.

Elena found me on the other side of the fence, huddled beneath a solitary tree, wild with anxiety. She leant down and talked to me, but couldn't reach me. Unable to get any response or reaction from me, she took me in her arms and I abandoned myself to her like a child.

3

I needed someone.

And Elena was there.

When death tries to suck the lifeblood from you, life has to react, or it will lose all credibility. That might be what happened to me. Hans's probable death had reactivated my survival instinct. By loving Elena, I proved to myself that I was alive. I was surprised to wake up in her bed. Surprised but reassured. My intimacy with Elena was more than a refuge for me, it enabled me to make peace with myself. Elena was embarrassed. Did she blame herself for taking advantage of the situation? She would have been wrong to think that. I needed support, and she was my rock. How could I have rejected her lips when they gave me back my soul? Hadn't she told me she felt lonely? In making love, we had formed a common front against all the things that had swept away our moorings.

She had made coffee, put the tray down on the bedside table and gone into the bathroom to get dressed. When she returned, her eyes wandered several times around the room before coming to rest on me. 'Now that you've decided to stay in the camp, what do you plan to do with your days?' she asked. I told her that if she had no objections, I'd like to resume my work. She assured me that the patients would be happy to be tended by me. I promised her I would join her in the treatment room as soon as I had taken a shower.

Elena had already examined half the patients by the time I joined her in the infirmary. I found her at the bedside of the old woman, who had miraculously survived and was still in intensive care. Her son, the young man with the cart, was in the next bed. He, too, was on a drip. He wouldn't take his eyes off his mother ... Elena introduced me to her patients. There were about thirty of them, from different backgrounds: old men, women and children, most of them survivors of raids. Orfane brought me a white coat and a stethoscope and gave me a row of beds to deal with. Within ten minutes, I had recovered all my old medical reflexes. A young boy grabbed me by the wrist. His case was clearly desperate. With his hairless skull, almost non-existent eyebrows and yellowish complexion, he was nothing more than a big head above a skeleton. The skin of his face crumpled like a sheet of paper when he smiled at me.

'Is it true that in Germany there are glass houses so high they reach the clouds?'

'Yes, it's true,' I said, taking his hand in mine and sitting down on the edge of his bed.

'And do people live in them?'

'Yes.'

'And how do they get to the top?'

'They take the lift.'

'What's a lift?'

'A kind of cage. You go inside, press a button with a number next to it, and the cage goes up by itself.'

'That's magic … When I'm better, I'll go to your country and see the glass houses.'

Still smiling, he lay down again and closed his eyes.

Orfane came and told me that the director was waiting for me in his office. I finished my rounds before going.

Bruno had got there before me. He was sprawling on the sofa, his legs crossed and his arms stretched out along the back. The Sudanese colonel saw us without either the captain or Pfer. We told him our stories from the beginning, the ambush outside Mogadishu in Bruno's case, the attack on the boat in mine, the terrible journey across scrub and desert, the disused fort where Captain Gerima had kept us prisoner, Chief Moussa, Joma the poet-pirate, the transfer of Hans, the final duel that had allowed us to escape, our meeting with Elena Juárez and her refugees. It was a detailed account, and the colonel didn't interrupt us once: I assumed he was recording our statements on the tape recorder that stood on Pfer's desk. When we had finished, he asked us to pay attention and went to a map of the region hanging on the wall. With an expandable pointer he pointed to three places, which he surrounded with little blue triangles: the place where Jibreel, the camp's guide and driver, had found Bruno and me; the place where the shepherd said he had received a visit from pirates with the wounded Hans; the place where we had been kept prisoner by Captain Gerima (based on our description of the outpost and the surrounding landscape). He admitted that he couldn't understand why the kidnappers had chosen such a bleak, hostile area instead of staying in Somalia where the trade in hostages could be carried on without too many obstacles, although he pointed out that rebels preferred to manoeuvre across borders so that if the worst came to the worst they could fall back on the neighbouring country to avoid being pursued by government forces. Bruno reminded him that we weren't there to follow a course in military tactics, but to find Hans Makkenroth. The colonel took no notice of his words and continued his presentation. Having finished with the map, he turned to his files. He began by telling us that the authorities had nothing on the so-called Captain Gerima and that no officer who had deserted matched his description.

'Gerima had definitely been in the army,' Bruno insisted. 'He isn't Sudanese or Somali. He's Djiboutian and speaks fluent French. He was in the regular army before being sentenced by a court martial for stealing rations and reselling them.'

The officer was exasperated by Bruno's intervention. He clearly wasn't accustomed to being interrupted and saw the Frenchman's attitude as insubordination and an insult to his authority. He waited for Bruno to be quiet before resuming.

'As for Chief Moussa, he's known to the authorities both here and in Somalia. He's being actively pursued in both countries. Now, with your permission, let's see if a few faces might point us in the right direction.' He turned his computer towards us. Photographs of men and teenage boys appeared on the screen. 'I should make it clear that they aren't all criminals. The one thing they have in common is that they've received gunshot wounds. Hospitals, clinics, dispensaries, all kinds of medical centres without exception are required to inform the police immediately of any admissions of that nature.

These people may be shepherds attacked by cattle thieves, lorry drivers intercepted by highwaymen, people hit by stray bullets, people wounded in the course of tribal feuds, but also dealers and bandits arrested during police raids, smugglers, rebels, terrorists and so on. I'd be grateful if you could take a good look at them and tell me if you see any familiar faces.'

We recognised Ewana and a second pirate, the driver of the sidecar motorcycle. Consulting his files, the colonel told us that the two suspects had been admitted to the same rural dispensary on the same night; that the first, whose real name was Babaker Ohid – thirty-one, married, four children, a cattle dealer by profession – had been shot twice, once in the thigh and once in the buttock; and that the second, Hamad Tool – twenty-six, married, two children, a former athletics champion who'd become a scrap merchant – had been shot in the hip. He asked us if we were absolutely certain we recognised them. We hadn't the slightest doubt, we told him. He switched off his computer, put away his files, asked us another dozen questions, noting down our responses in a register, and dismissed us.

Bruno went off to find his 'brothers', and I my patients.

In the evening, Elena offered to show me a quiet spot a few hundred metres to the east of the camp. We went there on foot. The sun hadn't yet set, and our shadows were long on the ground. It wasn't very hot. There was a cool breeze in the air. Elena untied her hair, and shook it so that it spread over her shoulders. She took my hand in hers and we walked side by side like lovers. She told me about an old school friend of hers, but I wasn't listening. Her voice was enough for me. It cradled my silence. Soon, the camp was merely a shimmering patch behind us. Coming to an area where the ground fell away abruptly, we stopped at the edge of the precipice. Below, at the bottom of a vast basin, shaggy shrubs grew alongside wild grasses and plants besieged by midges. The vegetation was green and luxuriant, hard to imagine in this part of the desert. A spring-like aroma filled the air, which was alive with the chirping of insects. Elena photographed me from several angles, then sat down cross-legged and invited me to do the same.

'The other day,' she said, 'I saw a group of antelopes grazing down there, with their young. It was magical.'

'It's a real haven of peace,' I admitted.

'I often come here to unwind. I put a hat on in order not to get sunburnt, have a flask full of cold water close at hand, and stay here for hours waiting for the antelopes to return. I've also seen a jackal. It had gone to ground down there. When it saw me looking at it, it stared at me suspiciously. I got the impression it could see right through me.'

'It might have attacked you.'

'I don't think so. Jackals are secretive, cowardly animals, who never take risks. If they aren't sure they'll succeed, they give up. Wild dogs, on the other hand, don't need to feel threatened to attack. An old night watchman discovered that to his detriment. He got lost in the dark and we found him torn to pieces not far from the camp.'

'Doesn't anything nice ever happen here?'

She laughed. 'Don't you think this is a beautiful place, Kurt?'

I wanted to tell her that *she* was very beautiful, but didn't dare. She took my chin between her pretty fingers, and looked deep into my eyes. My heart pounded in my chest. Elena noticed. She moved her face closer to mine and searched for my lips, but her kiss was cut short by the laughter of two little children who had just jumped up out of the undergrowth below us. They climbed the embankment as fast as they could, stopped to make fun of us, miming languorous hugs and kisses, and ran off towards the camp, laughing triumphantly.

'Where did they spring from?' I said.

Elena now also laughed fondly at the antics of the two kids. 'In Africa,' she said, 'even if God turns his head modestly away when two people are ready to make love, you can be sure there's always a little boy watching somewhere.'

A week had passed since the visit from the delegation. I had moved in with Elena. By day, I took care of my patients. In the evening, Elena and I wandered around the outskirts of the camp and only came back when night had fallen. Every now and again, Bruno would join us with one or two of his mythical 'brothers'. As far as the Frenchman was concerned, every African was a novel. But it was he, Bruno, who wrote it. Thus it was that he introduced us to Bongo, a teenage boy who had walked three thousand kilometres, without a guide and without a penny in his pocket, to see the sea. He had left his village in Nigeria in order to get to Europe. A people smuggler had promised to take him there in return for his mother's jewellery, but had abandoned him in the Ténéré. The boy had wandered for months and months in the desert, somehow getting by, until he had come upon the camp by chance. The day after we were introduced to him, he disappeared. He had stolen some provisions from the kitchen, a bag and some walking shoes, and had set off in search of the sea. Bruno had no doubt in his mind: sooner or later the young man would realise his dream. It was written all over his face that nothing would stop him.

One evening, Bruno came running into the canteen in a state of great excitement. He demanded silence, stretched his arms out wide in a melodramatic gesture, and with a lump in his throat declaimed:

> *I am a man of flesh like you*
> *And I have spilt blood*
> *As if pouring wine*
> *Into the cup of infamy*
> *I have dreams like yours*
> *Forbidden dreams*
> *That I keep within me*
> *For fear they will die in the air*
> *I am the sum of your crimes*
> *The funeral urn of your prayers*
> *The soul expelled from your body*
> *The twin brother you reject*
> *I am merely an old mirror*
> *A mirror cut to your disproportions*
> *In which you hope one day to see*
> *Yourself big even though you are small*

He gave a reverential bow, then rose to his full height to savour the applause, of which there was a little. '*Black Moon*, by Joma Baba-Sy,' he said, advancing through the middle of the room, where a dozen of us were having dinner.

He again asked for our attention and declared in a mocking tone, 'My dear friends, I am leaving you. I am leaving you to your struggles, your suffering, your miseries. I'm going. I leave you courage, sacrifice, the nobility of grand causes ... Yes, I yield them to you graciously. And if you wish, I bequeath you my virtues for they no longer make my soul tremble. As far as I'm concerned, the odyssey ends tonight. Tomorrow, I'll be back with my fat partner and we'll reinvent the world under a mosquito net ...'

A few people laughed indulgently. Bruno came over to the table I was sharing with Elena, Lotta and Orfane, grabbed a free chair and sat down astride it, between the gynaecologist and the virologist. His bulging, joyful eyes rolled like white-hot marbles.

'I've just come from Monsieur Pfer's office. Guess who I had on the phone? None other than the French ambassador! He told me officially that my case had been examined with the greatest care and that I no longer had anything to worry about. I'm going to be given a new passport and an entry visa to Djibouti. Tomorrow, I'm flying to Khartoum on the freighter aircraft. The pilot has received instructions.'

'Congratulations,' Lotta said.

'I've already told my partner the good news. She was so happy we cried like kids. My beard is still wet with my tears.' He turned to me. 'I'm going to miss you, Monsieur Krausmann.'

My throat was too tight to utter a sound.

He nodded his head and addressed the others. 'And you too.'

'You're a likeable person, Bruno,' Lotta said. 'A bit scatterbrained, but very likeable.'

'It's the African sun that's melted my brain. Which is all to the good. The less you think, the more chance you have of making old bones … Oh my God, how happy I am! I'm not going to sleep a wink tonight, and tomorrow will take for ever to arrive. I can already see myself at home, in my scruffy but comfortable little room … If you ever happen to be passing through Djibouti, come and see me. No need to tell me you're coming. There's no protocol in our house. Just go to the souk, ask after Bruno the African – that's what they call me – and any kid will bring you to me. You won't even have to ring the doorbell, because we don't have one. You open the door and you're immediately at home … Isn't that so, Kurt?'

I merely nodded.

'You will come?'

'I don't think so, Bruno, I don't think so.'

'You know what a marabout once told me? The man who sees Africa only once in his life will die blind in one eye.'

After dinner, Bruno took me to one side behind the canteen. 'If you'd like me to stay a few more days,' he said, 'it's no problem.'

'What for?'

'I don't know. The soldiers might come back and ask for more information.'

'They've already recorded our statements. No, you go. There's nothing more for you here. Go back to your nearest and dearest. They've already missed you long enough.'

'Monsieur Pfer told me the camp has received several

donations and that another plane is due next week. I could come to an arrangement with the pilot.'

'That wouldn't be a good idea, Bruno.'

'Are you sure?'

'Absolutely.'

He gave me a big hug and rushed off into the darkness.

The freighter aircraft landed at ten in the morning in a flurry of dust and noise. A monster of zinc and combustion, it trundled to the end of the waste ground, made a U-turn and bounced its way back to the camp. Some twenty men were waiting to unload the hundreds of boxes and crates fastened in its hold.

As far as I was concerned, the plane had come to rob me of my friend.

Bruno had put on a satin robe and had got Lotta to carefully trim his beard. His crew-cut hair shone and he had kohl on his eyelids. He gave me a broad smile and opened his arms to me.

'How do I look?'

'Apart from your bald patch, very handsome.'

He smoothed his hair. 'Baudelaire said that when imperfection looks good, it becomes a charming accessory.'

Bruno embraced Pfer, then Lotta, whose behind he pinched in passing. He had to stand on tiptoe to hug Orfane, then, holding back a sob, he clasped Elena to him. When he got to me, he cracked and big tears rolled down his cheeks. We looked at each other for a moment, as if mesmerised, then threw ourselves in each other's arms. We stood like that for a while in silence.

'Don't forget what I said, Kurt. The man who sees

Africa only once in his life will die blind in one eye.'

'I won't forget.'

He nodded, picked up a big bag filled with gifts and walked towards the plane. The pilot pointed to the hold and invited him to get on board. Bruno turned one last time and waved farewell. Once the unloading was finished, the door of the hold closed and the winged monster, in a din of propellers, moved onto the runway. We followed it from a distance, waving our arms. Bruno appeared at a window and blew us kisses until the dust enveloped the plane as it set off to conquer the sky.

I was pleased for Bruno, but sad to see him go. Our friendship had been sealed in pain and would never end. Neither distance nor time could lessen it. I knew that wherever I went, whatever my life held in store, whatever my future joys and sorrows, the indelible trace of those weeks full of sadness and fear shared with my inimitable French companion would always remain in a corner of my heart, a corner as sacred as a forbidden city. I would remember Bruno as a remarkable man, a good, sensitive man even when he was play-acting, always helpful and generous, closer to the poor than many a saint or prophet, and happy to be alive despite so many setbacks and so much ingratitude. I didn't know what he would represent for me in the future, but he had initiated me into the simplest of gestures, giving them a meaning, a strength, and a richness that was worth all the possessions in the world, and into a simple beauty, such as the beauty of fraternal signs that strangers send each other when they emerge from a tragedy or when they spontaneously rally round to deal with human disaster. Would I miss him? Yes, in several ways. For me, he would be Joma's 'twin', shamelessly consigned to oblivion. What would I have left of Bruno? What would I have left of Hans? All the things I couldn't hold on to: a tone of voice, a fleeting smile, situations distorted by the prism of years, absences that were like hangovers. Now that they were no longer around, I realised how insubstantial any truth was in this capricious world ... And what of later? ... Later, we come full circle, start again from the beginning and once more learn to live with what we no longer possess. Since nature abhors a vacuum, we create new reference points for ourselves. Out of pure selfishness ... Elena knew our relationship had no future, and so did I. That didn't stop us from taking advantage of the moment ... I had made friends among the refugees: Malik, the boy who had asked for my torch, and who came to see me regularly and made sure he never left empty-handed; Bidan, an amazing contortionist who could get his entire body into a box barely large enough for a puppy; old Hadji, who could read the future in the sand and spent all day long sucking on his pipe; Forha, the one-armed man who could put his clothes on faster than a sailor getting ready for combat; and the unstoppable Uncle Mambo, who was a bit of a mythomaniac and was absolutely convinced that Neil Armstrong had never set foot on the moon ... But the temporary is like a crazy moneylender who demands his due when he feels like it. And what I feared finally caught up with me. The previous day, three workers had fallen from scaffolding and been seriously injured. I spent the night assisting the surgeon who operated on them. In the morning, hearing the staccato buzzing of a helicopter, I assumed the men were being evacuated to a better-equipped hospital and buried my head under the

286

pillow. I was wrong. The helicopter was for me ... It was the Sudanese colonel in person who came and asked me to get dressed and follow him. From his crestfallen look, I understood. I had to cling to the handle of the door to stay upright. 'No, don't tell me that ...' I stammered. He looked at me without saying anything. There are silences that speak louder than words. I collapsed on my bed and struggled with all my might to keep a modicum of dignity. 'They're waiting for us, sir,' the colonel said. I got dressed and followed him ...

It was a dazzlingly bright morning. The night's slight drizzle had cleared the air and the sun was playing at being an artist. But who could stand its talent? Its light was garish, the clarity of the horizon overblown. It was a day that was playing to the gallery, trying to distinguish itself from all the others, making sure people took notice. It would be engraved for ever in my subconscious.

I walked to the helicopter, deaf to Elena's cries. I was in a parallel world. The inside of the aircraft stank of fuel. The engines started wheezing more and more loudly, then, like a huge dragonfly, the helicopter spun into the air. The colonel tapped me on the knee. I felt like screaming at him to keep his hand as far away from me as possible. I did nothing. My whole being was bowed like a weeping willow. The noise of the helicopter drilled into my eardrums. On the bench facing me, five armed soldiers looked out at the desert through the windows. They were the colonel's escort. Handpicked, probably expert marksmen. Young as they were, some beardless, they were battle-hardened. Their calm was like the lull before a storm.

'What happened?' I asked the colonel.

'An engagement between a detachment of the regular army and a group of rebels. Our soldiers didn't know there was a hostage.'

'A blunder, in other words?'

'Certainly not,' he exclaimed, outraged. 'Our detachment wasn't on active operations, it was carrying out a supply mission. It came across the rebels by chance, and they immediately opened fire to cover their retreat. Our response was perfectly appropriate. Our soldiers, I repeat, didn't know that there was a hostage among the criminals. And we are the first to deplore this … this accident.'

'Accident?'

'Absolutely, sir.'

'And you're sure it's Hans Makkenroth?'

'According to the two suspects you identified from the photographs, it was definitely him. They both confessed. And they took us to the place where they buried him.'

'When?'

'Yesterday afternoon.'

'Does the embassy know?'

'They were informed immediately after the discovery of the body. A plane went to pick up the ambassador very early this morning.' He looked at his watch. 'He'll get there the same time as we do.'

'Is it far from here?'

'About two hours' flight.'

'I suppose you're counting on me to identify the body?'

'I can't think of anybody else who'd be entitled to do so.'

I sat back and said nothing.

Below, pitiful hills, weary of sinking into the sand, formed lines to hold back the advance of the desert; scar-like anthracite patches told of the ages before the flood and their forests filled with game, which a cataclysm had decimated in an instant. Where was man in all this? What did he represent in the cosmic breath? Was he aware of what made him naked and isolated? Was the desert around him or inside him? ... I pulled myself together. I had to empty my head. I was in too fragile a state to venture into such unknown territory.

After two hours of noise and the stench of kerosene, the helicopter dipped to the side, straightened up again and started losing altitude. The colonel went into the cockpit to give instructions to the two pilots. Through the window, I saw a column of armoured vehicles parked along a track, soldiers and, further on, a little propeller plane beside which a delegation of civilians stood watching us land.

The German ambassador greeted me as I got out of the helicopter. He introduced the people with him, who included Gerd Bechter. They were all grief-stricken. There were no reporters or cameramen. A high-ranking Sudanese officer whispered something to me that I didn't catch. His obsequiousness maddened me. I was relieved to see him fall back into the ranks. I asked to be taken to see my friend. The ambassador and his staff set off after a young officer, and I trailed behind. I felt as if my shoes were sticking to the ground. A platoon of soldiers was mounting guard around a heap of stones, their rifles trained on two prisoners: Ewana, the former malaria patient, and the driver of the sidecar motorcycle. Handcuffed and in chains, they were in an indescribable state; it was obvious from the marks on their faces, limbs and clothes that they had been tortured. As I passed them, I looked them up and down. Ewana bowed his head, while his accomplice openly defied me.

We came to six makeshift graves. Some had been desecrated by jackals or hyenas, the soldiers had done the rest. The decomposing corpses were mostly unrecognisable ... Chief Moussa had his mouth open, exposing his gold tooth, a hole in the middle of his forehead ... Hans, my friend Hans, was lying in the same pit as his kidnapper. His head had been smashed in, and there were black stains on his chest. His white beard quivered in the breeze, his eyes closed over his final thoughts. I wondered what he had been thinking about just before he died, what last cry he had taken away with him, if he had died instantly or if his agony had been long and cruel ... My God! What a waste! What could I say in the face of such absurdity? All the words in the world seemed pointless and inappropriate. I could look at the sky, or my trembling hands, or the inscrutable faces of the soldiers and the officials, I could cry until my voice failed me, or say nothing and be one with the silence, it made no difference. And besides, what power did I have left, except for the strength to stare at my friend's body and the courage to admit that I had arrived too late?

'He came here to equip a hospital for the poor,' I said to the two pirates.

Ewana bowed his head a little more and stared at the ground. I lifted his chin to make him look me in the eyes and went on, 'He came to help the poor and the defenceless. Do you understand what that means? The man lying there gave his fortune and his time so that he could deserve to be called a human being.'

'Nobody asked him to do it,' the motorcycle driver muttered.

'I beg your pardon?' I said in disgust.

'You heard me.'

An officer slapped him, and the pirate reeled under the blow, but didn't flinch.

'Your friend is dead,' he grunted. 'Ewana and I will be joining him soon. They're going to shoot us. That's the price to be paid and we're not haggling. You haven't done too badly out of this so stop pissing us all off.'

Anger and indignation exploded in me like a geyser and I threw myself at him. I tried to blind him in the eye, to tear his tongue out, to crush him with my bare hands. I looked and found only emptiness: soldiers had grabbed me by the waist, while others jumped on the pirate and dragged him away from me and towards an armoured vehicle. He put up no resistance, but continued to taunt me: 'If you'd stayed at home in your nice silk sheets, nobody would have come looking for you!' he cried. 'Where did you think you were, eh? On a five-star safari? People who walk in shit shouldn't complain if they smell bad. Your friend knew the risks, and so did we. He's dead, and we're going to be executed. Why are you the one who's crying?' His coldness burnt me like the flames of hell. I struggled to reach him and make him aware of his own wickedness, of how everything he said and did was an insult to the day and the wind and the noise and the silence, to everything that made up life. My arms were like smoke, my rage was consuming me from within. I was my own cremation. I knew there was nothing more to be done, that the wonderful friend unravelling down in his hole saw nothing of my grief – maybe he wouldn't even agree with the way I was behaving, but what could I do? … I wanted to be somewhere else, a long way away, I wanted to shut myself up in my house in Frankfurt and resume mourning my wife. I wished I had never got on that damned boat or met anyone on my route. I wished for many pointless, ugly things, I wished to be invisible too, I wished there were oceans between me and the graves fouling the ground beneath my feet, but my demands were merely the expression of my refusal to confront the grim reality: men are the worst and the best of what nature has created; some die for an ideal, others for nothing; some perish from their own generosity, others from their own ingratitude; they tear each other apart for the same reasons, each in his own camp, and the irony of fate presides over that terrible drama, finally reconciling, in the same foul-smelling pit, the enlightened and the unenlightened, the virtuous and the depraved, the martyr and the executioner, all delivered to everlasting death like Siamese twins in their mother's womb.

taken ill. True, I was nothing but a ghost lost in the mist of its own emotions, but the trials I had been through were keeping me alert. Irritated by his interference, I had asked him if maybe he wanted to share my bed. He had apologised for bothering me and gone to fetch me a drink. We had drunk until morning and slept on the same sofa ...

A TV screen indicated the route the plane was taking: we had left Sudan, then flown across Egypt and along the Mediterranean. A hostess brought me a tray of food; I declined her offer and sank into my seat. Behind me, two journalists were dozing. A young woman who had been introduced to me but whose name I couldn't recall was leaning towards the window and staring out at the sea. Beside her, a cameraman was sleeping the sleep of the just. There were just eight passengers in the little plane, which had come specially from Berlin to repatriate us. An archipelago of eight islands separated by rivers of silence.

I imagined all the people waiting for us in Frankfurt. The Makkenroth family in full mourning. Friends of the dead man. His neighbours. His staff. The officials stiff with solemnity. The television channels. All the clichés wrapped in greyness. Closed faces. Empty eyes ... I couldn't see any place for me there. I had prepared nothing. I would say nothing. I would walk in the dead man's shadow and follow the funeral procession without asking any questions. I was in a state of shock. What I felt didn't matter. I would wait patiently for things to settle. Then I would take the plunge. Hans would be upset with me if I didn't survive him. Life is a succession of ambiguities and acts of bravado. You learn more every day, and every day you wipe the slate clean and start again. In reality, there is no irrefutable truth, there are only beliefs. When one turns out to be unfounded, you make up another and cling to it come hell or high water. Life is a shipwreck, and whether or not you survive depends not on providence but on stubbornness. There are those who give up and die, and others who rethink everything ... I recalled the image of the marabout dying on his camp bed, his face as pale as parchment. His tremulous voice reached me in a sigh from beyond the grave. What was it he had said? It came back to me: 'For a heart to continue to beat its defiance, it must look to failure for the sap of its survival.' Why had I fled that old man? Maybe because he could read me like an open book. Maybe because he had stripped me bare with his eyes. I had always hated exposing my nakedness to strangers. At Maspalomas, there had been a stretch of beach reserved for nudists. I could never bring myself to venture there. In a few hours, when I was thrown to the wolves on a runway swarming with important people and journalists, I would feel as naked and wretched as a worm, and I would hate the whole world ... Then interest would move to the coffin and the Makkenroth family, and there, too, I would catch myself resenting all those people turning their backs on me, already ignoring me and delivering me, with hands and feet tied, to the most pernicious of solitudes ... I wanted to have done with it all, to confront my tomorrows, which I guessed would be totally different from my yesterdays and wouldn't conform to whatever idea I might have about them, because another chapter, another episode, another story would make me a different man, someone I would find hard to grasp and to tame. 'What have we really learnt from what we think we know?' Hans used to say. 'Habits? Reflexes? Work during the week and a let-up on our days off? What do which a glorious afternoon was rolling out the red carpet for us. How to define the feeling that overcame me the moment the wheels of the jet touched my native soil? Impossible to describe it. Impossible to contain it. A remarkable alchemy took possession of my being, of every drop of my blood. I was millions of emotions … The jet rolled along a secondary runway, circumvented several small blocks, and at last stopped outside a structure that looked like some kind of grand reception area. Journalists were waiting impatiently behind a barrier. Flashbulbs started popping, and reached a peak as I got off the plane. The Chancellor and a few members of her government greeted me at the foot of the stairs. Not having eaten since Khartoum, I didn't feel well. Somebody whispered something to me, but I didn't catch it. Since everyone was smiling, I did the same. Happiness is contagious. Chests restricted my breathing, arms encircled my body, hands engulfed mine. The Chancellor was so moved she had tears in her eyes. She said something to me, but the yelling of the journalists drowned it out. I thanked her. I heard myself thanking everyone for everything. Behind the official staff, the Makkenroth family were having to grin and bear it; clearly, this media attention, these ministers, the whole performance was intruding on their mourning. I would learn later that they had wanted things to be done as privately as possible, but protocol had other requirements. I went up to Bertram, Hans's oldest son. I had known him for years. We threw our arms around each other. The hug was a brief one. His wife, hidden behind a black veil, lightly touched my fingertips. Mathias, the younger son, patted me on the back. I had met him two or three times, but couldn't remember where. He was a taciturn, the spectacle. She was wearing a sober tailored suit, and gave me a reluctant smile. Gerd Bechter offered me a lift in the back of his car. I told him I was going straight home. He tried to dissuade me, but I wouldn't listen to him and walked towards Claudia. At that moment, when my world was shrinking around me, she was my whole family.

A cluster of journalists were cooling their heels outside my house. I told Claudia not to stop. She did as she was told and took the first turning. She drove very badly. The emotion, perhaps. Earlier, when she had taken me in her arms, she had burst into tears. She was lost for words. She laughed and cried, grimaced and smiled, and shook from head to toe. The touch of her body against mine reassured me. Here I was, really here, in the flesh. I was in my country, in my city, in my element. The Frankfurt sun reconciled me to my feelings. I was free, I had my life back, and my suit had stopped chafing me. I lowered the window and couldn't stop breathing in the air, drawing strength and confidence from it. I looked at the buildings, the cars passing us, the lawns, the advertising hoardings, the street lamps, the surface of the road, and for the first time the hiss of the wheels on the asphalt silenced the hate-laden voices and the gunshots that had been using my head for sparring practice.

Claudia suggested we go to her place. I agreed. The journalists would have to cut me some slack in the end, and then I would go home and learn to live again.

Claudia lived on the third floor of a small building in Eckenheim. I had set up my first practice in that area, two years before I got married, and had really liked the place and the people, but Jessica had wanted me to move to Sachsenhausen, near where she worked, so that we could have lunch together. We had been very close at the beginning of our relationship. It was as if we were one and the same person. We would phone each other all the time, about insignificant things – we were just happy to know that we were only a call away from each other. The phone line constituted our umbilical cord.

Claudia preceded me into the entrance hall. There was no lift. We took the stairs as quickly as possible because I had no desire to be recognised by a neighbour. My photograph, along with Hans's, had been in the newspapers and on television for months.

'I sent someone to clean your house,' Claudia told me as she unlocked her door.

'Thank you.'

In the hallway of her apartment, she took my bag and helped me off with my jacket. 'You can stay here as long as you like,' she said. 'My mother will put me up for a few days.'

'That's very kind of you, but I really don't want to impose. I should go back to the house. It'll be night soon, and the journalists must have homes to go to.'

'Makes no difference. They'll be outside your door again first thing in the morning.'

'In that case, I'll go to my house in the country.'

'I don't think that's a good idea. You've been away too long. You need people around you.'

I asked her to show me the bathroom.

By the time I got back to the living room after my shower, Claudia had changed, replacing her tailored suit with flannel trousers and a sweater. She had also put on make-up and let her hair down.

'Let me buy you dinner,' she said. 'I know a nice quiet restaurant not far from here.'

'I don't really want to go out.'

'I don't have anything in the fridge.' She looked at her watch, thought for a moment, and decided to go out and bring us back something to eat.

It was the first time I had been in Claudia's apartment. The furniture was old, but well maintained. Everything was in exactly the right place, with no unnecessary extras. The living room was small and somewhat austere. There were no pictures on the walls, just a row of photographs on a chest of drawers, a faded rug on the floor and an old leather sofa in the middle. The window, framed by flimsy curtains, looked out on a sad little square with a giant tree in abundant leaf. Cars were parked on either side, but there was nobody about. No children played, not a sound betrayed a living soul. I sat down on the sofa and switched on the television. It seemed to have been years since I had last handled a remote control. It was the fact that Jessica had so often come home late that had made me a TV addict. Her absence would prevent me from concentrating on a book or on DIY, so I preferred to wait for my wife to return, pleasantly slouched in my armchair, a can of beer in my hand, and, sip after sip, I would count off the minutes like a priest his beads.

The TV news came on. The camera cut away from the newsreader and propelled me onto the tarmac, where I saw myself getting off the plane. I noticed how big my suit looked on me, and that I had stumbled on the last step of the stairs. Hans's coffin was taken from the hold and carried to the catafalque around which the Makkenroth family were waiting to recover the body. A young woman was crying on a relative's shoulder. Hans's two sons held themselves in a dignified manner, their black-clad wives by their sides. One can only gather one's thoughts in silence ...

I dozed off, or perhaps I fainted. It was probably just as well.

Five days after I got back, the funeral service took place in the Katharinenkirche, a Protestant church on the Hauptwache. The place was full to bursting. In the front rows, beside the Makkenroths, were the Chancellor and members of her government. People had come from the four corners of the world to pay their last respects to Hans. As well as the officials and national celebrities, there were people in turbans, Amazonian tribal chiefs, emirs in their ceremonial robes, ambassadors and nabobs. Hans had been not only a major industrialist, but above all a great man and a revered humanist. Outside, the street was packed with mourners. Thousands of anonymous people had been determined to celebrate the memory of this generous man who had devoted his time and fortune to the wretched of the earth. The ceremony was a very solemn one. After a speech by the Chancellor, who emphasised the dead man's courage and selflessness, Bertram read a poem by Goethe, of whom his father had been an assiduous reader, and reminded us of his father's principles and beliefs. By the time he rejoined his family, his face was drained of blood. Applause broke out when the coffin left the church.

The cortege set off for the crematorium. I had not been invited to this final farewell, which was strictly reserved for family members. My friend's ashes would be entrusted to the sea ... The sea he had loved so much, the sea that was his deliverance and his inner world.

I thanked Claudia for her hospitality and asked her to drive me home. The reporters had realised that I didn't want to speak to them and had gone back to their offices. Claudia offered to let me stay, just long enough for me to recover my strength. By that, I understood 'my spirits', and I deduced that I probably didn't look very good. I asked her if I had changed; she began by stammering some excuses before regaining her composure and asserting that I needed to have people around me, to get some distance from the events. Hadn't she asked for time off in order to take care of me? It was true that she had been looking after my every need, but her attention was starting to stifle me and I had to leave. I had been afraid to go out, afraid of being recognised in the street. All my life I had been discreet. Becoming an object of other people's curiosity overnight terrified me. But shutting myself up in Claudia's apartment was worse. I had been confined there for a week and it had worn me out. The nightmares that had undermined my sleep in Gerima's jail were again starting to keep me awake.

I had let my beard grow in the hope I wouldn't be recognised and I thought that if on top of that I wore sunglasses I'd be able to avoid curious glances.

I insisted on going home.

It was three in the afternoon when we parked outside

my house. Fortunately, apart from a plumber putting his equipment back in his van, the street was deserted. I didn't dare get out of the car. I had been impatient to get back to my own world, but now that I was outside my house, I became confused. An icy hand clutched my heart, and I felt intense pain when I tried to swallow. Claudia sensed that I was panicking and, wanting to show her empathy, did absolutely the wrong thing: she grabbed me by the wrist. I recoiled violently, opened the door and set foot outside. I didn't dare go any further. I stood there on the pavement, staring at that beautiful white house I had built with my own hands as a monument to everlasting love and life. Claudia realised I wouldn't move without an escort. She joined me, then walked ahead of me. I followed her. She took the keys from me. I felt as if there were a layer of ice on my back. I could hear my heart pounding in my head. I took a deep breath before venturing into the hallway. Claudia ran to pull back the curtains and open the windows. A blinding light flooded the living room. The cleaner had gone over the smallest nook and cranny with a fine-tooth comb. There were bright flowers in the vase. I saw my furniture, traces of my old habits, but the chasm left by Jessica was irrevocable.

Claudia kept me company for another quarter of an hour during which I remained indecisive, frozen, in a daze.

'Would you like me to make you some coffee?'

'No,' I said in a feverish whisper.

'I don't have much to do this afternoon.'

'Thank you, but I need to be alone.'

'Shall we have dinner together this evening?'

'If you like.'

'Good, I'll come and pick you up about seven.'

was so melancholy! The photograph of Jessica posing on a rock beset by milky waves still occupied the same frame but not the same memory. I opened the cabinet where my patients' files were stored, took one out at random, skimmed through it with a sense that I was desecrating other people's painful secrets. Emma informed me that Frau Biribauer had been unable to overcome her depression and had taken her own life a month earlier. And whose file should I have in my hands but hers; I immediately put it away with a gesture as lacking in courage as a desertion.

I took some sleeping pills. At four in the morning, I jumped out of bed and walked round and round in the darkness. I switched on the television then immediately switched it off again and went and stood by the window. Outside, the wind was tormenting the trees. A car passed, then there was silence, as blank as a truce. I went and fetched a beer from the fridge and sat down in front of my computer. My inbox was full to bursting with spam, unanswered messages of condolence going back to Jessica's death, and a hundred pending emails. A message from Elena with an attachment drew my attention. I moved the cursor over it, but didn't click – I was afraid to open a Pandora's box; I wasn't ready yet. I went back to my bedroom and waited for daybreak. After an improvised breakfast, I realised I needed to go out. I couldn't remain a prisoner within four walls, imagining hidden doors that led nowhere. I needed to breathe, to clear my head. Not that there was anything in my head. My thoughts were like pebbles at the bottom of a river ... or like sleeper agents, maybe. I was in a state of vague expectation. I was afraid of what I was holding back ... I decided to try a diversion, to go into town and melt into the crowd. I had to renew acquaintance with my city, see the old landmarks, the places that had meant something to me. I urgently needed to recover what my African adventure had taken from me, to plug the gaps that those I had lost had left around me ...

I was soon disillusioned.

Frankfurt was full of Jessica. My wife's ghost was everywhere in the city. It walked beside me on the wide streets around the Hauptwache, was reflected in the shop windows on the Zeil, played hide and seek in the Palmengarten, took the place of the walkers outside the Römer, and made an exhibition of itself in the Opernplatz. It appropriated the space, the shadows and the lights, tried to be the pulse of every neighbourhood, which only sweated, only felt, only trembled through it. Jessica was the flesh and memory of Frankfurt. In our favourite French restaurant, Erno's Bistro, she was already at the table, her hands clasped under her chin, her eyes as blue as a summer sky. She smiled at me, refusing to vanish when I blinked. Her perfume filled my nostrils. I beat a hasty retreat, wandered about some more, got back in my car, parked somewhere, walked up and down the pavements, entered a bar ... Jessica was at the counter, half shaded by the subdued lighting of the wall lamps, recalling the woman I had loved, the woman I had rushed to meet after work so that we could go to the cinema together. I didn't have time to order a drink before I was again on the avenue, hurrying to get away from those queues outside the cinemas, where every person waiting had something of Jessica about them ...

I couldn't stand it any more.

I went back home.

To shake off the voices pursuing me, I made my bed, tidied my wardrobe, polished my shoes, wiped the blinds, waxed the mahogany of my bedside table, then, without leaving my room, swaggering in front of the mirror, I put on my suits one after the other, checked my ties, the creases in my trousers, the stiffness of my shirt collars before going through my pyjamas with so little enthusiasm that it almost made me cry. Once that nonsense was over, I collapsed on the edge of the bed and took my head in both hands, aware that I was losing the thread of a disjointed story which had absolutely nothing to do with me.

I ordered a pizza and sat down in front of the television. I avoided the news bulletins with all their tragedies and disasters, skipped a reality show, lingered over some models strutting on a catwalk, endlessly, like a firework display. I wanted to continue channel-hopping, but couldn't. I focused on the fashion show. An absurd anger came over me. I felt as if I were under attack, but found myself unable to switch to another channel. An unknown force kept me watching the models sparkling beneath the lights. The theology of the image said that photographers' flashes made sequins brighter than the sun and stars. Bling flaunted itself, proud of its panache and exuberance. A few steps on the catwalk, and the whole universe threw itself at the feet of these made-up, redrawn silicone muses. I looked for some merit in their narcissism and found none, only the unbelievable practice of voluntary starvation in the quest for so-called perfection. In Africa I had seen people who were no more than skeletons, with bloated bellies, chests devoid of breath and open mouths that let out no sound. Over there, I thought, the catwalk was less attractive, with all the contingents of the damned who trod it – a catwalk riddled with deadly traps, strewn with unburied corpses rotting in the open air and in such a poor state that even the vultures recoiled from them in horror. Here, things were different: here, beauty was a confirmed talent, hip-swaying an art, the closing photo a magic moment that granted posterity to the makers of compromise … A few dance steps, a smouldering look, a sensuous pirouette as lap of honour, and all at once you are the height of celebrity. No need to waste your time in academia; all you have to do is flash your beautiful mascaraed eyes to supplant whole galaxies. What money decides, the gods validate: those same gods who, in Africa, show no sign of life, who pretend not to be there when the poor pray, who look away and deny any responsibility for the wars decimating the land … At the fashion show, those same gods clap their hands and stamp their feet. This star earns enough to feed a thousand tribes just for putting in an appearance at a swanky night club; that diva sells her smile for millions in a commercial as fleeting as a thought. And what hope for decency, when the rulers of this world do all they can to avoid it; morality nowadays is just for nuns and virgins … I pulled myself together. I was rambling … Kurt, Kurt, what's happening to you? Why all this anger? Since when have you set yourself up as a judge? I quickly switched off the television. Soon, in the silence of a sleeping Frankfurt, if I listened carefully, I would hear the day complaining of having to set itself alight once again … No, no, no, I told myself, you have to get a grip, Kurt, before it's too late!

At midnight, I came to the conclusion I had to leave Frankfurt for a while. I thought about the friends from university I had lost touch with. Then I thought about my mother: I hadn't put flowers on her grave since her funeral. I realised how quickly the time had passed, how ungrateful and selfish I'd been. My mother, my sweet mother who had died at the age of forty-four of vain prayers and terrible solitude. I could still see her in her pale dress, half mad, wandering in the cancer ward, her prematurely white hair absorbing the light filtering in through the French windows behind her.

At five in the morning, I took my car and set off for Essen.

I wandered the length and breadth of the cemetery without finding my mother's grave. It was the caretaker who pointed it out to me. I placed a wreath on the granite stone and stood there for a while, collecting my thoughts. I had hoped to revive my memory, to summon up distant recollections, but strangely, not a single image came to mind. How was that possible? ... I didn't stay long in the cemetery. What was the point? I went to have lunch in a restaurant overlooking the lake, then called Toma Knitel, a childhood friend. His jaw must have hit the floor when he recognised my voice at the end of the line. He could barely speak for laughing. He gave me his new address in Munich and asked me to drop by the university, where he taught mathematics. I got to Munich an hour late because of an accident on the autobahn. Toma was waiting for me outside the front entrance of the university. He was pleased to see me again. His embrace felt good. He directed me to his place, a small house in a modest neighbourhood on the outskirts of town. Toma's wife had hair as red as a maple leaf and a slightly plump figure, and was very pretty. Her name was Brigitte, and she was a Frenchwoman from

Strasbourg. Her welcome immediately put me at my ease. She was delighted to meet me and to introduce her two children, twin girls who were clearly not used to strangers. We ate in, because Toma was determined that I should discover his wife's culinary talents. Then we talked about the good old days. After a few hours, we had run out of subjects to mull over and spent the rest of the evening in a slightly alcoholic haze. As Toma had a class in the morning, I took my leave. He wanted me to stay over – I could sleep in the guest room, he said – but I had booked a room in a hotel. We said good night at about eleven; Brigitte was already in bed.

At the hotel, I didn't take any sleeping pills. My reunion with Toma had done me a lot of good. I felt at one with myself and it occurred to me I could repeat the experiment with Willie Adler, another friend from university, who lived in Stuttgart. I would look for his phone number and call him in the morning.

Willie was happy to welcome me to his home. He had been successful in life. He owned a thriving company, lived in a beautiful house in the most fashionable neighbourhood in town, and had a lovely wife. He entrusted his two children to a babysitter and drove his wife and me to a superb restaurant on the banks of the Neckar. During the evening, he talked endlessly about his career, the astronomical contracts he was negotiating, his ambitious plans. I noticed that he had aged quite a bit: he had deep, sallow rings under his eyes, and premature baldness had deprived him of the fine head of hair he had been so proud of at university, when he played guitar in an amateur pop group. He wasn't the same person he had been when we were twenty. He barely listened to anyone else, and his laughter rang out like a bugle. His wife watched us in silence. She seemed to be bored and constantly looked around to see if her husband's loud voice was disturbing the other diners. It was once the wine had started to take effect that Willie really came out with it. He admitted that he was the one who had smeared my desk drawer with grease and urinated in my bed on the evening of the graduation ball. He glared at me as he told me this. I realised to my surprise that the young man I had thought was my best friend hadn't really liked me, that he'd been secretly in love with the girl I was going out with at the time, and that he'd hated me for putting him in the shade. When he became aware that his rants were bothering the couples having dinner around us, his bitterness only increased and he became even more aggressive. His wife begged me with her eyes to put her husband's bad behaviour down to alcohol. Willie had never been able to handle his drink, but that evening he had gone too far. I listened to him without flinching, out of respect for his wife, wishing he would shut up. After dinner, we went out into the coolness of the night. Willie was dead drunk. He could barely stand. He yelled at the valet who had taken his time bringing him his car, then leant towards me and whispered in my ear, 'No hard feelings, Kurt. I've always preferred to put my cards on the table.' His wife helped him into the passenger seat and, before taking the wheel, said to me in an embarrassed tone, 'I'm truly sorry. Willie's like this with most people.'

I closed the door on her and let them go.

Then I walked around the city until the rain forced me back to my hotel.

The next day, I went to Nuremberg, where I spent two days wandering the streets, then to Dresden for a spot of sightseeing. During the night, I thought about my father. I hated him so much I thought I had wiped him from my memory for good. He had been nothing but a drunkard and a brute who spent most of his time hanging around in shady bars and his nights terrorising us ... A year earlier, the telephone had rung in my consulting room. The call was from a nursing home in Leipzig. The lady at the other end of the line informed me that a man named Georg Krausmann had just been admitted. He required detox treatment and had asked if I would agree to bear the cost. If I had been hit over the head with a hammer, I couldn't have been more stunned. I had been speechless for quite a long time, then said yes and hung up.

I can't explain my thought process. It was as if an irresistible force drew me to my car and sent me heading straight for Leipzig. On the way there, I wondered what I could possibly say to my father, what rational motive I could find for the visit. It made no sense, I kept telling myself; my father wouldn't even recognise me. I was fourteen when he broke all ties with us. Even at that time, he had almost never looked at me. He would come back late at night, and disappear in the morning. He was never home on special occasions, and he wouldn't remember my birthday or my mother's. Often, he would vanish for weeks on end without a word and without an address where he could be reached in case of emergency. When he came back, he would bring storm clouds with him. I could still see him, staggering in the hallway, saliva dribbling from his mouth, his hand ready to strike. They were turbulent homecomings: the neighbours would knock on the walls, and sometimes call the police. I would lock myself in my room and pray for him to go away and never come back

... One night, finding his packet of cigarettes empty, he turned the house upside down in search of a cigarette end. He was like a junkie desperate for a fix. After knocking my mother about – he held her responsible for every misfortune that befell us – he had left and never come back. That night, I knew God existed, because my prayer had been granted.

I got to the nursing home at about eleven in the morning. Luckily, the sky was cloudless and a sun as big as a pumpkin shone down on the establishment. The director received me in her austere office, reassured me about my father's state of health, asked me a lot of questions about my relationship with him, asked if I planned to leave him permanently in her care, because, she said, he couldn't manage on his own and would be better off at the home with its well-trained and highly devoted staff. I asked her if I could see my father. She called a nurse and told me to follow her.

We crossed the verdant grounds, where the patients were getting their supply of sunshine and fresh air. There were old people in wicker chairs with blankets over their legs, sickly figures walking up and down the paths, staff bustling back and forth. A sombre melancholy cast a veil over the daylight. The nurse led me into a dormitory block that looked like a place where people were left to die. A few ghosts dragged themselves along the narrow corridors, some with walking frames. My father's room was at the end of the corridor, near the stairs. The nurse opened the door without knocking and stood aside to let me in. An old man sat huddled in a wheelchair. It was my father, or what was left of him: a bundle of bones wrapped in a grey coat. All I could see of him was his unkempt hair, the chalk-white back of his neck and his thin arm dangling over the side. He didn't turn round when he heard our footsteps behind him. Nobody had been to see him since he had arrived here, the director had told me. When he had been informed that I was coming, he hadn't said yes or no; he had remained as inscrutable as the Sphinx ... The nurse withdrew. Her heels clicked in the corridor. I closed the door behind her. My father kept staring out through the French window. I knew he wouldn't turn round. He had never had the courage to confront things. Whenever he came back from one of his drinking sprees, I would hide in my room and cover my ears in order not to hear him yelling and overturning the furniture. Had I ever loved him? I suppose I had. Every child sees his father as a god. But I must have become disillusioned very early when I realised that you don't have to be a hero to procreate, that it doesn't take much and can even be an accident. Had my father loved me? He had never given me the impression that he had ... Now, as soon as I entered his room, he had opted for withdrawal; he wasn't looking at the grounds, he was running away. He had sent me a letter. Just one. It dated from the day he was admitted to the home. A kind of *mea culpa*. He must have been afraid I would refuse to pay his bills. *Your mother was a good woman*, he wrote. *I left because I couldn't hold a candle to her.* He wasn't telling me anything new. He'd been a loser, sponging off a devoted wife who had martyred herself in the observance of her marriage vows and had always hoped for the best while coping with the worst. *I didn't abandon you, I left you in peace.* I hadn't read his letter to the end. It had fallen from my hands. It had sounded as false as the bells of paradise.

I waited for him to stir, to show signs of life. My father

become an inescapable milestone on my road map? Why had I gone to look for forgiveness at my mother's grave, when I hadn't laid flowers on it for years? And what magic formula could my old university friends possibly have had that might allow me to bounce back when adversity laid me low? … The dullness of the village was startling. I had to find out where I was and how to get back to Frankfurt. I looked in the glove compartment for a map and found a packet of cigarettes that someone must have left. Without being able to stop myself, I lit up. The first puff went to my head. I had quit smoking the day I graduated as a doctor, a lifetime ago … The mist on the windscreen saddened me as much as my thoughts. A pharmacist's sign blinked on the façade of a small shop. A little girl in a hood ran across the road. A few drops of rain hit the roof of my car … Essen, Munich, Stuttgart, Nuremberg, Dresden, Leipzig, and then what? … Even if I visited every city in Germany, where would it get me? I knew I wouldn't shake off either my grief or my shadow. The sickness I was fleeing was inside me. Wherever I went, it would be there, rooted in my flesh, playing on my weaknesses and thwarting my attempts at diversion. I needed to ward off the old demon, to drive it out of my body. With my bare hands or with forceps. Because there wasn't room for the two of us.

I stubbed out my cigarette on the pavement and walked into the bar. A woman stood behind the counter, her face in her hands and her eyes staring into space, paying no attention to the two young men sitting at a table at the far end of the room. She jumped when I ordered a beer and a cheese sandwich. After serving me half-heartedly, she went back to her corner and resumed her daydreams.

'Is there a hotel around here?' I asked.

She shook her head.

I left a banknote on the counter and went back to my car. The sky had darkened; a faulty lamp was flickering at the end of the street. The memory of my father came back to provoke me. I got in and thought about what I should do: find a hotel for the night or keep driving. An old man with a newspaper under his arm walked past me, dragging his leg. He reminded me of Wolfgang walking away in the rain, weighed down by grief. Wolfgang! Why wasn't he on my list? Had I forgotten him, or had I deliberately left him out? There was no rhyme or reason to this trip. All these unlikely reunions, this whole laborious itinerary intended to somehow purge my mind, were merely a desperate manoeuvre to get away from what I couldn't accept. It was pointless to look for a hotel. The answers to my questions were buried somewhere in my house.

Somebody was ringing the doorbell. The noise drilled into my head. My hangover was so bad I found it hard to get up. The daylight hurt my eyes. The sun was at its height. I don't know how many hours or days I had slept. My mouth furry, my movements laborious, I slipped out of bed, looked for my slippers, couldn't find them, and went barefoot to the door. It was the postman. He was surprised to see me in vest and pants, looking quite untidy, and handed me a registered package. I signed for it and slammed the door in his face. I hadn't done it deliberately. It was a mistake, due to my drunken state, and I immediately realised how rude it was. I opened the door again to apologise, but the postman had already disappeared. I staggered to the kitchen – I didn't dare go to the bathroom yet – stuck my head in the sink and let the water from the tap lash me, then went back to my bedroom and tore the wrapping off the package. Inside, I found a small book with a letter in it. The book was *Black Moon*, Joma's collection, dedicated to his 'desert rose, Fatamou'. In the letter, Bruno had written:

My dear Kurt,

I think of you every day. I hope you're well. For my part, things have settled down. I'm reunited with my partner, and I'm living in her house, in Djibouti. Her name is Souad, like the other one, except that she's too huge to be a dancer and she snores like a diesel engine. But when she gets up early in the morning, she lights up my life. I hesitated for a long time before sending you Joma's book. I'd never forgive myself if the only memory you had of Africa was a jail and a gang of idiots. We never become battle-hardened, and I know how false the concept is. Often, it's those who have triumphed over misfortune who are the least ready to confront it a second time. I thought I knew everything about Africa, its hardships and about-turns, and yet, with every false move, I don't merely stumble, I fall like a child learning to walk. But whatever nasty surprises are lurking around the corner, I refuse to believe that Africa is nothing but violence and poverty, just as I refuse to believe that Joma Baba-Sy was merely a brute with a narrow mind and no heart. I would be at peace with you if you read his poems. They say what we did not deign to hear; maybe one day they might block out the voice reminding us of the wrongs we endured.

For you, in the name of the suffering we shared, I will

always keep the faith of those who have come through the
same ordeal with greater wisdom than anger.

Fraternally yours (in Africa, we are all brothers)
Bruno

At the bottom of the page, there was an email address and
a telephone number.

Claudia insisted that I emerge from my 'lair'. 'You look like
a peasant,' she said. Not having the strength to resist her, I
gave in. She took me to a restaurant just outside town. The
subdued lighting soothed me. We sat down at the far end
of the room. There were only three other couples having
dinner. Nobody recognised us. Claudia ordered the dish
of the day for both of us. We ate in silence. She seemed
hesitant. Every time she was about to say something, she
changed her mind and dropped it. We were in the middle
of the meal when a dapper, plump-faced middle-aged man
came and said hello. He was wearing tortoiseshell glasses
and a gold wristwatch. I didn't know him. Claudia invited
him to join us. He pretended to hesitate before accepting.
The smile he gave me went right through me. I didn't
appreciate the liberty Claudia had taken in imposing a
stranger on me.

'Let me introduce Dr Brandt, an eminent psychologist.'

The man hastened to hold out his hand. 'I'm delighted,
Dr Krausmann. Claudia assures me you're reacting very
well after what happened to you.'

So she had told him about me.

I signalled to the waiter and asked for the bill. I couldn't
stand the thought of spending a minute longer in the

company of someone who had a head start on me.

Claudia realised she had upset me. In the car, she sat silently, wringing her fingers. I drove carefully, but inside I was seething. When we got to her building, I switched off the engine and turned to face her.

'That shrink of yours wasn't there by chance.'

She dabbed her forehead with a small handkerchief, convulsively swallowing her saliva. 'You've been through a lot, Kurt. You've had a terrifying ordeal. But being a doctor, you should know as well as I do that there's nothing humiliating about consulting a psychologist.'

'What I find humiliating is that you assume the right to decide for me. You could at least have said something. You know me, I prefer swimming to football: I don't like dribbling, tackles from behind or dives. I've always swum in my own lane and taken care not to stray into anyone else's.'

She was on the verge of bursting into tears. Her face was twitching. 'You're not the same as you were before, Kurt. And every day, you give the impression you're becoming someone else. You tell me off for staying too long in the shower, for wasting water needlessly. You get angry with people who leave food on their plates. You almost threw a fit when you saw that giant poster of that pop star in a dress made from animal skins. You've been back a month, and all you're doing is making your case worse ...'

'My *case*, Claudia?'

'Yes, Kurt ... You worry me. I'm only trying to help you. Dr Brandt is an old friend. Trust me, he's a good person ... Please, tell me what's wrong, Kurt.'

'Why, do you think there's something right?'

'Don't you?'

She clenched her fists. 'You've changed a lot, Kurt.'

'Do you think so?'

'I see it.'

'And what do you see?'

She weighed up her answer, and said, 'A man who's been through a terrible experience and refuses to move on.'

'And what is he like, this man who's been through a terrible experience and refuses to move on?'

My questions threw her; she hadn't anticipated that I would badger her in this way. Caught by surprise, she had to think fast to avoid making things worse. She had surely not been expecting to find me with my guard up and ready for battle. That morning, when she had phoned to invite me to the restaurant, I had waited calmly for her to hang up so that I could get back to my old demons. Solitude suited me. I had private conversations with myself, and there was nobody to question me. For some weeks now, holed up in my house, I had been spending my time pulling myself to pieces, and this unconstrained exercise perfectly suited my state of mind. I conducted my trial in total freedom, being the judge and the defendant best suited to this kind of therapy. There was a sense in which I could no longer bear to listen to other people; they were crowding me, denying the essence of me. When I was alone, I could choose to tell myself all or nothing, without the need to weigh my words or suffer because of them; I was in my element and had no desire to share it or reveal it to anyone.

Having thought over my question, Claudia had to admit defeat. 'I don't know what to say,' she sighed.

'Then don't say anything.'

She must have been wondering why I was behaving

so unreasonably. Seeing no justification for my rudeness, she retorted, 'You left Africa to its wars, and brought its misfortunes with you.'

'You've never been to Africa, Claudia. What do you know?'

'I know what it's done to one particular man.'

'A man who's seen what you'll never see.'

'I'm not blind,' she said in her defence. 'You're the one who's become blind … You remember the other day, on the terrace of the restaurant, that drunken beggar who stood there watching us eat until a waiter chased him away? You put your fork down on the table, you wiped your mouth with a napkin, and then what did you do? You shook your head irritably, ordered a beer and carried on with your lunch as if nothing had happened.'

'It isn't the same.'

'It's exactly the same, Kurt. Except that in that restaurant the world was reduced to the four of us: you, the beggar, the waiter and me. And it happens the same way all over the world. On a larger scale. That's the way the world is, and nobody can change it. There are people who suffer, and people who get by as best they can. That's the nature of things. Nobody's supposed to take other people's misfortunes on himself, because everyone, rich or poor, has his share of them. Good luck and bad luck are both tests we are destined to get through. Nature has its rules: we don't blame a millipede for having more legs than it knows what to do with while a worm doesn't even have a claw to scratch itself. And a turkey can't claim it's unfair for a partridge to fly away when a predator approaches while he can only stand there like an idiot. There's a morality in what we consider unfair, Kurt.

The real question is whether to deal with it or ignore it. Your problem is that you think you embody that morality when you have neither the calibre nor the weight to do so. You're one person among seven billion other people, with no special authority to demand a fairness that nature itself can't conceive of.'

'There's an African proverb that says: "He who doesn't know that he doesn't know is a disaster."'

'What does that mean?'

'Exactly what it says, but I assume you're not one for riddles. Don't you see, Claudia? What happened to me in Africa has at least taught me something, something that may seem like nothing to you, but to me is very important.'

'I wish you'd enlighten me.'

'Sorry, I'm all out of enlightenment.'

I leant across her thighs and opened the door for her.

She pursed her lips, sniffed loudly and got out.

I switched on the engine and drove off.

The wind blew along Schaumainkai. The neon signs streaked the river with different colours. A few islands of greenery stood out on the soot-black river banks. I walked as far as Theodor-Stern-Kai, wandered through Niederrad, then returned to the river. I couldn't accept what Claudia had done, let alone forgive it ... I felt alone. My legs were like lead, my breath like fire. Jessica's ghost was pursuing me. It had been limping behind me since I had got out of my car. I was downcast, but I kept going, swept along as I had been the day I decided to confront the valley of shadows rather than rot in Gerima's jail. I had the feeling I was changing ...

Lost in his own thoughts, a man sat on a bench, talking to himself and watching his cigarette end burn out at his feet as if watching a caterpillar die. His coat was torn at the shoulder and through the tear you could see part of his sweater. He didn't look up when I passed him and continued to mutter and box the air. Like him, I despaired of finding a cure for my depression. I sat down on another bench and threw my head back, and my mind was invaded by a plethora of images like a speeded-up film, flashes of Jessica on the beach, in the forest, coming out of a hotel, lounging on a sun-drenched terrace, hailing a yellow taxi, sitting on a plane, kissing me on the lips. The images followed one after the other, led to more flashes, collided with another reel that was out of control. My skull was seething with noises, voices, laughter, smashing glass, the clicking of high heels on marble floors, waves rolling on white sand. I started to feel dizzy. *Why?* ... The man on the next bench jumped. I realised I was shouting.

The next day, I left my house for my home in the country. The peace of the countryside and the freshness of its groves would cheer me up, I thought ... I was wrong. My 'exile' merely made things worse.

The days went by, all totally empty. I didn't want anything. I didn't know what to do with my time. I sometimes spent the whole day sitting in an armchair, staring at the wall. I felt adrift, a stranger to myself. Sometimes I found myself standing with my nose up against the window pane, looking at the rain-drenched grove without seeing it. Whenever a hiker crossed the clearing, I would rush out to see him, but by the time I got outside, he would be gone; only his boot prints in the mud proved to me that I hadn't been dreaming. One morning, a car stopped at the end of the path. I had hoped it was Claudia; it wasn't Claudia. I realised how unfair I had been to her ... The solitude was worse than the misunderstanding. The day before, I had gone for a walk among the trees. The gloomy weather infected my mood. By the time I got back to the house I was in a terrible state. I lit a fire and sat down so close to the fireplace that my clothes steamed. In a flash, I saw again the old man standing in front of his burning hut like a lost soul at the gates of hell, and I grew afraid of my shadows, which the fire projected around me in a tremulous dance. On the table, alongside an apple core and a dirty plate, I lined up ten bottles of beer and started knocking them back one after the other, at regular intervals, until I could no longer see clearly. Then I walked all over the house. A comb left lying about, a nightdress, a piece of jewellery forgotten on the dressing table: any trace of Jessica was a torment. Without her, I was nothing but the raw expression of my widowhood, my interrupted mourning, my grief – a grief that was irrational and unrestrained. My legs unsteady and my mind numb, I went to the bedroom. The bed, once so narrow, now seemed more vast and arid than the desert. I fell asleep and woke up a few minutes later, sure that I would not close my eyes again before daybreak. A recurring image kept passing in front of me: in a funeral urn overflowing with ashes, a haughty vulture posed phoenix-like on a pile of cigarette ends. I tried to grasp the symbolism of that surreal image, but couldn't. I hugged the pillow to me, in the absence of another person, and let myself be overcome by the sweet lethargy of depression.

*

After a week, I returned to Frankfurt. As crumpled as an old sheet. Sick. My hair sticking up on my head. My furrowed cheeks covered in beard. A neighbour must have told Claudia, because she showed up within the hour.

'What are you doing to yourself, Kurt? … And now you're even smoking! Your house stinks of cigarettes. Look at yourself, you're an absolute state.'

I knocked back my drink and threw the glass at the wall. Startled, Claudia raised her arms to protect herself. I laughed, amused by her bewilderment, swaying in the middle of the living room, defying the portrait of Jessica that I was daring to confront for the first time since my return from Africa.

'I have a beautiful house, don't I?' I asked her. 'It cost me a small fortune. And what about these curtains, what about these sofas? Even a prince would envy me. And what about me, aren't I handsome? Is there anything wrong with me? I'm healthy, I have style, and I'm of sound mind. Any diva would fall into my arms like a shot.'

'Kurt,' she begged me, 'calm down, please.'

I stumbled over a pouffe and almost fell flat on my back. I declaimed:

> *We were lovers*
> *We were two volcanoes*
> *Burning with a thousand fires*
> *From summer to spring*
> *We were but one season*
> *We were lovers*

'Kurt, for heaven's sake …'

'What's heaven got to do with it? It's what happens down here that matters, on this filthy earth where everything decays ... I need reassurance, Claudia. Am I still handsome?'

'Of course you are.'

'Then why do I hate myself so much?'

'What are you talking about?'

'I'm talking about her,' I screamed, sweeping away with my hand the photograph of Jessica, which fell to the ground and smashed. 'I'm talking about Jessica, Jessie, my other half, my dream that went up in smoke ... How could she do that to me? In Africa I saw people who were nothing but skin and bone, who had nothing to eat and nothing to expect, and who fought for every second of life. People who'd had their lands stolen from them, people who were persecuted, reduced to the level of their own beasts of burden, chased from their squalid villages and wandering among bandits and disease, and yet, just imagine: poor and helpless as they were, they didn't give up one scrap of their wretched existence. And Jessica, who had everything to make her happy, *everything*, a beautiful house in a wonderful city, lots of friends, money in the bank, a luxurious office, a job with a major company, and a husband who wouldn't have let a speck of dust touch her, what does she do, what does she do to us? She deliberately takes her own life! And why? Over a promotion ...'

Claudia picked up the photograph, put it back in its place, and ran her finger over the star-shaped crack in the glass. Then she walked around the armchair that was between us, took my hand, and pressed it to her breast. I hated anyone to feel sorry for me. What she assumed was part of a nervous breakdown was only legitimate, clear-headed disapproval; and this misunderstanding, rather than bringing us together, placed a thick barrier between her and me, leaving us engaged in an absurd dialogue of the deaf. I had the feeling I was making a spectacle of myself to a blind woman.

I took back my hand; she took hold of it again and kept it. Her breath fluttered against my face. I suspected she might try to kiss me. Her eyes questioned mine, searched for my quivering lips, while her half-open mouth offered itself in an imperceptible movement of her head.

I recoiled.

She lowered her eyelids with their curved lashes. From the touch of her fingers, I sensed that my reaction disappointed her.

'These things happen, Kurt. We live in a crazy world. Things get too much for us and we rush about thinking we can catch a moving train. It's no wonder some end up on the wrong platform.'

Again, her eyes met mine and her scarlet mouth, as vivid as a wound, again brushed my lips. Her breath was burning my face now.

'Not many people can control their anxieties,' she went on, 'and even fewer know what they really want.'

I pushed her away. Not violently, but firmly enough to make her let go of my hand.

'You're a great girl, Claudia ... I'm sorry if I went too far. I have nobody else to let off steam to, but I mustn't take advantage ... I need to be alone. I have an account to settle with myself. Man to man.'

'Are you sure that's what you want?'

'Yes.'

She nodded, a little lost, tried to say something, gave

up. After looking at me with infinite sadness, she picked up her bag from the table and left the house, leaving the door open.

I felt much better. I had lanced the boil; now all I had to do was wait for it to heal. The guilty party had been identified, and it was Jessica. How can you take your own life over a deferred promotion? How can you believe yourself incapable of surviving failure when that failure is merely the kind of hiccup that's supposed to make you stronger? How can you dare to fall short of your ambitions and think for a single second that there is an objective stronger than love, or more important than your own life? So many skewed questions designed to divert us from the only answer that matters: ourselves. Since time began, suspicious of anything that doesn't make him suffer, man has been chasing after his own shadow and looking elsewhere for what he already has within reach, convinced that no redemption is possible without martyrdom, that any mishap is a mark of failure, when his greatest strength is his ability to bounce back ... Man, that prodigy failing to make the most of his chances and fascinated by his own vanities, constantly torn between what he thinks he is and what he would like to be, forgetting that the healthiest way of existing is quite simply to remain oneself.

After Claudia had gone, I pulled back all the curtains, opened all the windows and let the light of day flood my house. Never had rays of sunshine seemed so bright. The weather was magnificent, weather that makes you feel alive and eager to chase the dreams you've allowed to languish.

I went to the bathroom, sober, sure-footed. There wasn't a corpse in the bathtub! Or any skeletons in the closet. There was only me, Kurt Krausmann … I undressed and threw myself under a burning-hot shower; my skin was soft to the touch. After shaving and putting on aftershave, I dressed in my best shirt, my best trousers, my best jacket, and set off to do what I had promised myself as I watched the sun go down over the valley in my hostage prison. I had dinner at Erno's Bistro, without the shadow of a ghost around me. Late that night, refreshed and sated, I got home, took a beer from the fridge and switched on my computer. This time, I clicked on Elena's email. No message, just an attachment that I opened without hesitation. I no longer feared Pandora's boxes. Some twenty photographs appeared. Photographs that Elena had taken of me in the camp. I was standing on the site of Hodna City, sitting on the steps of a cabin, smiling at the back of the canteen, lying in an unmade bed, standing with my arm around Bruno's neck, examining a child in the infirmary, letting Lotta cut my hair while a swarm of children watched and laughed … Happiness flooded through my being.

I wrote to her, moved but not sure what to say. *Thank you for these beautiful memories, Elena. How are you?*

I pressed *Send*.

As I stood up to go and change, a sound came from my computer. Elena had answered me. It was as if she had been waiting for my email. It was 11.45 p.m. by my watch. There was at least an hour's time difference between Sudan and Germany. I couldn't get over it. I sat down again and clicked on the message.

Elena: *I'd be lying if I told you I miss you and am*

331

constantly thinking of you. You mean nothing to me. You never existed ... I'm a woman, you see? The truth would offend my modesty.

I didn't understand at first. On the second reading, it hit me head-on that it was a declaration of love. All at once, I realised that I had misunderstood what it was I was lacking, that it wasn't Jessica I missed, but Elena, that my trauma had skewed my perception. All I could see was the blankness of the bad patches I had gone through. In the harshness of my inner winter, the forest of my concerns had gathered into a vast funeral pyre and had been waiting stoically for a merciful sun to descend from its cloud and set it ablaze. But in the evening, there was never any fire. My anxieties closed ranks to get me through the night, and the sun, as pale as the moon, withdrew noiselessly like a false dawn. If I had been unhappy since my return from Africa, it was because of my inability to put things in perspective. I'd been beating myself up, blaming myself for a crime I hadn't committed, a crime of which I was the victim and the evidence. I had been holding completely the wrong trial. I had been going round in circles in an artificial maze, looking for a way out where there wasn't one. Only someone who knows where he's going can find a way out. I had to learn to live with what I couldn't change and find my own path. But I had lacked the presence of mind to do so. How could I have been so thoughtless? ... I reread Elena's message, over and over, and each reading reduced the insidious brew that had crept into my subconscious. As light shone in on my dark thoughts one after the other, my brain was filled with dazzling sparks, and an unaccustomed clarity made the slightest detail around me stand out. 'Why of bread into which he had slipped Hans Makkenroth's note. *Stand firm. Every day is a miracle.* And again on that fateful track, trying to reason with Joma. Joma who was doomed to seek elsewhere what he had within reach; Joma, that twisted poet who had thought that with the Word you could overcome adversity and who, if he had listened to himself, would have realised that no rifle carried further than a good word ... The plane took off. Beside me, a young woman leafed calmly through her magazine. A child started crying. I closed my eyes and projected myself across an African desert as hot and disturbing as a strong fever. Beneath the marabout tree, Bruno was naked; he was dancing like a djinn and showing me his pale buttocks. *That's Africa*, he cried, pointing to the young man with the cart who was carrying his mother on his back and who, at that moment, in his absolute generosity and courage, embodied selflessness. Good old Bruno, nobody knew better than he did how to look beyond the surface of things and give a fallen land its nobility. I was in a hurry to see him again, to once more experience his old-world romanticism, his exuberant chauvinism, his incorrigible optimism. I could already see him opening his arms to me, arms as wide as a bay, generous and proud of being what he was, with his saint-like forbearance and his opiate daydreams. We would sit by a campfire, and as I looked in the sky for a constellation made to measure for me, he would tell me about Aminata whose eyes shone like a thousand jewels, Souad the dancer who hadn't hesitated to sacrifice love for a pimp's promise, the low dives where he slept off both his binges and his sorrows, the indomitable peoples wandering where the desert winds took them, the filthy huts where you had board and lodging at any hour of the day or night, the human beings whose rags I saw but not their souls … I thought about Lotta, and Orfane, and Bidan the contortionist, and Forha the one-armed man, and that old veteran Mambo with his giant body confined in his makeshift bed, his disconcerting comments, his elephant-like indolence and his categorical refusal to admit that men could walk on the moon without offending gods and wolves … As the plane emerged from the clouds to conquer a sky as blue and limpid as a cherub's dream, the sun hit me full in the face. Like grace. As if emanating from the light, Elena's face appeared on the horizon. I laid my head back against my seat and let the memories take over. I recalled points of reference, gestures of help, an outstretched hand, another hand caressing, a face smiling in the middle of the night, a lip melting into a beloved lip and the song of a griot transcending prayers. Then I thought about Elena, about the days and nights ahead of us, the brand-new paths opening up to us, and I told myself that the desert is not finite but virgin, that its dust is pure and its mirages stimulating, that where love sows, the harvest is limitless because everything is possible when heart and mind combine. As my flesh remembered every one of Elena's kisses, as I felt her slender fingers running over my body in a multitude of happy quivers, and her mouth pouring its intoxicating nectar into mine, and her arms carrying me higher than a trophy, and her eyes absorbing my anxieties, and her breath ruffling my senses with millions of vows, there suddenly flashed into my mind these redemptive lines of Joma's which I had learnt by heart: